D0435440

F
Healy, Marti.
The rhythm of Selby

the RHYTHM of SELBY

A gently mysterious novel of the South

MARTI HEALY

ISBN 978-0-9791277-3-1
Printed in U.S.A.

First Edition
Copyright © 2008 Marti Healy

Design by Barry Doss.

Photography by Shelly Marshall Schmidt.

The Design Group Press, LLC
832 Brandy Road
Aiken, South Carolina 29801
803.644.4610

DEDICATED

To the town of "Selby"
– both real and imagined.

WITH DEEP GRATITUDE

To my father, who said I should write this book.

To Barry, who made it happen.

PROLOGUE

Do you believe a place can have its own distinct rhythm?
I do. Just as surely as the pulling of tides. Just as
meaningful as a beating heart. And just as mysterious as the
throaty purr of a well-stroked cat.

I believe every place has its own unique rhythm. And I
believe we are either in or out of sync with it.

I live in a town called Selby, tucked in the midlands of
South Carolina. Selby has a very definite rhythm. A lovely,
low-keyed, soft Southern charming rhythm.

When people greet each other here, they hug. Not always,
of course. But a lot. They hug or shake hands or pat an
arm or pet the dog. This leads to smiles and "how are yous."
There's no rushing into the topic at hand. No business first.
Warmth and hospitality are a part of Selby's rhythm.

People up North say "hi." People in Selby say "hey." It's

slower and sweeter and carries a touch of good humor with it. That "hey" is a part of Selby's rhythm.

People in Selby go to church. And places of business don't open until after. This is not to say that people here have more faith than in other places. Or that they live a faithful life any more consistently. And not all people in Selby do attend a place of worship. But most do. And all can. And hearing church bells, and sitting quietly and listening, and pausing to think of something larger than oneself is a powerful way to feel a spiritual rhythm in Selby.

Here, manners matter. People say "please" and "thank you," "Ma'am" and "Sir." They hold the door and hold their tongue. They wait for their turn, and then more often than not, they give it to someone else. They hold hands. And it's hard to rush along in a self-absorbed world when you're holding someone else's hand. This is a part of Selby's rhythm.

There are so many other ways about this town that contribute to its rhythm and pace and cadence. There are horses' hooves and multi-course meals, art shows and music recitals, soft summer nights with crescent moons, and rain drops that slide over scented trees.

There are carriage wheels on dirt-packed streets and there is pine straw underfoot. There are dogs that bark at sunset and horses that work out at dawn and a train that whistles at midnight.

Church suppers and parades and dance classes. Trails in a thick, cool forest. Music in a lush public park. More night stars than numbers to count them. And this, too, is the rhythm of Selby.

There are heroes in the town of Selby. Men and women who give their lives for their neighbors and people they love.

The rhythm of Selby was broken once to prove it.

I am, admittedly, a newcomer here. But I have felt in step with this place ever since the day I arrived. Now, whenever I am away, I feel out of sync, out of place, out of pace.

I believe in the rhythm of Selby. It has become like the rhythm of my own heart.

But now, of course, I know. There are secrets hidden as well – within the rhythm of Selby.

ONE

Reverend Ridley Knox leaned in closely to the dying lips, trying desperately to hear this poor man's words. He'd known Dennis Robecheaux all his life.

Dennis's last coughing spasm had been a rough one. Ridley, a hospital chaplain for more than 20 years, judged it would, indeed, be the last. The chemical stench of chlorine still rose from Dennis like a public pool. It came from his hair, his breath, the very pores of his skin. Twelve had already died. Dennis would be number 13. Dear God, let him be the last, Ridley prayed.

Five days and 12 hours ago, at exactly 12:06 a.m., a Southern Railways freight train, carrying 70 tons of toxic liquid chlorine, had been sent by mistake to a side rail, ramming three stationary rail cars and spilling a cloud of deadly fumes over a 2-mile radius just outside of Selby, South

Carolina. The epicenter of the accident was less than 100 yards from the town's primary industry, a brick production facility, Carolina Bricks.

The night shift at Carolina Bricks, 25 men and 18 women, were trapped. Heroic efforts by the plant workers themselves, as well as Selby's Public Safety officers and the County Sheriff's Office, got them out. And then they evacuated the town's northwest side of more than 6,000 residents. But 11 died in the process. Eight employees and three rescue workers. The train's engineer made 12. And now, one bystander, bringing the toll to 13.

In those first horrifying hours following the crash, Ridley remembered thinking about the Biblical passage, John 15:13, "Greater love hath no man, than he would lay down his life for his friends," because that's exactly what happened. No one died in the accident as a result of a selfish act. All who perished were thinking of, or trying to help, someone else. They laid down their lives for each other.

Even Dennis, who wasn't a safety officer and didn't work for Carolina Bricks, was found with his body wrapped protectively around a stray dog. He succeeded in saving the dog's life, but was losing his own – here, today, after suffering untold misery for 5 days and 12 hours. For the most part, Dennis had been incoherent. But within the last 24 hours, he had become surprisingly lucid. Then, about an hour ago, he asked repeatedly for Reverend Knox. Ridley had been at his side ever since, but Dennis had slipped in and out of a merciful coma.

While Ridley waited, his mind went lovingly over the memories of those lost in the tragedy. Harry Jackson, Carolina Bricks' night foreman, had been the first to grasp what was happening. He rang the alarm, dialed 911, and called to his co-workers to run to the break room – the farthest, most air-tight part of the building. Jenna Busbee, who lived just a few blocks from the plant, tried instead to reach her home, her sleeping husband, her two kids, and their four dogs. The Coroner thought Jenna was probably the first of the eight plant workers to die. She was found in the parking lot just a few feet from the exterior door.

Robby Cadwalader, a night-shift regular, was found behind the wheel of his jeep. Everyone knew he lived with his only brother, a man who "never grew up" the townspeople said. His brother, called John-John, depended on Robby for everything. No one was surprised that Robby's first thoughts were to get to John-John. But the car's systems reacted as fatally to the fumes as human ones. It simply died in the middle of the street, Robby with it.

Despite the employees' attempt to seal themselves into the break room, the toxic gas crept through every crack and crevice. Its choking effects were instant. Breathing was impossible. Uncontrollable vomiting compounded the other hideous bodily reactions to the poison. Panic was as hard to fight as the tears that blinded eyes shut as tightly as humanly possible. Flesh burned as if it had been in a raging fire. Even deeply colored clothing bleached in the saturated air to a faded, ghostly white.

Death came soon to five more. Of the Carolina Bricks employees, Jules Thompson was next. Father of a newborn, Jules' wife and their infant daughter were still in the hospital a safe 5 miles away. Jules tried to find out if there were other workers outside of the plant. Twice, he left the relative safety of the room, and came back with at least one other person.

The third time, he never returned.

Then came Bubba Newcome. Bubba was six months away from retirement. His boat was sitting in his driveway a few blocks away. It was his pride and joy, his retirement dream. He spent hours polishing and primping that boat to shining glory. By the time Bubba was buried, the chlorine gas had completely corrupted the finish on the boat and even compromised the structure of its Fiberglass. Paint bubbled and peeled. Wiring corroded and disintegrated. Bubba's wife just left it where it stood, a crumbling memorial to Bubba, their dreams, and their lost future together. They said he kept encouraging everyone to hang on and tried to pray for them, until the fumes prevented him from speaking at all.

Public Safety volunteer, Big Jake Dooley, was the first rescue worker to arrive on the scene. He knew the drill; you wait until you have protection for yourself before you enter a dangerous situation – and never, ever, go in without backup. But he also knew just about everyone that worked at Carolina Bricks. And he knew they were dying. He carried 10 to safety in his truck, but it gave out on the way back. On foot, he staggered in one more time. Reaffirming his name "Big Jake" with honors that morning, he carried one more out on his back, got her to a clean air pocket, then collapsed and died on the spot.

Deputy Carrie Jo Tanner had only been on the job for less than 6 months. No amount of training could have prepared her for this. And no amount of instruction could have taught her the kind of courage she demonstrated. Without regard for her personal safety, she began hosing people down with water, covering their faces with wet towels, and pushing them toward streets that would lead them out of the chemical massacre.

She was 21 years old. She was personally responsible for saving at least eight lives.

Johnson Aubrey was working night shift to finish putting himself through school. He, too, had called emergency 911, but could barely speak through the choking poison. His recorded blurred words and pleas for help for his coworkers were played over and over on the television newscasts with heartbreaking regularity in the days that immediately followed the accident. He died trying to help two others: Esther and Estelle Jameson.

The Jameson sisters were finally pulled unconscious into the break room by foreman Harry Jackson. It was his last act on this earth. Esther and Estelle were among the first to be transported to the hospital, but died later that day. In life, they had been devoted to each other. Neither married and they fought like only sisters can – constantly, cruelly, yet always just short of doing any real emotional harm. When Estelle fell, Esther refused to leave her, and was destined to prolonged inhalation of the chemical. In death, they were still inseparable, and died within two hours of each other.

Marcus Antony Vawter, a 15-year veteran of the volunteer rescue workers, and a survivor of Desert Storm, died two days after the event. One by one, he led or carried half-a-dozen people from the plant, and then went door-to-door in the surrounding neighborhood waking people up, telling them to close all their doors and windows, to bring their animals inside, and to turn off any air-conditioning or vents. He promised he'd be back to help them to safety as soon as he could. Ruthie, his wife, said Mac kept trying to get out of his hospital bed to keep that promise. His burned lungs eventually gave out, but not his will. His eyes were blinded, but he still could see the faces that needed him.

At exactly 12:04 a.m., Jonathan Tolbert, the engineer of the Southern Railways freight train carrying the load of chlorine, finished a second cup of coffee and came into view of the lights of the Carolina Bricks facility. Rounding the bend, he carefully checked his speed – the required 30-miles-an-hour in a populated area. He thought about how much he would hate a confining plant job like that. No excitement of traveling through the night air. No discovering new places, new people. He loved how his family greeted him every time he came home after being gone for days, sometimes weeks.

In the last minute before impact, John had time to realize something was very, very wrong; the train veered to the left instead of traveling straight. The lights were green. The train hadn't jumped the track. His brain ticked off the possible causes. Someone must have left the switch open by mistake. Then he saw it. There was something ahead in the darkness. Something on the track.

In the final seconds, John prayed for the people in the plant. He was the first to die that night.

Reverend Knox brought himself back to the moment as Dennis' hand tightened on his. He leaned forward again. What was Dennis trying to say?

"Not real," Dennis whispered. "Blood isn't real. Forgive us."

"Dennis, I'm sorry, I don't understand," Ridley replied. "What blood? Forgive who?"

All he could think of was that Dennis was somehow asking for forgiveness for the three railroad workers who had been responsible for not switching the track from the side back to the main after they had off-loaded the empty cars. The three men who had to live with the idea that the loss of more than a dozen lives rested on their shoulders. Two men, now. The third had not been able to live with the guilt, and had taken his own life just days later.

Ironically, in his sad and remorseful note, this man had found the one bright spot of the tragedy. "Thank God," he had written, "that it was not a few hours later. Thank God, the children were not in school. But God forgive us for causing them to lose their mothers and fathers." His hunting rifle had put his anguish to rest. He was never counted in the official death toll.

He was right. Within a few hundred yards in the other direction of the track was Lincoln Elementary School, with over 150 students. Less than eight hours after the crash, the bell rang for the first class. It sounded haunting and hollow in the empty halls and playgrounds. And people thanked God.

But Dennis had no connection with these men or the crash, as far as Ridley knew. So why was he asking for forgiveness for them?

Dennis struggled to raise his head a few inches and whispered even more desperately into Ridley's ear: "Please ... tell Big Jake ... I'm sorry ... sorry."

Ridley remembered the words. Pondered them. Wrote them down on a piece of yellow paper a few days later, and put them carefully in a drawer. And then went to bury poor Dennis.

Dennis was laid to rest in the old cemetery next to the Presbyterian church where six generations of Robecheauxs preceded him.

TWO

It was approaching dusk. That time between late afternoon and early evening when most of us are adjusting our lights and clothing, appetites and mindsets, to make the transition from the end of the day to the beginning of the night. A time when both sun and moon can share the sky. One of my favorite times.

I was in downtown Selby. Stores were closing, but restaurants were bustling. Automobile traffic was minimal, while walkers and even bicyclists happily shared the streets, alleys and sidewalks. I was alone. Hearing the laughter and spirited conversations of the "alfresco" restaurant patrons, and having been passed by a few politely preoccupied groups and couples lost in light banter and camaraderie, I was probably feeling a bit lonely. New to town. No family to hurry home to. No friends with open invitations to join them.

A slight breeze flirted with me as I turned the corner, and suddenly I was smiling. A few steps ahead was an enormous and handsome Great Dane. Her companion at the other end of her leash was a man wearing a tuxedo. Both of them were stopped to exchange a few words with a mounted police officer on a calm and lovely chestnut horse.

I was no longer alone. My passion for animals long ago removed any semblance of shyness (or even good manners) when it comes to greeting such creatures without reservation or invitation. Put something in fur on four legs, put it in front of me, and I am never among strangers.

And here were two delightful animals, placed in my pathway – in the middle of a busy downtown, surrounded by other people's friends – just when I needed them. It was as if God, sensing my pending loneliness, had said: "Just walk a little farther ... just around the corner ... just for you."

There is something very compelling to me about the way animals allow us to communicate when we would not otherwise have done so. Turning that corner, the breeze may have just felt chilly to me. The man in formal wear perhaps would not have even been there. The police officer would probably have been isolated in a car. If not for the animals.

I stopped to pet the dog.

"Her name's Claire," the gentleman said. We spoke for a few minutes about the love of dogs in general, and the Great Dane breed in particular. He told me how he was drawn to the Dane because of its great inherent gentleness and intelligence – as well as its dignity of size. He also spoke about how he had rescued Claire from an inappropriate life, and I appreciated that he didn't share the details. But the way Claire looked at her human friend, watching his every movement and body language, told me the dog would never forget whatever it was he had done for her.

"Please excuse me," the man said. "I have dinner guests arriving soon." As he began to walk away, he said good night to the mounted policeman, then turned back to me and said, "Welcome to Selby. Be sure to stop into the Hancock Art Gallery sometime." And then he and Claire disappeared down an alley that backed the block of restaurants, shops and businesses along Main Street, where I had just been walking.

I thought about how I hadn't told him I was new to town. But he knew it. And then my attention turned completely to the police horse still standing there.

Throughout the sidewalk conversation with Claire, her human, and the man on horseback, the mount had stood quietly, patiently – as if he were a silent participant in the exchange. And, to my mind, he had been. To me, animals are always as much a part of any group where they are present as the humans. And here, in Selby, this seems to be the prevailing attitude as well. This town obviously loves its animals.

The horse's name was Rowdy, although he was anything but that. He politely breathed up my nose. I had learned many years ago that this is the preferred greeting of most horses. They like to breathe up your nose. Especially when you're first introduced. In fact, this particular bit of animal observation was, in a way, how I came to be here – standing on a curb, stroking a horse's neck, in downtown Selby, South Carolina, on a balmy late summer evening, at the age of 59.

Just two years earlier, I had been taking a Bible study class in my church in Indiana. We had been reviewing that part in the Book of Genesis where it talks about God giving

Man "the breath of life." And our group leader asked us what that meant to us. Since I always learn better when I put new information into terms and context of something I already know, I immediately translated it into animal behavior. The first thing that came to my mind was how a horse likes to breathe up your nose when it gets to know you. So I shared this opinion with my class. Out loud. In spite of the silence that first met the observation – followed by a good deal of good natured laughter – I couldn't let go of the idea. And the more I thought about it, the more "connections" I began making between animal behavior and a great number of faith lessons and principles.

Having been a professional copywriter for more than 30 years, my natural inclination was to write it all down. Less than a year later, the book "The God-Dog Connection" was published and enjoying modest success. Enough success, at least, to allow me to move out of Midwestern winters and into the most beautiful, charming, small Southern town I had ever encountered.

It was a chance meeting, this town and I. It was a move on faith. And it was becoming the best thing that had ever happened in my life.

Rowdy's nose was velvet and warm. I suddenly remembered to ask the rider's name. Officer Joseph Tanner had been part of the mounted patrol for about 10 years, he said. He'd been in Public Safety for almost 25. I asked him why all the police and firefighters here were called "Public Safety Officers." The phrase was printed on all the patrol cars and fire engines, on signs, and mentioned in the local newspaper. He explained that it was because all of these people – both professional and volunteer – are cross-trained to serve in either capacity. Whoever is first on the scene in any type of crisis situation can respond with knowledge and ability. I told him I thought it made perfect sense. And I wondered why more towns – of all sizes – didn't operate accordingly.

I also asked him about the black band he was wearing on his left upper arm – the arm closest to his heart. He told me about his only daughter, Carrie Jo, a deputy in the County Sheriff's office, who had given her life in the great train wreck and chemical spill six months earlier. I had heard references to the tragedy before, but hadn't talked to anyone so closely associated with it. He said he would wear the band in her memory – in memory of all the victims – for as long as there was grief in his heart. He expected he would never take it off.

He gave me a gentle smile and wave as he nudged Rowdy and they continued on their way down the street. I watched them both for as long as they were in sight – speaking to everyone they passed, stopping to say "hey" to old friends and visitors, Rowdy lowering his head to greet a dog and gently breathe up another nose.

The old-fashioned globe-topped streetlights were beginning to glow deeply as I made my way home a few blocks from downtown.

THREE

I have heard or read somewhere that you should always live in a house that is older than you are. I don't know the reasoning behind that philosophy, but I rather like the idea.

My house in Selby doesn't quite fit the requirement. But we're within the same general decade of each other. And we have close to the same amount of nicks and flaws and uneven places. For both of us, I like to believe it adds "character" and interest. It's a part of the patina that comes only with knowing a bit of life.

When I first fell in love with Selby, and knew that I would be living here, I determined I would live as close in to town as I could afford.

One of the things that had attracted me to this town in the first place was the amazing residential area in and around downtown. From stunning mansions to delightful cottages.

Gorgeous estates to quaint and rambling almost storybook houses. And what impressed me most was how Selby revered its old homes.

In Selby, people celebrate the past that is represented by its architecture. Rather than tear down and rebuild, they just keep adding on. Changing bits at a time, over time. Admittedly, sometimes a house may have been added on to so continuously and extensively over several generations, that the original parts have been absorbed entirely. But even then, it has been done with caring and grace and respect. And perhaps just a touch of eccentricity.

My search for my house ended on a street a handful of blocks out from the heart of downtown. On a street with the unlikely name of Gardenia. Its surrounding sister streets also reflect the obvious influence: Magnolia, Jasmine, Hydrangea, Wisteria, and similar Southern garden specialties. And, as if somehow compelled to live up to their curb-side namesakes, the houses themselves all seem to be draped in color, scent and natural beauty most of the year. It makes walking in the neighborhood a sensory adventure.

Architecturally, the neighborhood is well established, sturdy and loved. My own house, two down from the corner, is a brick, single-story structure, with hardwood floors and lots of windows. It was well thought out and thoughtfully built.

But what attracted me most to this particular house were its bits of nonsense. Doors that opened the wrong way; cupboards that were not symmetrical. The unexplained window in the laundry room door. The doors that were out of alignment or missing altogether. A light switch that is half hidden behind a cupboard. And another one that is so high up I have to stand on a chair to reach it. A doorknob that refuses to stay put. The funky kitchen cupboards made of maple and trimmed with scalloped edges of wood.

Interestingly, the fireplace chimney tilts somewhat. And most of the floors sag and squeak reassuringly. But, overall, it's a solid, well-loved home that made me smile immediately the first time I saw it.

I have also experienced a great sense of not exactly "déjà vu" here – but a certain "knowing." I just knew the TV room should have two glass-paneled doors at either end; and out behind the guest cottage were leaning two old glass-paneled doors. I had dragged a large double roll of wallpaper with me across the country that I purchased more than 20 years ago and had no where to use; but it's perfect in one of my bathrooms here. Stained glass panels that collected dust in my last attic fit in a double window here as if they were custom-made. I knew exactly where to put the piano and my bed and the cats' dishes. It was "mine" from the day I moved in.

I thoroughly appreciated the specialness of the homes and other buildings in Selby from the first time I stumbled upon the town. This old house was empty then. Somehow, I can believe it was waiting just for me to find it, and smile, and come home.

That night, however, I came home to the house itself, two cats, and little else. For yet another day, my moving van had not arrived. It had been overdue for almost three weeks. Each day would start with the same obligatory phone call: "Where is my furniture?" With the same inevitable answer: "It will be there tomorrow." But more than 20 tomorrows had come and gone without the van – and all my worldly possessions.

I had become acutely aware of how much we depend on our "stuff" – the things that tell us who we are and define where our home is. I had also become rather embarrassingly aware of how little I really needed to exist, compared to what I knew I had accumulated in the boxes and boxes that were waiting – somewhere – to come to me.

Deep inside, I had the nagging conviction that perhaps this was God's way of poking me in the ribs a bit to say, "See ... you really don't need so much now, do you?" And so I would wash and dry my single dish, glass and fork that I had brought with me, and I would wash and dry my two changes of clothes that I had packed, and I would sit on the single folding chair that I had purchased here, and read the two books I had carried in the car. And I would lie down on the hardwood floor, cushioned only by the two small throw rugs and one bath towel that I had tucked in the car for the cats for the road trip. And I would say: "Yes, Lord, I've learned my lesson. May I please have my stuff now?" But this day, again, He apparently had answered, "Not yet."

Tonight, however, I would at least sleep a great deal better. With visible bruises on my back and hips from trying to sleep on the floor too many times, I had finally purchased a new box springs and mattress, and they had been delivered that afternoon. A new set of sheets, and it was bliss.

Then, with a warm and grateful cat on either side of me, I slept deeply, soundly, and more appreciatively than I had in ages. The van arrived on the 21st "tomorrow."

FOUR

The moving van was pulling away from the curb. It was just getting dark. Molly, the young teenager from across the street, came hurrying over to catch me before I went back inside. I had met her family shortly after I arrived. They had graciously brought me some banana bread as a "welcome to the neighborhood" gesture.

Molly's dad, Ed Cinkowski, was editor of the local daily newspaper; her mom Ruth Ann was a third-grade teacher at the elementary school. It had been an interesting first meeting.

Ed shook my hand and immediately said: "I know you from somewhere." I thought he may have seen my book jacket photo and recognized me from that, but he hadn't.

He then said: "Ruthie, don't you remember? She was having dinner at Shoney's last Thursday night when we were there with David." He explained to me, "David's our grandson, our oldest daughter's boy, and we have him every Thursday night."

Ruth Ann's blank look said, no, she didn't remember. But Ed went on to describe exactly where I had been seated, that I had been there alone, what I had ordered, and that I eat left-handed. I thought he was either the most observant man I had ever met or he was starting to disconcert me a bit. Fortunately, it was the former. A short conversation later, and I had agreed to write a weekly column for the paper. It was to be about any topic I wanted – mostly, my experiences as a newcomer to Selby. I appreciated that he had said "newcomer" rather than "outsider" or even "Northerner," which was the way most Southerners would have described me. The term Yankee is passé, I believe; Northerner is the politically correct term nowadays, and a true Southerner is nothing if not polite.

I greeted Molly and could tell she was somewhat agitated. She said her dad wanted to know if they could borrow an empty box.

"It's for the snake," she said, knowing that I would understand.

I had heard the story in detail. About two weeks earlier, Ruth Ann had come across a very large but harmless snake while clearing a new plant bed. A consummate animal lover and teacher, her first instinct was to capture the snake, and take it to her classroom before eventually releasing it. She called to her husband to get a box or bucket or something in which to contain it.

"Leave it alone," Ed had advised.

"But I want to share it with my class," she responded.

"That's great – now leave it alone," he repeated.

After the snake was trapped, it was gently placed in a large cardboard box, with grass clippings, water and air holes, and carefully left on the workbench in the garage for Ruth Ann to put in her car the next morning. The next morning, the box was predictably empty, and for two weeks the family had cautiously entered the garage, looking up at rafters and around corners. The snake was never sighted again. Until now.

"Where did you find it?" I asked.

"Behind a garbage can," Molly reported. "But we don't have the box anymore, and it didn't do a very good job of holding him the first time, so Dad wanted me to see if you had one we could use," she explained.

"Your mom's taking it to school then?" I guessed. But she said no, that her dad had won out this time. They were going to take it to Selby Woods and release it there.

Selby Woods is 2,100 acres at the very heart of the town. It is cared for by an endowment, and loved intensely by all the town's inhabitants. No motorized vehicles are allowed within its borders. No bicycles, either. Just walkers, horses and dogs. The only wheel tracks ever permitted in the Woods are from horse-drawn carriages – a long-time heritage of the town. The plant life is amazing in the Woods: great live oaks, fragrant pines, citrus-scented magnolias, shadowy ferns, aromatic wisteria and honeysuckle and much, much more. There are mossy dirt-packed paths winding throughout its depths. And a few sun-dappled clearings with gentle jumps established for steeplechase horses in training. The wildlife is abundant, too, and would soon be expanded by one more snake.

My mind suddenly retrieved a bit a trivia I had read

someplace. I told Molly to wait while I wound my way through unopened boxes and found one marked "linens." I broke the seal and pulled out a pillowcase. I told her that I believed this was the best way to move a snake, because they couldn't push their way out, as they could with a stiffer-sided container. Together, we took the potential transport system across the street to her garage. The lights and action were in full force, as was the camera. Ruth Ann had felt if she couldn't deliver the real thing for her class, that she ought to at least get video. But Ed was not such a willing co-star.

It took three adults, one teenager, one extremely excited dog, and an hour, but the snake was at last inside the pillowcase. Ed got behind the wheel of the car and made Ruth Ann sit in the passenger's side of the front seat, holding the top of the pillow case like a sack out the open window. "That thing's not getting loose in my car," he stated more than once.

A little after 10:00 p.m., Molly and I stood in the driveway watching the taillights of the car as it drove off in the direction of Selby Woods – slowly, steadily, with the vague outline of a human arm protruding stiffly from the passenger's side, a strange, squirming bundle at one end.

Molly went to settle the dog, who was convinced there were undoubtedly more snakes to be found in the garage. And I returned to my house to begin writing my first column for the paper.

I decided to write about my downtown encounter a couple of days earlier with the man in the tuxedo, Claire the Great Dane, and the mounted Public Safety Officer. I titled it "The Noah Factor."

When the column was published the following Wednesday, I received an excited call from my neighbor whose property backs up to mine.

"I know who that is," she claimed. "That man and dog you wrote about in your column … his name is Hancock, Jonathan Hancock – yes, like the signer of the Declaration of Independence – an actual descendent of the family as a matter of fact. He owns the Hancock Art Gallery downtown. The dog's name is Claire."

Sally Houseman, my neighbor, is possibly one of the nicest people living. She had welcomed me immediately to Selby and took it upon herself to help me feel loved and less lonely in a totally new environment. She loaned me ladders and tools while I was trying to fix up the house, before my own things arrived. And she was the best audience ever. If I got a new faucet for the kitchen sink, or painted the walls a warm wheat color, Sally was always there to admire the effort and tell me it was "perfect" – just what the room needed. She hugged me a lot, too. And in those first few days and weeks, the hugs kept me going. I had wanted whole-heartedly to come to Selby. But leaving a place you've called home for 30 years is still hard. And I had known no one here at all.

It was a happy coincidence that Sally was also a pet-sitter. I was required to travel a bit for the book – speaking and book-signing engagements. And my cats adopted Sally without hesitation. Even Sparkey, the boy cat who was so shy he wouldn't let most people see him, had let Sally coax him out from his favorite hiding place and curled up purring in her lap. Katie, the female calico, was a fan from the moment they met.

When she isn't charming animals, Sally works as a nurse,

specializing in eldercare. A gentle, nurturing, compassionate person with a genuine servant's heart. Everyone should have at least one "Sally" in their lives.

With small town ease, other people also soon let me know about whom I had written my column. But it was still a pleasant surprise when the phone rang later that day and a voice said: "Claire would consider it a privilege if you'd join us for coffee." Jonathan Hancock introduced himself and told me to stop in at the Hancock Art Gallery anytime.

I took advantage of the offer the next day.

The entrance to the Gallery is through a slender blue door at street level, fitted between the drug store and a small coffee shop. The sign is subtle and sophisticated. But a slim dark blue awning sheltering the entrance adds a bit of visibility.

The door opens onto a narrow, steep flight of bare dark wooden stairs that climb straight up to the second floor. Grasping a side handrail, I smiled as each stair creaked and groaned with abandon, as if a thousand feet had trod there before me as, indeed, they probably had. A group of visitors started coming down at about the same time. Neither of us wanted to turn around or back up and repeat the journey. So we laughed and made obvious jokes as we sidled past each other in the tight space.

Reaching the top, I paused to catch my breath. Claire was there in an instant to greet me, as it was her self-appointed duty to do so. I spotted Jonathan at the back of the main room, waved, and he came over immediately.

"I had telephone calls all day yesterday about your

column," he began. "And Claire and I are quite flattered to be mentioned. Please ... have a seat," he said as he motioned me into a small room to our right.

"It's Miss Harris, right?" he asked.

"Please, call me Macy," I replied.

"I'm Jonathan Hancock. And I answer to any number of variations, including John, Jack, Jonathan. My father even calls me Nate," he added.

"Would you prefer tea or coffee?" he asked. He nodded to a small, overstuffed chair for me to sit in. It was among a cluster of unmatched but very comfortable-looking chairs surrounding a low table filled with coffee cups and steaming pots. At the center, a slightly chipped platter of exquisite Haviland china held an array of small cookies.

Claire positioned herself discreetly behind Jonathan's chair and kept her ears alert in case her name was mentioned, or for any opportunity to contribute to the conversation. I waved to her, she blinked and yawned back, we were instantly old friends.

I liked Jonathan immensely from that first encounter. Since then, I have found him to be one of the most honorable and comfortable men I've ever met. He was born in the South, left for a short time to be educated abroad, then returned to his roots and eventually settled in Selby after a few years in Savannah and Charleston. He is passionate about two things: art and horses, not necessarily in that order. And dogs are a close third. Nothing pleases him more than the combination of all three, so his attraction to Selby was a matter of natural selection. I could tell by the art surrounding us in this small area of the gallery that he had varied tastes, or at least represented a diverse selection of artists. But his favorites seemed to be various interpretations of the equine world.

He is amicably divorced from a woman who now lives on the East Coast. He is incredibly proud of his one daughter, a financial advisor also residing out East. His father is over 90, still going strong, and living in his own private residence near downtown Selby. Mr. Hancock, Sr., is one of Selby's treats. Between the two of them, they know just about everyone in town. The father likes about half of them. Jonathan is much more accepting.

Jonathan lives in a cottage almost immediately behind the Gallery, with a fine stable and a few modest paddocks. It's not unusual in downtown Selby. The town grew up around horse aficionados. But he holds most of his private dinner parties, which are frequent and renowned in the area, in the Art Gallery itself. And, if you're ever invited to "eat in the gallery," you can consider yourself one of the insiders in Selby. When I got such an invitation the next week, I felt as if I had been asked to sit at the popular kids table in the high school lunch room. Apparently, I had been "interviewed" during our coffee together, and had somehow been approved.

I accepted immediately, and wondered what one wore to eat in the Hancock Art Gallery. When I had first met Jonathan, he had said he was expecting dinner guests – and he had been wearing a tuxedo. But that, I learned, had been a special occasion – his father's birthday, in fact. Typically, fashion simply takes a back seat to great food, excellent wine, one-of-a-kind personalities, and unforgettable conversation. And on the night I first attended one of Mr. Hancock's dinners, the conversation would unknowingly pull the first thread that would unravel a century-old secret.

FIVE

The night of the party, Jonathan and Claire both met me at the top of the Gallery entrance stairs, and he informed me that they were beginning to become worried about me. I looked at my watch; it was 7:30 p.m. on the dot. He had told me 7:30-ish, but I had yet to learn that in Selby, that means you get there at least 15 minutes before.

I tried to apologize, but Jonathan would not hear of it – saying he was at fault for not better informing me. We wound our way through the small gallery rooms still open to a few patrons – whom Jonathan greeted by name and commented to individually as we passed: "Harvey, heard you had a great vacation … welcome home. Glad that knee's doing better, Charlie … Mary Louise, congratulations on the silver cup … Ridley, why don't you just buy that print – you're going to wear it out looking at it."

"I'll have to introduce you to Ridley Knox. He's good people," he said to me, but we kept walking.

The Gallery itself was a work of architectural art. It had been changed little – if at all – from its original use as office space above the retail shops below. The long flight of entrance stairs topped at a large landing and a continuation of uncovered wood floors. Six rooms radiated off of this central area. Each room was small, perhaps 8 feet by 10 feet. A larger main gallery was at the very back of the building.

Each room had its own proportionate fireplace – probably the original sole source of wintertime heat. Not much artificial heat is needed in South Carolina. But winter nights can dip surprisingly low at times. Remarkably, these fireplaces still had their original tile work, and each was different. From delft blue scenes to green and black checkerboard, they were marvelous to behold. Tin ceilings that were 12 and 14 feet high, hanging globe light fixtures, transoms above the doors. It was all still there.

"LuRay, Mr. Jackson is in the Adams gallery," Jonathan spoke quietly to his assistant manager as we reached the door to the main gallery. "Please see to him, then, go ahead and close up for the evening," he said. How he'd known about Mr. Jackson, I'm not sure. But I would have bet he could probably have told me exactly how many people were in the entire place at any moment, in which rooms, and if they were serious buyers or not.

Each of the smaller rooms had their own gallery names. The main area we were now entering was called the Prince Rivers gallery. I had read about Mr. Rivers earlier. He had been a remarkable local hero of the Civil War era. Born into slavery, he had been second-in-command under Colonel

Thomas Higginson of the First South Carolina Colored
Infantry Volunteers. It was the first regularized all-black
Union troop, formed in 1862. After the war, Mr. Rivers was
an elected member of the South Carolina State Constitutional
Convention, and then became a State Legislator. He
also served as a trial judge and as Chairman of the State
Republican Party.

The Gallery had been established in his name to showcase
local African-American artists. But, in the true spirit of
equality, it now represents work by both blacks and whites.
It also held the ongoing and fascinating art restoration
work being done on the premises. And it was the site of the
Hancock dinner parties.

The room was both sophisticated and homey at once, and
outfitted much more like a private living room than an art
gallery. Only the incredible works both framed and unframed
that surrounded us in the dim light gave it away. Much of it
was hanging on all four walls, casually, yet not irreverently.
Some canvases were simply propped on the floor, leaning with
a sort of uncomplicated self-confidence against the walls and
each other. It all reflected a society that lived among its art as
casually and expected as others live with wallpaper.

The floor was heart of pine, polished and buffed to a
brilliant sheen over the scars and discoloration of decades and
decades of use. Two of the walls were covered with a paneling
that was a combination of old oak, bee's wax, and years of
exposure to smoke and humidity and the breath of a thousand
lives that had passed through its doorways.

The third and fourth walls were brick and plaster, the one
opposite the doorway held a massive fireplace.

The ceiling-high windows were covered with wide-slatted,

dark-stained shutters. Slow-turning ceiling fans circulated the air at both ends of the room and another was immediately over the table.

A long table in the center of the room was set for eight and glittered with glass and silver. The other guests were gathered near the fireplace, with wine and drinks, appetizers and laughter.

Jonathan called to everyone that I had finally arrived. He introduced me to the group at large and then excused himself to check on the food. But everyone greeted me individually, introducing themselves, making me feel comfortable and as if I were the most important person at the party. It's a singular Southern talent.

I was seated in the center of the conversation on a low, extremely comfortable, down-filled hassock that was covered in a wonderful old English chintz. Claire settled at my feet.

A couple was seated on the sofa opposite me. They were Lydia and Shelby Deveraux: Lydia, a life-long resident here; Shelby, a native of Savannah. They had been here since they married, about 30 years before, and resided in the home in which Lydia had grown up, inheriting it from her family some 20 years back. The home is one of the important mansions in Selby: "the Montgomery place" on Magnolia Avenue. It could be lived in by Deverauxes from now to eternity, and it would still be known as "the Montgomery place."

Margaret Ann Lawton was curled up in a large, overstuffed arm chair to my right, a cat draped over the back of the chair, next to her left ear. She was absently scratching his chin. She was dressed in riding clothes – the kind that serious steeplechase horsewomen wear as casually as the rest of us wear a pair of jeans. Her feet were bare, a pair of well-worn moccasins close by. I couldn't stop looking at her hands. While the rest of her could have stepped out of a Ralph Lauren advertisement – model-perfect teeth, skin, hair and figure – her hands were rough and worn, leather brown, sinewy, and strong as tree roots. She was a real horsewoman. She mucked stalls. She helped foal babies. She groomed and carried water and had handled reins all of her life. I guessed her to be about 55, but she was one of the ageless Southern beauties I had come to admire in Selby.

Margaret Ann's husband, Brooks Lawton, was perched on the arm of the chair to my left. He could have been 10 years her senior. A retired lawyer, Brooks had exceptional eyes. They told me he took very little seriously, but missed nothing and gave nothing away. Intelligent, just a little arrogant, and quick as the devil. This is a man who is used to being in charge, I thought to myself. And this is a man who knows things – about situations and people. He is a great secret-keeper.

The unofficial bartender serving wine and mixing drinks at a small side table was a friend of Jonathan's from when he had first lived here: Drew Henderson. Drew is a published author and expert on Southern architecture in general, pre-Civil War in particular. He is not dependent upon his royalties, however. Andrew Lee McGovern Henderson is a Southern Gentleman in every sense of the word. He was born and raised in Charleston, but had for some unexplained reason chosen Selby as his adopted home. No one really knew why. No one asked. To a typical born-and-bred Charlestonian, there is Charleston, and then there is the rest of the South. And the rest of the Union does not particularly count for much. A Charlestonian accent is distinct. A

Charlestonian outlook on life, society, and "that great unpleasantness with the North" is wholly unique. Drew is a fabulous conversationalist who knows a great deal about a great deal, is soft spoken, kind, and chivalrous. He is a preferred member of any dinner party, and a regular at Jonathan's.

Chance Montigue made up the final member of the eight present. He was seated slightly apart from the group, but a definite part of it – as the others would all turn to him to reinforce what they were saying or to get his input. A highly respected stable owner, Chance had settled here about 25 years ago, already well established in the Thoroughbred horse industry. Chance had originated the idea of syndication or partnerships relative to race horse ownership. The costs had simply become too high for a typical individual to own, train, and race a Thoroughbred any more. But Chance found a way. Share the costs. Share the risks. Share the rewards. It was simple and brilliant. Chance is a lovely man, warm and friendly, thoughtful, quietly understated. A wonderful storyteller. I liked and trusted him immediately. He is married to an equally respected and accomplished woman who was not with the group due to an out-of-town conference she was chairing.

The group was finding out a great deal about me through polite questions and observations. But I was becoming rather embarrassed from the focused attention and one-sided conversation so far. The combination of Southern graciousness and small-town curiosity can be almost lethal at times.

At that moment, Jonathan reappeared, followed

immediately by the caterers bringing the food to an antique sideboard.

Without breaking the conversation flow, everyone moved to the table, Jonathan indicating where each of us was to sit. I had the seat of honor to his right. He gave a short welcoming toast, an old Scottish blessing, which served as our grace.

One of the servers brought forward a large icy pitcher from the sideboard and began filling our water glasses. Slices of orange floated among the ice cubes. Watching the strain of his muscles, I guessed it to be leaded crystal. It was gorgeous and very old. I noticed a rather significant chip was missing from the base, but that didn't mar its inherent beauty or usefulness. Another Southern tradition: quality matters, quality lasts, beauty transcends the chips and scars of the years. Perhaps such flaws even enhance it, by proclaiming a history of appreciation for quality.

The food was outstanding. Grilled salmon. Freshly roasted tomatoes stuffed with couscous. Corn-on-the-cob. Field greens. Wine carefully selected for the food. The simple dessert of a small scoop of peach ice cream, topped with another spoonful of sorbet, finished the meal perfectly. By the time fresh-ground coffee was served, I was quite sure I would never want to leave that room again.

The conversation had been lively, dancing from one topic to the next: horses and travel, books and concerts, the improvements planned for the old library, the needful state of the town's oldest cemetery, the value of preservation vs. restoration vs. re-creation when it came to architecture. Who bought what property, the terrible influx of traffic (it takes over 10 minutes now to get from one side of town to the other), and personality profiles drawn just for my benefit of those discussed but not yet met.

"She's wonderful, a terrific animal psychic."

"He's one of a kind – more money than Canada, and he wears the same pair of pants every day … every day."

"Her family's one of the original Winter Colony – that big old house on Hunter Street. Her grandfather started the free clinic and she supports it practically single-handedly. But don't ever mention that to her."

I had already heard the general outline of Selby's history. It had been founded about 30 years prior to the Civil War. The natural springs and fresh air – much less humid than in the coastal cities of Charleston or Savannah – were prized by its inhabitants and drew regular visitors even then.

There had also been a pivotal battle fought in Selby during Sherman's march to Atlanta. Decidedly Southern in their position, Selby residents had soundly turned the Yankees away from a targeted powder and ammunitions stronghold a few miles to the west. It's still talked about. Guidebooks mention it. Historians write about it. Authors enhance it. And every spring it's relived; reenacted with astounding energy and detail. A movie company once recorded the modern version, but I never have found out for which film.

But for all the Southern pride in this historical victory for the Confederates, there is equal emphasis and enthusiasm for recalling and celebrating the famous underground railroad that passed hundreds of slaves to safety through members of some of the older churches in town. Wounded Union troops separated from their units were also secreted away, nursed, fed, and returned to the North. Even more than a century and a half ago, even in war, Selby was disarmingly hospitable and generous.

The most colorful period in Selby's past, however, came about 35 years after the "unpleasantness" subsided. And this is the heritage Selby reflects and refers to most today.

Around the turn of the last century, Selby became a unique and wonderful Winter Colony. A treasured escape for families of wealth and significance from the North. In Selby they found a warm sun and soft air and ground that never freezes. They found healthy waters and hospitable neighbors and each other. They brought with them their entire households, children and staff, dogs and horses. They brought their art and music and theater and sports. They brought a love of education, and a sense of commitment to community. And they brought their money. They came year after year, generation after generation, and have been here ever since.

Eventually, the evening's conversation turned to one of the old family tales. All have great stories. But some are better than most.

"Has she heard about the Faith Ruby – the Carolina Star?" someone asked, and they all looked at me expectantly. I remembered having heard of the famous gem at some point in my life – most people probably have. But I didn't know of any Selby connection to it, I had to admit. So I got the complete and fascinating story on the spot.

Jonathan refilled our wine glasses as I got a brief tutorial on the stones known as "rubies." They are closely related to sapphires, it seems, both variations of the mineral corundum; only the ruby color classifies it as its own type of gem. The color of a ruby can range from light red (but not pink) to orange-red, to a deep almost purple-red. This latter, most valued color type is typically found in Burma.

That interesting bit of information segued into a brief geography lesson on rubies, including the surprising fact – at least to me – that there are several active and formerly producing ruby mines in our sister state to the north – North Carolina.

The Carolina Star ruby was actually mined not in North Carolina as the name would suggest, but in Burma. It was a 90-carat, "pigeon blood red" – that is its official color classification – and had a rare 12-point star at its heart. Such stars are created, I learned, when inclusions of tiny parallel needle-like substances cause an effect called an "asterism" in the polished stone, and they are usually six-pointed. A 12-point is exceptional.

The remarkable stone was named the Carolina Star because it was bought at auction by a Charleston, South Carolina, jeweler in the early 1900s. It was purchased by him on behalf of a private buyer, Mr. Abernathy D. Faith, as a gift to his then bride, Charlotte Louise. The Faiths resided in New York City, but were one of the original families of the Selby Winter Colony.

Charlotte Louise – affectionately known as Lottie or Lottie Louise – was a beauty. A turner of heads, a charmer of hearts. Since childhood, her dimples and smiles and curls and easy laughter won her many friends and admirers, and taught her she needn't develop any other skills or mental abilities of her own. By all accounts, she was a very sweet and loving person, generous and kind, and scatty as a bat. These endearing qualities became even more so as she aged.

Long after her husband's early death, Lottie Louise continued to return to Selby, season after season, with her twin daughters in tow. Many times, one or the other of the young girls was seen wearing the precious ruby as they played in the garden or rode their ponies around the estate.

Lottie Louise herself was in the habit of wrapping the gem in the toe of an old stocking and stuffing it in the silverware chest or the back of the linen closet. Once, it was found by a maid in the speaker of an old gramophone player. She wore it on the most unlikely occasions and with a seemingly complete disregard for its sizeable worth. She often forgot it, leaving it in an empty Selby house from one season to the next. Or she would send it by mail to herself at her New York address weeks before leaving Selby, with no one at the other end to claim it.

Then, in 1964, two equally precious and fabled stones were stolen in an infamous burglary: the 100-carat oval DeLong Star Ruby; and the Star of India, a sapphire of over 500 carats.

They were ransomed together for $25,000. Remarkably, they were returned intact. The DeLong Ruby was placed in a designated phone booth drop in Florida. The next day, the Star of India was found in a bus terminal locker in Miami. Two days later, police were directed to a church in Savannah, Georgia, where the Faith Ruby was in a brown paper sack behind the altaår.

"So it was stolen at the same time as the others?" I asked a little confused.

"Oh no, that's the mystery," I was told. "The Faith Ruby was never stolen."

While the original 12-point, 90-carat Carolina Star Ruby was carelessly, yet undeniably, in the custody of its rightful owner, 84-year-old Lottie Louise Faith, an absolutely identical gem was being "recovered" in a small church more than 200 miles away. The two stones were indistinguishable from each other. Experts found no variances.

I marveled that I didn't remember hearing anything about it at the time. And then I was reminded of the times – assassinations, peace marches, space travel, civil rights. A small town mystery and a ruby that wasn't stolen were easily dismissed by most of the world.

SIX

To the residents of Selby, the past is more than history, it is ancestry. It is simply a compilation of family stories, told and retold, from one generation to the next. It's old brown photographs framed in silver on the piano. It's grandmother's dishes and the family home and ancient trees planted ages ago that still shade the porch and scrape the knees of children who climb them today. It's stables that have never been without horses and hay and Jack Russell Terriers. It's gardens that have their roots in the 1800s and their fresh-cut blossoms on this evening's dinner table. It's an unbroken thread of memories and families and love.

Because of this continuous flow of time in Selby – indeed, throughout the South – the distinction between past and present often becomes blurred. Sometimes, a residue of the past becomes superimposed over the present in a decidedly unique manner.

I had been in the midst of some of the most intriguing old family remembrances that evening, and was enjoying the short walk home, hearing them again in my mind. Ever the gentleman, Jonathan had offered to walk with me to my door, but being safe even on the street late at night was another benefit of life in Selby. So, with sincere thanks, I left him under the blue awning at the Gallery front entrance. As he turned to ascend the stairs again, I began walking south on Main Street.

At the edge of downtown, I looked up to admire the old post office building, now housing a wonderful antiques shop. The air was thick with compressed heat and crackled with lightning. Approaching thunder told me the storm would be with us quicker than I may have wished. It would be good to have the cleansing release of an old-fashioned Southern storm. But I hoped it would hold off for just a few more minutes, until I made it to my front porch.

Just then, a particularly bright flash of electricity lit the post office from behind. I saw its classic dome outlined in the brilliance. Even the ornate carvings around the base of the dome itself were etched in deep contrast. As was the human figure standing at the top near the flagpole.

I had only a few seconds to see him – or her – and in the next instant all was pitch dark. Had I really seen someone? The next flash showed me, indeed, I had. The figure was moving cautiously toward where the slope of the dome became treacherous. The obvious danger made me hold my breath. And then, the blackness again. I turned to see if I could still call out to Jonathan. But in the third lightning crack, there was no one. No human figure above or below. There may have been a light in one of the top story windows beneath the roof line of the building. Perhaps not.

Great drops of pelting rain began to hit me, and I raced to the front entrance of the post office for cover. The storm was coming out of the north, the direction the building faced, so I received little protection. Water poured over the edge of the overhang, beating the marble steps with such force that it was difficult to hear the voice at the other end of my cell phone. I had dialed 911.

I tried to explain what I had seen, but wasn't sure I was being understood or even heard. Someone must have gotten the message, however, as a patrol car pulled to the foot of the stairs less than a minute later.

My rain-drenched clothes soaked the back seat as I explained what I had seen. The two officers – one male, one female – exchanged glances. The woman smiled at me and said, "Darlin' you've just been seein' the ghost of Mr. René Robecheaux."

Apparently, Mr. Robecheaux lived in Selby and acted as its postmaster in the early 1900s. Every morning, he climbed the 37 steps from his office to the roof of the building, and then the additional 13 steps to the top of the dome, and dutifully raised the flag. At sundown, he repeated the trip to lower it.

One fateful night around 1915 or '16, René forgot. No one knew why. It was second-nature to him. But that night, the flag was allowed to remain out in the elements after dark. Sometime in the night, he must have remembered and returned to the building to correct his oversight. It had been a hot summer night, pouring rain, and very dark. He was found the next morning at the base of the front marble steps.

Always under similar weather conditions – like tonight

– about once-a-year or so, somebody reports seeing a figure on top of the old post office dome near the flagpole. The sighting only lasts a few minutes, and then the figure is gone – as if it has slipped over the edge, repeating the tragic accident of so many years before.

I was still trying to grasp what they were so calmly telling me, when I saw a light moving around inside the post office second floor.

"Look," I pointed to the window, "There is someone there, there really is."

But the officers said that the light always followed the sighting. There was never anyone there. Just the light.

Just to make sure, however, they dutifully checked the premises while I waited in the car. When they came back they said, yes, it was the ethereal light they expected. It would be gone now, as the storm was passing.

They kindly drove me home and welcomed me to Selby.

SEVEN

A lovely, aromatic rain drizzled away most of the night.
By morning, everything was freshly washed and colored. Part
of the magic of the South is how there is always something
new blooming every season – sometimes every month and for
weeks on end. After a good soaking rain in particular, there
is a virtual explosion of new blossoms and scents, which the
birds especially seem to celebrate. I awoke to a pre-dawn
party of them. They were having such a good time, it was
hard not to smile along with them, regardless of the hour.

I had to be at a book signing later that day – my first in
Selby. But it wasn't for hours. I got up anyway, and, a cup of
coffee in hand, walked the front yard.

My feet, clad only in flip-flops, were pleasurably wet from
left-over rain drops. A hint of mist was waiting to say good
morning and then disappear. The rapidly rising sun glistened

off the grass and branches that leaned low with moisture and blossoms. But as the early morning shadows began to take shape, I reconfirmed what I already knew: the entire yard desperately needed attention.

Decades of growth had taken its toll. Overgrown bushes lined each side of a lovely curving brick walkway to the front steps. But they had been allowed to have their way with the little walk, and had almost lost it entirely. Across the front of the house, on both sides of the small brick porch, stretched massive plantings. Some were brown, leaf-dead remnants of themselves. Others were so prickly it was hard to get near them. A strong offensive odor was also emanating from them, reminiscent of a visiting male cat. With a sigh of financial concern, I admitted to myself that, to begin with, all of the bushes simply had to be removed.

Then I turned my focus to closely evaluating the exterior of the house itself. Red brick with black shutters. I walked to the curb, and looked both ways up and down my street. And I saw house after sturdy red brick house.

The impressive manufacturing facility on the northwest side of town – Carolina Bricks – had been established in the late 1940s, as the post-war demand for brick, and the natural abundance of red Carolina clay in the area, offered a wonderful employment opportunity for Selby residents returning from the front. They had obviously been kept quite busy filling orders in Selby itself. In this neighborhood in particular. On this block.

I looked right and left again, on both sides of the street. Red brick with black shutters. Red brick with black shutters. Red brick with black shutters. Red brick with white shutters. A rebel among us. Red brick with black shutters. Red brick with black shutters.

Each house was architecturally different. Each yard was lovingly landscaped with individuality. But the fact remained, there were plenty of red brick with black shutters on this block. I would paint my house white. White brick with naturally stained wooden shutters – stained a warm honey-colored oak.

Returning inside, I first wrote my thank you note to Jonathan for his wonderful dinner party, and told him about my excitement on the way home. Then, I started making a list from the phone book of both house painters and landscapers to contact. I called and got some appointments scheduled. And, by then, it was time to get ready for my very first book signing in Selby. I was surprisingly nervous.

I rather like book signings. I know some authors find them tedious, but I honestly enjoy talking to people who share my love of animals and faith and books. And this one was particularly special. Because it was in Selby. And because it was for the public library.

For as long as I can remember, libraries have been an integral part of my life. It is one of the first places I go when I move to a new town. It was one of the first lessons I learned about sharing as well as the honor system. We borrow only as much as we can use – and then we bring it all back for someone else to have a turn. It's one of the few experiences in today's society that shows us we don't have to "own" something to enjoy or benefit from it. And everyone can participate.

I always thought that if I could ever write a book that would be on loan in a public library – well, then, I would truly be an author. Selling a book is wonderful. But seeing it on a long, full shelf in a public library is an experience almost beyond words. The first time it happened to me, I asked the librarian for a favor. She smiled, looked it up on the computer, and said yes, it had been checked out – several times, actually. It made my entire day.

Shortly after I had arrived in Selby, the Selby County Public Library had written to me and asked if I would join them for a "gathering of authors" that they were hosting. I was incredibly honored. Selby celebrates a large community of arts practitioners – from writers to painters, photographers to musicians. There is never a lack of opportunity to showcase one's work here. And all abilities and levels of professionalism are welcome and encouraged.

On that Saturday morning, I pulled into the library parking lot, and admired the massive old building. It had been built as the town's public high school. It had subsequently been used as a middle school, and had become the library in the late-1970s. Like so many buildings in Selby, both public and private, it had never really been remodeled; it had simply evolved from one life into the next, one purpose after another.

It still had faint well-worn school smells that greeted you hospitably at the entrance. Floor wax and old wood. Damp wool and new pencils. Rain boots and sack lunches. A musty scent, now mingled with the lovely, unmistakable smell of books.

Brass banisters were bright from repeated moist rubbings by countless young hands. Voices echoed down steep stairwells and lengthy hallways. Milky white light globes still hung suspended from heavy black chains.

The display cabinets in the entrance hall held an array of books and publications, where once they had proudly exhibited hard-won sports trophies and medals, along with long, horizontal photographs of winning teams and revered coaches and young heroes rightfully enjoying their moments in the sun. I half expected the bell to ring, warning me that it was just minutes before I was supposed to take my seat. The floorboards creaked from years of students rushing to classes, and now me – hurrying to find where I was to be located.

This time, I had arrived the prerequisite 15 minutes before I was scheduled. And I marveled at the number of people who were already there. "Great turn-out," I thought to myself. "The other authors must be much more well known than I am." As I entered the room that had been designated for the writers to be present with their books, I realized: we were all there with the same purpose – we were all "the writers."

Between 25 and 30 authors, that call Selby and its surrounding areas home, were there to sign their books. I humbly took my place at the end of one of the rows, and put out a few copies of "The God-Dog Connection." Poetry was deep on my right. Fiction was across the room. Our side outnumbered them about two-to-one, mostly with memoirs and histories of every aspect imaginable about Selby life, from horse racing to houses, Civil War days to last year's Polo Tournament. Mine seemed to be the only faith-based animal book, although there was one volume of photos featuring churches in the area and quite a few books about horses.

The atmosphere was noisy with camaraderie and mutual respect. If there were any feelings of jealously or competitiveness, it was not evident in any way. Gracious Southern manners, generous spirits, and a hint of "show and tell" filled the room. By the time the public began to arrive, I had already signed and traded several copies of my book with other writers around me.

To my immediate left, across a narrow aisle, was the editor of a marvelous little collection of "Ghosts Stories of Selby County and the Midlands of South Carolina." I couldn't wait to talk to him about my sighting the night before at the old post office.

"Macy Harris," I said, extending my right hand.

"K.C. Korngold," he replied as he accepted the handshake.

"Any relation to the composer?" I asked, referring to a once-famous Hollywood film score writer from the early and mid-1900s.

"Oh, probably," he laughed. "With a name like Korngold, we're bound to be related. But I haven't researched it very thoroughly yet. Too busy with dead people." He nodded to his book by way of explanation.

I didn't think it was probably necessary or particularly nice to point out that Korngold the composer had himself been a dead person since the late 1950s. So I told him, instead, how much I would like a copy of his book, and asked if he would be interested in trading for one of mine. He agreed, although I could tell he thought my book would not be much to his liking. So I emphasized that it made a good "gift book," and then he thought he might know someone who would appreciate it.

The exchange of goods thus accomplished, and with no one near our respective tables at the moment, I repeated the events of the evening before to K.C. in detail. He smiled and nodded throughout the entire recital. "I would love to see that for myself sometime. I'm quite jealous, you know," he said in response. For all his research and gathering of data and stories, K.C. has never actually sighted a spirit first hand, and he considers it a great disappointment in his life.

At that moment, two women arrived at our tables asking for autographed copies of each of our books. And for the next several minutes, we were both occupied with requests. It surprised me greatly, but a small queue even began to form in front of me. With my ear still not completely in tune with the melody of a Southern accent, I had to concentrate rather closely to make sure I was understanding the names correctly for inscribing the books. "Janna Steele" turned out to be "Jo Anna Still." And "My Ling" was actually May Lynne. But, for the most part, I did pretty well.

By the time I turned my attention back to my fellow author, K.C., he was deep in conversation with the person on his left. His round-lens glasses were perched on top of his head, white wisps of hair curled around the frames and over the tops of his ears. He, himself, was slightly round in build. And his skin was a soft nut-brown color, probably from living years in the Southern sun. Thumbing through his book, I discovered that he had been a professor of marine biology, and that the spirit world had only become of interest to him later in life. A hobby that took hold and wouldn't let go. His eyes glittered off the back cover photo just as they did in real life.

"You know, there's still quite a bit of controversy over what René Robecheaux was doing on the dome of the post office at that hour – and if, indeed, it was an accident that he fell." K.C.'s words startled me, as I hadn't noticed that he had finished his other conversation and was picking up ours where we had left it at least 30 minutes earlier.

"Really?" I responded with genuine surprise. "I thought he had just gone back to take in the flag, because he had forgotten to do it earlier," I said, repeating what I had heard.

"That's what most people believe," he said smiling, inviting me to ask the obvious about what he believed.

"Well," he confided, "he did have quite a 'thing' for one Miss Lottie Louise Faith at the time. Do you know about her?"

I said, yes, that I had heard all about her and her famous Carolina Star Ruby just the night before. He seemed disappointed to not be the one to acquaint me with this rich bit of historical gossip, but made up for it by telling me a titillating part of the story that had not been discussed at dinner.

Throughout a number of interruptions at both our tables to sign books and chat with people, K.C. managed to complete the tale in pieces. Lottie Louise Faith and René Robecheaux had met when she was a bride and arrived for the first time in Selby with her new husband, Abernathy – whom she called Abe. René's family had already been here for several generations.

René had spotted Lottie Louise in church, and fell head-over-heels. I could easily imagine the sun shining through a tinted, leaded-glass window, the light softly diffused and highlighting her rich auburn hair. René, as Postmaster, commanded a certain amount of respect in town, but was still considered "working class" by the majority of Winter Colony residents. Somehow, he had been introduced to Lottie (a must in society of the early 1900s), and she had greeted him as an equal thereafter. It won his heart completely. I remembered what I had heard about her kind personality and lack of adherence to certain social standards at the time. I wondered if she was just being Lottie – or might she have also been attracted to René?

The two were often seen in deep conversation – sometimes at the post office, sometimes walking in the town's lush

Laroque Memorial Gardens. Often, they were seen together at sporting events – Lottie was extremely active with Steeplechase and Riding to Hounds. These times together seemed to increase rather noticeably after Abe's unexpected death around 1910.

René was also married, but not particularly happily. In those days, however, couples typically remained married, regardless of personal feelings. K.C. didn't know much about Mrs. Robecheaux. Apparently, she didn't play a very significant role in this human drama, as far as most people were concerned.

There was some talk at the time. But nothing definite. And if the topic was ever broached with Lottie Louise, she responded with a quizzical blank look – an utter lack of understanding – followed by a flash of charm and innocence. I could just imagine, with steady blue eyes, she probably smiled politely and asked if the caller would care for a cool glass of sweet tea or lemonade. To have pursued it any further would have been very un-Southernly, lacking in good taste and manners.

The night René died is still shrouded in mystery. No amount of research on K.C.'s part could ever uncover anything more than the recorded facts. He had died of massive head injuries, as a result of a fall from the dome of the post office.

Townspeople at the time remembered seeing the flag still flying after hours – even when the storm hit. This alarming oversight and lapse in protocol was on its way to becoming a minor scandal in its own right, when the death of René superseded it. The authorities concluded that René had been trying to correct his mistake, slipped in the storm, and fell to his death. The books were closed.

But what made him "forget" the flag in the first place, K.C. wanted to know. And what was he thinking to go up there during a storm in the middle of the night? Did he want it to look like an accident? Did someone else want it to look like an accident? And then, of course, was it actually no more than a simple, tragic, unpremeditated fall?

Lottie Louise had attended the funeral for René. Most of the town did. And afterward, she had resumed her life as before; as did most of the town. Perhaps she was just a bit more eccentric. Perhaps she cut her stay in Selby a bit short that year. Perhaps it only seemed that way in retrospect.

All told, I sold 37 books that day (not counting those traded for other works). It had been a decent book signing. There would probably be more residual sales over the next few days and weeks as a direct result. But mostly, I came away from the event with an arm load of wonderful new books, an interesting new acquaintance, and a fascinating new story about this town. A town that was capturing my heart and imagination more deeply every day.

EIGHT

Over the next few weeks, I had several house painters and residential landscapers come look at my house and the bushes in the front yard. After much measuring and note-taking, "Yes, Ma'am" and "No, Ma'am," and "Are you sure you want to do that, Ma'am?" the painters sharpened their pencils and gave me some pretty good quotes. The landscaping folks, however, only wanted to remove the bushes if they could also have a rather significant contract to redesign and replant the property. But budget wise, I couldn't do both.

Then, I met William. William Jones was a highly skilled house painter who assured me he would be the most expensive, "but worth it." I never told William, but his quote was actually quite competitive with the others. I was leaning toward choosing him on self-confidence alone, and then he offered to take out all the old bushes for free. "Or maybe for

$60.00." I have no idea where he came up with that amount. But it suited me fine.

William couldn't have been over five-foot-two on his best day. And wouldn't have weighed more than 110 pounds soaking wet. But he was wiry and amazingly strong. He had been an exercise rider in his youth. A back injury had ended his career, and he seemed to accept it without rancor. The pain still plagued him at times, though, and he even missed a few days of work on my house because of it.

William was also a good talker. He could carry on a conversation with a doorknob. So I tried not to keep him thus occupied, and was glad I was paying for the job, not by the hour. If no one was around to talk, William would play the radio – but only talk shows. His personal favorite was Rush Limbaugh. I think he liked talking back to him, which he did frequently.

William was as good as his word when it came to the bushes, too. He had a friend help him – who was every bit of six-foot-six and at least 250 pounds. Despite the size difference, William was obviously in charge, giving orders to his workmate, who often did what he was told. And they had a ball.

Hedges and bushes were ripped from their roots through an ingenious method of tying a rope to the bumper of a pickup truck – dirt and rocks flying everywhere. The lawn would never recover. And the bumper came off once. But it was successful and fast and I had a pile of bushes at least six feet high and 10 feet deep at the curb by the end of the second day.

When it came to the bushes lining the walkway, however, we were confronted with a unique challenge. When the first plant was pulled loose – very reluctantly – from its 50-year-old position next to the porch steps, the entire brick walkway started to cave in. After all these years, a deep system of complex roots was probably the only thing holding it all in place.

It was finally determined to cut the bushes off as close to the ground as possible. This was not nearly as much fun. But William was committed, and did his best. Unfortunately, it left me with significant dead "stubble" lining the now wide-open little walkway.

My neighbors in the area were extremely supportive throughout this entire process. Every day, someone would come over or call out as they rode past on a bike or walked the dog:

"It look's great."

"Glad to see the change."

"You're doing a wonderful job."

I greatly appreciated the kind words of encouragement, even if I was rather alarmed about what was happening with the landscaping.

My neighbor Sally consoled me by claiming it was obviously a work in progress and that by the time we entered cooler weather, she was sure I would have a wonderful plan to begin implementing. Ed and Ruth Ann Cinkowski (who had the worst view, dead-on across the street from my property) reminded me that new planting is just as prevalent in fall as in spring in the South. They said that I had to remember I would have considerably more months yet in which to create the front yard of my dreams.

Aside from my concern over the vacant lot appearance of the front yard (the paperboy actually stopped delivering at one point, claiming he was sure no one lived there), the newly painted house itself did look grand. William was as good as he said he was. A master house painter.

And, then, there were the shutters. I could picture them perfectly in my mind, but they were proving to be rather difficult to find. Shopping is not always easy in a small town.

Then, one day, on a trip to the hardware store to see if they could recommend any new sources, I drove a slightly different route, down a street I hadn't traveled regularly, and a yard sale drew my car to the curb. I don't remember anything that was for sale that day. I was completely taken with the uniquely artistic fence that surrounded it all. It was wooden, about 4 feet high, painted barn red, and featured cut-outs in every-other slat. Hearts and birds and a variety of other shapes were outlined with great imagination and obvious love.

I commented to the man in charge of the yard sale about the wonderful fence, to which he replied: "Thanks. My wife designed and made it. She's designed a lot of fences around here. She's the artist, I just do the grunt work – the heavy stuff."

I had to ask: "Would she make some shutters, do you think?" He thought she would. And I called her that afternoon.

Rosemary is amazing. She's the kind of artist that other artists would invent, if they could. She has red hair that's naturally curly and escaping constantly from a bun gathered on the top of her head. She has at least two slender water color paint brushes and the odd pencil absently stuck in her hair most of the time. And she sports a touch of different colored paints on her knuckles and elbows. There's typically a smudge on her chin as well. She has hands that are large and creative and built to build things. Fantastically imaginative things. She wears bib overalls and sandals or shorts and plaid shirts. She's all freckles and laughter and full of fun. Her favorite word is "magic" – which she uses to great effect. And, after 15 minutes in the company of Rosemary, you do, indeed, believe in "magic."

Rosemary Johansson built my shutters just as I had imagined them. And became a lovely new friend.

9 NINE

Before Rosemary started crafting my window shutters, she shared her portfolio of artwork with me. I was so taken with her talent that I made an appointment for her with the Executive Director of the local Art Museum. It has an auxiliary arm that is deeply involved in the development and promotion of local artists and crafters. Oils, watercolors, pottery, woodworking, jewelry, pen-and-ink, photography, books (even mine), and more are all carried in the small gift shop and featured on display in the gallery. Rosemary's energetic originality seemed to be a better fit with this exhibit situation than a more formal gallery, such as Jonathan Hancock's.

I had become acquainted with the Museum's Director, Crispin Demerist, when I first took my book in to see if they wanted to carry it. Crispin had been very welcoming to me personally. She had not been in town much longer than I had, and I think she felt an affinity with someone else who was still finding her way.

I accompanied Rosemary to the gallery to make the initial introductions, and Crispin immediately agreed that Rosemary's work should be shared with a broader audience. As they began to talk seriously with the director of the local artists' gallery, I left them and wandered out into the main display room where there was an interesting new featured show.

It was primarily watercolors, some acrylics. Almost primitive in approach. There was a vivid use of color and imagination. Mostly landscapes. Haunting titles. There were multiple artists displayed. There was one in particular that caught my attention: simple clouds against an impossibly blue sky, which was called "Freedom." I found a printed brochure telling more about the hanging.

All of the works were by local patients with Alzheimer's disease. Each individual had been paired with a local artist to develop his or her original painting. The framing had been donated by all the local framers and art galleries in town. The paintings were for sale to benefit a neighborhood Alzheimer's care facility.

I walked slowly around the room and fell under the spell of each masterpiece. Regardless of its degree of professionalism, there was an originality and passion and poignancy about each of them that kept the viewer intrigued. A forest of greens, a confusion of colors. A farm scene of forgotten memories. A beach of white sand and blue-green sea that stretched into an uncertain future, a single small boat symbolically adrift. A Christmas tree.

I kept returning again and again to "Freedom," all the more meaningful now that I knew. I learned later that the artist had died peacefully just two months after she had produced this work of love. She had found her "Freedom."

As the painting was being carefully packaged for me at the gallery counter, Crispin and Rosemary joined me again. Rosemary would be bringing some of her work in for display immediately.

It was late in the day, the gallery was closing, and Crispin suggested dinner. Rosemary had to be getting home to her family, she said. But I accepted readily. I had been wanting to get to know Crispin better. She was a recent transplant from somewhere out East, but that's about all I knew.

We chose the Selby Hotel dining room, where they produce fabulous suppers six nights a week. Multiple small tables were covered in thick white table cloths and deep green cloth napkins. Vintage hotel silver complemented old-world French china. Not everything matched. It had that wonderful look of finery that has been lovingly gathered over many years. The small candle-lamp on our table leaned comfortably against the wall, one brass leg missing but still completely functional. The aromas would encourage even the most reluctant appetite. Wine was racked against the entire back wall – an obviously extensive selection. Staff moved expertly between tables and each other. They moved fast but served deliberately, as if you were their only customer.

Crispin – or "Cris" as she preferred to be called – had, indeed, moved here from Philadelphia to take the Executive Director position at the Art Museum and had some exciting plans for the not-for-profit facility. I also discovered she has a way of talking in a sort of shorthand and rather fast.

Somewhat like audible text-messaging. Actually, the speed of her speech isn't inordinately rapid, it's how she moves from one thought to the next without transition that makes it hard to follow. And she often just assumes that the listener is already familiar with an author or composer or artist or other topic that she references. I'm doing better at keeping up, as I've gotten to know her. That first evening, however, I batted about 500; I only understood half of what she was talking about. But the part I did understand was very interesting. And I could tell she was intelligent, gracious and kind. It's a first impression that has become reinforced ever since.

One of the programs in which the Museum had become a central figure is something called "Selby Nights." Held on the first Thursday of each month, all of the downtown merchants, restaurants, and art galleries stay open late into the night. The various art-based facilities have featured artists on hand to talk about their work. Wine, cheese and other light refreshments are available, too.

Spontaneous street music and plenty of alfresco dining add to the festive atmosphere. The fine South Carolina weather allows for only a few months of the year when people have to scurry from shop to shop to avoid a rain or chill. Most of the time, it's rather like one great street party. And Selby – a true town of the South – embraces any good reason to host a party. Happily, the next evening was the first-Thursday night for October.

Cris and I left the Hotel dining room just under two hours later. And, when we walked out the front door, we realized we were the last of the patrons to leave.

We also discovered that Cris rents a house just a few blocks beyond mine and had driven in, so she gave me a ride home. She drives like she talks, so we were at my door in about two minutes and I wasn't sure how we got there.

On my voice mail I had two messages waiting: One was from Rosemary, thanking me for introducing her to Cris and the Art Museum and asking me if I wanted to join her family the next night. They were going to take a walking "Ghost Tour" of downtown Selby during "Selby Nights." The second message was from my neighbor Sally, asking me if I wanted to join her the next night for a walking "Ghost Tour" of downtown Selby during "Selby Nights." It did sound like great fun, and was obviously quite popular. So I called and said yes to both of them.

Then I fed the cats and hung my new "Freedom" clouds and blue sky. I lay in bed looking at it in the soft light of a street lamp that casts a warm yellow glow through my open bedroom window. And I was lulled to sleep with a gentle Southern breeze and all the sweet Southern night sounds of Selby.

TEN

K.C. Korngold, the ghost story author from the library book signing, was the Ghost Tour guide. I should have guessed. He was the perfect blend of authority and imagination. All of the stories in his book were presented as "what if" and "could it be possible that." He never came right out and said it was absolute fact. He was, after all, a retired scientist. But one got the feeling he was a hopeful believer. In his heart at least, ghosts walk among us.

"Hello, K.C.," I said, reintroducing myself to him. He remembered me, and I also presented Sally Houseman, Rosemary Johansson, her husband Tim, and their children.

Appropriately, we had gathered for the beginning of the tour at the gate to the town's oldest cemetery. It was dusk. An evening breeze lifted leaves and shirt tales and stirred imaginations.

The gate was ornately wrought iron, squeaked perfectly and on cue. K.C. led us to the heart of the old graveyard, respectfully walking on stone pathways between the grave sites themselves. The fading light made it difficult to read the markers, but it was all I could do to pull myself along with the crowd. I wanted to stop at every one. Sally grabbed my sleeve with a tug. "I'm coming," I whispered. We were all whispering, even the children. So when K.C. started talking in a normal voice, we all jumped a bit.

"Late in the Civil War, a fierce battle was begun right here where we're standing now," K.C. stated. He then gave us a brief overview of the times, because it was important for us to understand the stage upon which this drama took place. It was February 1865. It was uncharacteristically cold. Bitter, wet, with heavy-laden fogs and red-clay mud that could swallow men and wagons whole. By this time in the war, most of the Union troops on the front lines in the South had become woefully lost from their original honor and principal. They were just tired and angry and mean. They hated South Carolina because it had been the first to secede, in essence causing the rest to follow, and for its heretofore insulated position. On their way up from Savannah, Georgia, they stole everything from food and horses, to family portraits and children's toys, to church funds and silver communion chalices; they called it "foraging." That which they couldn't carry they burned and destroyed. They readily captured people of color, free or not, and sold them into Jamaican slavery. This was the standard during that saddest of times. This was the fear that preceded them into Selby.

K.C. resumed his story. "Right where we're standing now, the dreaded Blue Coats entered Selby. They sauntered into what they thought was an inconsequential little town – a village that would provide them with food and other supplies, while they quickly disposed of significant Confederate mills and a large ammunitions stronghold a few miles to the west. The townspeople of Selby and one Confederate brigade were all they faced.

"But men and muskets hid silently behind these very trees," K.C. described, as he pointed to the giant live oaks that still encircle the cemetery and stretch great boughs of shade like a dome across the grounds. "They extended down both Pine Avenue and Oak Lawn," he continued, noting two primary east-west parkways in downtown that border the cemetery.

"When the first of the Yankee troops were well within the center of town, the soldiers stepped out and surrounded them. Desperate, hand-to-hand fighting ensued. The Yankees were driven back, away from the munitions and other targets, and away from the town. It was a terrific victory – but dearly won. Casualties on both sides remain in this cemetery and churchyards throughout town.

"This battle occurred in February. Two months later, in April of 1865, General Robert E. Lee signed the conditions of surrender. And today, passers-by and those who live near this churchyard hear a faint, yet unmistakable, Rebel Yell – just at sundown and just at one time of year. It seems to be coming from the headstones themselves – coming from all directions and no direction. As I said, it happens at just one time of year – not in February when the battle took place – but in April, the anniversary of the surrender of the South."

We stood silent. Perhaps listening for that hauntingly sad echo from the past, even though it was October. Then someone said softly, "Wow." And the spell was broken. And

K.C. told us to follow him to the next ghostly stop on the tour.

The spirits of Selby seem to particularly favor a few select ages in the town's history – at least according to K.C.'s research and tour. They include the time of the town's founding around 1830, the Civil War era in the early 1860s, and the bustling expansion years of the Winter Colony from about 1900 to 1925.

The next Ghost Tour stop that night found us peering over the edge of a bridge that drops 30 feet onto a railroad track. We followed the beam of K.C.'s industrial-strength flashlight as it eerily illuminated the tracks below.

A working railroad line travels along the edge of downtown Selby, which has been there since the beginning. In fact, most historians give credit to easy accessibility by rail for Selby's early prosperity. But there were natural elevations with which to contend, and less-than-powerful train engines at that time. In the end, ingenious and determined engineering found a way to reach the desirable high ground of Selby, without building any major inclines. To lay the tracks, they sliced down into the ground creating deep furrows – somewhat like long toaster slots. The tracks themselves remain virtually level, while the ground around them swells and rises and dips with its natural topography. Near the outside edge of the town limits, the ground lowers again to expose the tracks at surface level. Under the bridge on which we were standing is the steepest point of descent in town. The rocks and vines that cling to the sides of the topless tunnel below cast thick and very black shadows in the artificial light. We all clutched the bridge railing like a bunch of sick sailors, cautiously leaning over the edge – perhaps to see better, I suspect also to enjoy a bit of height-induced thrill.

Then K.C. told his story. In the late 1830s, a young woman from Boston, suffering from weak lungs and general ill health, was brought to Selby by her family for the healing waters and fresh air. Her name was Sarah. Sarah and her family took a house just up the hill from this bridge, K.C. pointed out. Not far, although it no longer exists there now.

Sarah left behind her an anxious fiancé, who had been her best friend since childhood. His name was Charles. In an attempt to keep in close contact with her, Charles wrote to Sarah every day, and visited regularly with her cousins and extended family in Boston seeking any news they might receive.

Because of her precarious health, however, Sarah's father decided to withhold the young man's letters from his daughter until she was stronger, to avoid the possibility that they would make her miss her young lover all the more, which might agitate her condition. Of course, this attempt to calm her had the opposite effect, and she began to weaken from depression. To complicate matters, word did reach her that Charles was spending a great deal of time in the company of her cousins – one of them a beautiful young woman their own age. Sarah became inconsolable and developed a frightening fever.

At that same time, Charles decided to leave Boston and come to Selby to see Sarah for himself – regardless of what her father had to say about it. He took the first train out. The trip took longer than two days by rail back then and, as he traveled, Sarah's condition worsened. On the second night, she became extremely agitated, and rose from her bed. Somehow slipping past her nurse and the servants, clad only in her thin white nightgown, she walked out into the damp night air – falling into the deep abyss of these very train tracks

– directly in front of the engine that was bringing her young man to see her.

Her long white gown can sometimes still be seen whipping in the breezes of a passing train, descending closer and closer to the tracks. While the broken voice of her devastated lover calls her name, echoing on the wind after the train whistle blows in the distance.

Fortunately, no train came by just at that moment.

The next stop on the tour was the old Selby post office. K.C. related the history of René Robecheaux, the rainstorm and René's subsequent fall, just as it had been told to me. He even invited me to add my bit of recent experience, and for a few minutes, I was quite the celebrity.

The post office was followed by two stops with fascinating stories involving fires. Then, we heard about one mysterious curse, two suicides, an ill-fated love triangle (complete with an Old Southern duel at dawn), and even one ghost dog – a beloved pet that had passed quietly from old age and had been buried under a favorite tree on the property, but whose familiar bark still alerted the family to impending danger.

Perhaps the most intriguing tale that night was one that is cloaked in mystery even today. A lone woman moved to Selby in the early 1910s. She was exceptionally beautiful, but appeared to be very, very sad. No one knew her or anything about her. She brought no formal introductions. And in the South, in a small community, in the early 1900s, this was naturally a subject for much speculation and discussion at dinner tables and on porch swings all over town.

The woman apparently had means; she purchased one of the largest estates in the area with cash. She lived there alone. Her clothes and shoes came from New York. And she received occasional letters from abroad. But while she was in Selby, she never went to parties, never had guests, always dined alone. Even her staff was minimal and silent about their mistress, if, indeed, they knew anything about her themselves. She was, however, a talented and dedicated horsewoman. She rode daily, for miles, for hours on end. Her favorite mount was a large, all-white mare.

One day, she rode out as usual, but when dusk came, she didn't return. Her staff alerted the neighbors, and people went out with torches, on foot and on horseback, and called and looked all night. The next morning her horse came back lame but with no sign of her rider. For days, the town continued to search. Authorities were called in. Even other towns sent dogs and riders and hikers, but with no result. She had simply disappeared.

The estate eventually fell to ruin, with no inheritors, no will, no hard evidence that the owner was actually deceased. I could well imagine the cobwebs and spiders and thick, dank vines that might have invaded the house and eroded the bricks and mortar. Weeds would have filled the once fragrant flower gardens, and wrapped around lampposts and fences. I could almost smell the damp as it must have crept up the walls from un-mended roof leaks. Rugs disintegrating on the floors. Furniture molded and warped. Windows broken by loose pebbles and passing boys on their way to school. Perhaps it became a child's dare.

K.C. said when the property legally reverted to the town, sometime in the 1930s, it was sold off in three smaller parcels. Then, with the tearing down of the old, crumbling buildings, and the construction of new homes and landscapes, the sightings began: A woman on horseback – on an all-white horse.

It continues even today. Just before dawn, the mysterious woman can be seen riding back and forth across the very place where the original stables had stood. She rides to the old home front steps and back. She rides as if she is searching for something, looking for a place to dismount. She rides as if she is trying to come home.

And with that, K.C. bid us good night.

We all shivered and called out our thanks – as we walked ever so quickly to the nearest bright lights and gathering of people on the street who were enjoying some of the other attractions of "Selby Nights."

Some of the brightest lights were reflecting from the Art Museum and its local artists' gallery, so we went inside there first. Cris was busy greeting visitors and talking to potential patrons; I just waved as we made our way to the refreshments table. Cheese and crackers, mini quiches and cookies were all attractively displayed and quite popular. Wine and soft drinks were available at a cash bar, and punch was free.

Rosemary and her family ran into other friends and began talking. Sally was captivated by the Alzheimer's hanging. So I excused myself and slipped out to visit the Hancock Gallery again just down the street.

Jonathan was also busy greeting people, giving short tours. But he took the time to greet me personally and make me feel as if he had been waiting just for me.

Four or five artists were present in front of their works. Most were engaged in conversations with admirers or prospective investors or each other. One stood apart, alone. Jonathan nodded to him and whispered, "Go meet him. I think you'll like his work."

The artist was about 50 years old. He looked as if he would rather have been anywhere on earth other than standing where he was tonight. He gazed down at the floor. He stuck his finger in his drink glass and stirred the melting ice cubes. He sighed. He wore a plaid shirt buttoned to the collar but with no tie. A worn brown jacket topped dark trousers that drooped alarmingly over his scuffed shoe tops. His hair may have been cut at home. No one would have looked twice at this man in a grocery store checkout lane. The sign near his work introduced him: Darrell Pickins. In an apparent attempt to add a bit of legitimacy and sophistication to the name, a middle initial had been added. It didn't help: Darrell P. Pickins.

Because of Jonathan's cryptic urging, as well as a combination of curiosity and courtesy, I walked over to Mr. Darrell P. Pickins and said: "Good evening."

He said, "Hey."

"Is this your work?"

"Uh-huh."

I began to look at his paintings. They were amazing. They were surreal, but used an almost "old masters" realism approach to the individual elements within them – mostly single or paired pieces of fruit or flowers. One orange. Two pears. A single dying rose. A strawberry coiled with a bit of satin ribbon. For the most part, each of the paintings was on a field of solid black, with the richly colored fruit or flower offset in a corner or within the top one-third of the canvas. None was framed. To do so would have ruined their stark beauty.

None of his canvases was over 18 inches square. And most were square. Somehow, there was a very dark-side humor about them. An off-center loveliness. A purity. Even the fact that the forms rarely varied – oranges, pears, roses, ribbons – gave the entire body of work a great "Alice in Wonderland" kind of appeal. I was an immediate fan. But they were priced well beyond my reach. I had the feeling Mr. Darrell P. Pickins didn't actually care whether he sold his paintings or not.

"I love your work," I told him.

"Thanks," he said.

"Do you have a studio nearby?"

"I have a barn."

"You really do hate being here, don't you?" I sympathized.

"Yes, Ma'am."

"You'd rather be painting?"

"Yes, Ma'am."

"Well, I wish I could afford to buy something. I really do like it."

"Yes, Ma'am."

"It was nice meeting you."

"Yes, Ma'am."

I left poor, uncomfortable, talented Mr. Pickins and went to look through the rest of the Gallery. Lots of new and interesting work. But nothing to compare to the originality and appeal of Darrell P.'s, I thought.

I was looking for Jonathan again to tell him thank you, when Sally found me and told me the Johanssons were taking the kids home to bed. We went back downstairs and decided to get a slice of handmade pizza in one of the Alley restaurants.

Back on the street, the unmistakable aroma of boiled peanuts wafted down from the corner where a vendor was selling steaming sacks full for a dollar.

"Oh, boiled peanuts," Sally said turning toward the source. "Want some?"

"I'll wait for the pizza," I told her. So she said she'd be right back and headed for the small, red, wheeled cart.

Boiled peanuts are an acquired taste, I have decided. Most long-time Southerners absolutely love them, associating them with fond childhood memories. But for some of us newcomers, the dark musty flavor and consistency of an over-cooked lima bean isn't an immediate hit.

Suddenly, there were sirens – increasing in sharp intensity – interrupting conversations and capturing the attention of just about everyone on the street. First blue then red swirling lights swung into view and came to an abrupt stop just half a block up from where I was standing. There was a black and white patrol car, then a ladder-stacked fire truck. Then another fire truck. And yet another.

Officers ran into Trotters Pub. Almost immediately, patrons started walking rapidly out. Most of them were clutching their dinner plates and beer glasses as if they were at some over-ambitious cocktail party. With napkins tucked into belts and over arms, they continued to eat standing on the sidewalk. There was some waving of forks and pointing of knives as they obligingly described to an anxious gathering crowd what was happening inside.

Soon, word filtered down the block that smoke had been detected on the second floor – possibly an electrical problem. They were evacuating everyone as a precaution. Yellow tape appeared, enclosing the front sidewalk and entrance to the

Pub.

Just then, the manager of the Selby Hotel came out of the hotel dining room leading some of their staff. They began laying fresh tablecloths on their unused outside tables, and the manager walked up to invite the dispelled patrons to come use their facility – where they would be comfortable, out of harm's way, and out of the way of the firefighters. Hotel employees helped the diners re-lay their places, while staff from the Pub simply walked the two doors down to continue serving them. It was probably the most precise, gracious and thoroughly Southern show of hospitality I had ever witnessed. And it was utterly Selby.

In downtown Selby, the historic buildings touch and lean against one another along entire blocks, with wooden frames and floors and old shingled roofs. A fire could be tragic. It could happen in a heartbeat. It could devastate us. I thought about what a fire could mean to a place like Jonathan Hancock's Art Gallery where I had just been. But the Selby Public Safety officers know our vulnerability. And they are quick to react and they are conscientious. And they kept us safe that night.

Soon, the caution tape was removed, the trucks were reloaded, and a couple of the still-yellow-clad firefighters were studying the menu taped in the Selby Hotel window, discussing where to bring their families to eat on Sunday.

Sally and I continued on our way to order pizza.

We walked a short distance to the mouth of a wide brick alley between two Main Street stores. It's called, appropriately enough, "The Alley," and it's lined with some of the best little restaurants in town. It's about a car-width wide, with sidewalks on both sides. Although it is an approved throughway for auto traffic, very few cars venture down it. It's typically frequented by people on foot and the occasional horse or carriage.

The two-story solid brick walls of the buildings that flank the entrance to The Alley provide huge canvases for imaginative and colorful murals. No one seems to remember when or by whom they were done. They've just always been there. Permanently painted. More fun than professional. Now, flower-filled climbing vines compete with them for attention.

Past the open courtyard of one restaurant, past the open front door of a bar and grill, past another small slit of an alleyway that runs from a side street into the main Alley, sits a small Italian pizzeria – all red and white checks and neon signs and marvelous smells. It's nestled low under tree limbs and ivy and one old-fashioned street lamp. In front, a bike was resting against the trunk of a tree. A cat was lounging in a windowsill. There were more customers eating at the tables in the fenced side yard than within the little shop itself on this fine October night.

"Hand-tossed ... homemade ingredients ... sold by the slice," the sign said. A tall, slender young man called out a welcome as we walked through the door. Another brought us ice water in large plastic glasses. We sat in mismatched chairs at a table that wobbled just right. I don't remember when any food ever smelled so good. And tasted better than it smelled.

When neither of us could hold another bite, and the tabletop was filled with sauce-stained napkins and an embarrassing number of empty plates, we paid our bill, complained about eating too much, and both yawned at the same time.

"I think I need to go home," Sally confessed. I would have joined her, but I had spotted a used book table in front of the local book store earlier, and wanted to swing by it before I called it a night.

"See you tomorrow," Sally called out as she waved over her head and started the short walk home.

"See you," I responded as I headed in the other direction toward the bookseller's.

I chastised myself that I should have come earlier, as I looked at the picked-over remains on the table. There were a couple of children's books that looked unimaginative even on the covers. There was a travel book that was incredibly dated, but not old enough to be fun or historically interesting. There were several "how-to" paperbacks – home improvement, body shaping, and auto repair. And a few fairly recent releases about former presidents and business moguls. Almost lost, at the bottom of the stack, there was an old hardcover book without a jacket. Just the kind I like. It was slim and the color of washed denim. It was about the Underground Railroad. I had been wanting to study the topic more thoroughly since moving to the South. This would be the perfect way to begin.

I had just snapped the book shut from a quick review, when a fellow late shopper at my side said, "Not much of a selection left, is there?" I looked up into the handsome face of a very tall, very elegant gentleman with just a hint of an equally elegant Southern accent.

"Not much," I agreed smiling back.

His gray-white hair was trimmed neatly. His blue eyes were perceptive and intelligent, with laugh lines etched deeply at the corners. He had an even, light tan, artistic hands, and white teeth that filled a charming smile.

"My name's Charlie McEwan," he said offering me his hand. I introduced myself, too. I told him I was new to town and how much I enjoyed life in Selby. He welcomed me, and said he was glad I had chosen this place where he had grown up, and then he recognized my name from the newspaper columns. He was complimentary and gracious.

"What book have you chosen?" he asked. I showed him the title. To which he reminded me that Selby had quite an active part in the underground process. He said for me to be sure to check out the local historical museum as well as several of the churches relative to the topic.

He quickly picked up one of the biographies of a former president: "One of my passions," he explained.

"Biographies or presidents?" I asked. He replied that they both seemed to be.

We walked into the store to pay for our respective finds at the same time. The Southern gentleman held the door and preferred that I go ahead of him.

I paid my two dollars, turned to tell him good night, and then left. Just as the shop door was closing shut behind me, I heard the clerk say: "Hello, Mr. Mayor. Nice to see you tonight. Another biography I see."

Mr. Mayor. Of course. Charlie McEwan. The honorable Charles McEwan. I had heard the name, but had forgotten it, and had never seen him before in person. "Idiot," I threw at myself. "You dolt."

What I regretted most was that I had missed my chance to tell him what an admirer I am of his work as Mayor of Selby.

One of the things I noticed when I drove around downtown Selby for the very first time was a series of dark blue flags that hang from the lampposts at every corner. On each flag are the words: "Character First" – followed by a list of character traits: Sincerity, Respect, Self-Control, Responsibility, Attentiveness, Loyalty, Compassion, Citizenship, Truthfulness, Courage, Patience, and Forgiveness. Under the leadership of Mayor Charlie McEwan, Selby had declared itself a town of Character. And dedicated itself to these qualities. It touched my heart so deeply then, as it does still today. I wanted to tell him that. I wanted to let him know how meaningful I thought that was in today's world. I wanted to tell him thank you. It's a small town, I thought. Perhaps there will be another opportunity.

As I walked home in the night, a breathtaking full moon lit my way. Contrary to what we know about astronomy and the laws of nature, I swear the moons in South Carolina are either perfectly crescent-shaped or perfectly round and full – they don't seem to go through all the stages in between. Here, they seem to simply alternate, one to the next and back again, each as magnificent and romantic as the other. Even the stars here appear more numerous and brighter and closer somehow.

The thick smell of pine all around me and a rich yellow full moon above slowed my walk to a stroll as I traveled the few blocks to my porch. I sat on my front steps awhile and listened and watched and tucked this night away in my memory for safe keeping.

And I reflected that, from this evening alone, there would be no shortage of topics for my columns for weeks and weeks to come.

ELEVEN

About a month after "Selby Nights," another after-dark feature came to town. And I was soon to discover the flip side of Selby's night life.

Her name was La Femme Angelique.

La Femme Angelique was a wonderfully flamboyant and effective female impersonator who had become nationally famous from a convincing bit part she played in a movie set in her hometown of New Orleans. She stole every scene she was in. Almost overnight, Miss Angelique rose from being a star in the back streets to stardom in the mainstream. And she was coming to perform in Selby. She was appearing, for one night only, at Selby's one and only gay bar.

I had somehow missed the announcement in the paper. So when Sally called, she caught me by surprise. "We have got to do this," she began.

"Do what?"

"Haven't you seen today's paper?" she asked.

"Yes. But I still don't know …"

"Didn't you ever see that movie that takes place in New Orleans where that guy gets killed? It was a mystery… a really dark thriller. You remember, that one where there was that performer La Femme Angelique?" she kept prodding. "That female impersonator."

"Oh yeah," I remembered, even though I realized that pretty much any movie set in New Orleans is going to be a mystery, really dark, and someone is going to get killed. But the name triggered the memory. It was – she was – rather unforgettable.

"We have got to do this," Sally repeated. "We have to go see her for sure. It's this Saturday night, and it's at Lucky's on the other side of town."

I agreed immediately that it was an opportunity not to be missed. I had never been to Lucky's – or "the other side of town," for that matter. But Sally said she knew where it was, and would drive, and suggested we get some more people to go with us and make it a party. I said I thought that, too, was an excellent idea.

Apparently, just about everyone else in town had the same excellent idea. Everyone had seen the ad. Everyone thought it would be great fun. Everyone seemed to be going. With a few exceptions.

I had called Cris to see if she wanted to join us, but she was concerned that someone in her position as the Executive Director of a "rather conservative organization" probably shouldn't be attending a performance of that nature. Of course, she was right, but I was glad I didn't personally have any image to uphold. I had also asked Jonathan if he wanted to come, but he said the Southern gentleman equivalent to "not with a ten-foot pole." He also advised us to sit or stand near a fire exit. He didn't elaborate.

Ed and Ruth Ann Cinkowski were going to be out of town. But when I contacted Rosemary Johansson, she and Tim both said they absolutely wanted to be part of the group. Sally had also gathered together an ex-sister-in-law, Barbara, and Barbara's sister, Patty, who was visiting from Chicago.

The performance wasn't scheduled to start until 11:00 p.m. And that was the early show. So we met at 8:00 p.m. for a leisurely late supper.

Everyone agreed on a small bar and restaurant near Lucky's. I had not even been aware of its existence before that night, but it looked friendly and fun and full of patrons. As we entered, a long-haired white cat walked in with us. The hostess picked him up and gently set him down outside again. This became a ritual throughout the evening. He would wait patiently until someone entered or left through the front door, he would walk in without even trying to be unseen, someone would pick him up and set him outside. In the process, however, he attracted much sympathetic attention. Consequently, he received much sympathetic food. A con-cat.

We were seated at a large table near the front window. The hostess said someone would be taking our drink orders shortly. Ten minutes passed. We were having fun, talking, laughing. Fifteen minutes passed. We started looking around. About half the other customers were also waiting. And we didn't even have our menus yet. Twenty minutes passed. We talked some more and laughed some more. Almost 25 minutes. The hostess kept disappearing for long periods of time into the kitchen and, aside from one over-extended bartender, there seemed to be no other waitstaff on the premises.

Tim got up and found some menus and brought them to us. He also good-naturedly provided them for people at other tables. Rosemary then asked each of us what we wanted to drink and she and I went to the bar to fill the order. On the way back, another patron jokingly said, "We'd like some ice tea, please." So a different customer who was sitting near the ice tea pitchers picked one up and served everyone who raised their hand.

Finally, one rather frantic waitress came hurrying in and apologized for the long delays. She started taking orders, and everyone remained inexplicably patient and kind and good natured. It had become rather like a private dinner party – or a private joke – that everyone was invited to enjoy.

An hour or so later, we were served rather mediocre food. Most of it was what we had ordered. We were still having a great deal of fun, and we had plenty of time to fill before the evening's entertainment, so it all seemed appropriate somehow.

By way of dinner conversation, I began to tell our little party about the book I had just bought and the research I had been doing about the Underground Railroad. I asked if any of them knew about the existence of the organization in early Selby.

Sally, Rosemary and Tim were aware that the practice had existed here. But Barbara turned out to be an unexpected source of real knowledge. "Kind of a pet interest of mine," she explained.

"So tell me," I encouraged.

"Well," she looked around the table and encountered

interested faces, so continued, "one of the places where it got its start in Selby – well, all over the country, really – was through the Quakers. They were very opposed to slavery, and were a tightly knit community made up of people that could trust each other."

Based on my own research, I added the observation that many Quakers were also on the move at that time – out of the South to the new frontiers of the West.

"Right," Barbara chewed, swallowed, and nodded. "And some of the escaping people were sent along with Quaker families who were already moving or in a wagon train, so they got them smuggled away relatively safely that way."

"But I didn't know Selby had a Quaker church," I said.

"It doesn't now," Barbara responded. "But back before the Civil War there was a prominent Quaker community here. It was way out in the country back then. And it's really sad to realize, but they eventually all left because of the slavery issue. South Carolina went with the Confederacy, remember. They really kind of started it all."

"But the Quakers weren't the only ones," Tim chimed in. "A lot of other people helped, too."

"Oh, sure they did. Sometimes, whole churches got involved. But mostly, they were just individuals who had compassion and felt morally obligated to do something. Or someone was just in the right place at the right time."

"And some did it for money," Patty added.

"That, too," Barbara admitted. "But mostly it was done by prominent members of several of the local churches – although there aren't any records that I'm aware of, so it's kind of hard to know to what extent. Rumor has it that members of the Presbyterian church were some of the more active."

"Yea!" I said. "I'm Presbyterian," I explained to the looks I got. "First Pres. ... downtown ..."

"How about the Methodists?" Rosemary asked.

"And the Catholics?" chimed in Tim.

"Yes ... and ... don't know," Barbara answered them respectively with a laugh.

She turned to me again, "Seriously, I'm pretty sure the Presbyterian Church did play a part in the Underground Railroad in Selby. You ought to look into it, if you're really interested."

"Are we ever going to get a bill," Tim finally broke the thread of conversation and brought us back to the present.

We had already been served coffee by the couple sitting two tables over. And, looking at our watches, we decided we needed to be on our way to Lucky's. But the hostess and the one lone waitress had both disappeared again. So we sought out the bartender, individually told him what we had had to eat and drink, and he rang up a bill for each of us. The waitress even got tipped in absentia. And, of course, con-cat got a variety of takeout.

We walked the two additional blocks to Lucky's.

The club was set in the midst of a number of small, weed-encrusted warehouses and seemingly abandoned businesses. Here, the same globe street lamps that grace downtown proper with vintage appeal just looked old and dusty and dim. They created deep, dark shadow pockets and hidden doorways. Our voices sounded too loud. Our feet crunched across a partially graveled, uneven parking area between giant old tree trunks.

Some of the parked cars seemed to have been there for a very long time. Rust, flat tires, cracked windows. But, squeezed in among them that night, there were an impressive number of BMWs, Lexuses, and a Mercedes or two. Big luxury cars, small economy compacts, SUVs, pickup trucks, PT Cruisers.

"Look," Tim pointed to a handicapped license plate.

"Here's another," Sally laughed.

We decided La Femme Angelique had a wide and age-diverse following.

The music was both muffled and loud, and filled the night air approaching the door. An old-fashioned barn light hanging high on the wall threw circles of harsh halos to show the way. We entered through the back door to the building, which was actually the "main entrance" to the club. A haze of smoke billowed through the open doorway. I thought about Jonathan's warning, but smelled only cigarettes and cigars.

We stepped into a small cubby hole. About five feet across from the exterior door were interior swinging doors, barely closed around the bodies already pressed inside. To the left a few feet was a glass-fronted counter where a man was taking money for the cover charge. It had been raised to $10.00 that night in honor of the famous performer.

We made our way to the counter, paid our fees, and got our hands stamped with something that was red and smudged, but it was too dark to see anyway. "Ah, yes. Something with which to embarrass myself in church tomorrow," I thought.

Once inside, strobe lights emitted dizzying flashes of glaring colors, giving an unreal ambiance to everyone and everything. Music throbbed against our eardrums and chests. Small tables and a few dozen chairs were filled beyond capacity – with two people sharing each chair where possible.

The rest of us stood on the bare concrete floor anywhere we could.

A small dance floor was marked off with large-linked plastic chains at the far end of the room; an even smaller stage was at the far end of that. A few couples were dancing self-consciously. Behind the stage hung a collection of homemade curtains – black and glittery and dusty and rather sad, with worn hand prints and duct-taped holes. A make-shift dressing room was draped not far behind. It was all somehow reminiscent of children putting on a talent show in their parents' basement.

The music was sourced by a live D.J. playing recorded discs and tapes from a slightly raised platform to one side of the stage.

Along the left side of the room was a long bar crowded two and three people deep. Three or four bartenders were hustling madly, but were woefully outnumbered by would-be customers.

Tim shouted something that was probably asking if anyone wanted a drink. We hollered back and shoved money at him, but it would be interesting to see what he brought to us. And when. Rosemary decided to help him and squirmed her way through the crowd in his wake. So Sally, Barbara, Patty and I inched as close as we could to the stage. In honor of Jonathan, I kept my eye out for the nearest fire exit.

Since casual conversation was out of the question, I had a chance to look over the crowd around me. A more incongruous, unexpected, and eclectic mix of individuals was probably never gathered in one room before. The man right next to me looked like someone you would cast to play a school principal. The man on his right was dressed all in black and had more tattoos than bare skin. There were grandmas and grandpas with white hair and hearing aids, wearing Bermuda shorts and sandals. Twenty-somethings graciously gave up their chairs to them. There was a gorgeous blond black woman dressed for an elegant evening out. At least I was pretty sure it was a woman. Height suggested not, but cleavage said yes. Lots of middle-aged, middle-class couples – both gay and straight, black and white, dressed in khakis and jeans and polo shirts. Young gay men in tank tops and tight pants. Young gay women in tank tops and tight pants. And all were having a wonderful time.

Those who appeared to be straight vastly outnumbered those who appeared to be gay. And, by the size of the room, it was obvious that this was a huge influx in patronage. So what impressed me the most was the way in which the "regulars" of this club welcomed those of us who crashed the gates this evening in search of something out of our ordinary. Barely invited, we took their seats and tables and made them wait in line. And, in return, they were gracious and patient and showed us thoughtful and good natured hospitality.

Eleven o'clock had come and gone. The music was unceasing. The air was becoming increasingly choked with body heat, smoke, the smell of beer and whiskey, and anticipation. Everyone was anxiously watching the stage, but there were no announcements, no warm-up acts, and no La Femme Angelique.

In spite of the unexplained delay, we were a well-behaved crowd. No one was even complaining about the standing-room-only or the closeness of our fellow patrons. And no one was leaving. More and more people were dancing. Individuals were asking others to dance whom they seemed not to even know. And the invited accepted. Singles danced in groups. Groups did a form of line dancing. A very large family wedding on New Year's Eve couldn't have put on a better floor show.

One man who had been sitting in front of me turned and looked me over. He stood up with a smile and shouted in my ear, "Why don't you stand on my chair so you can see better." I took him up on the offer.

At one point, Rosemary thought she saw the diva winding her way through the crowd toward the dressing room. A tiny bit of a thing she was. Dressed to the teeth. We caught a glimpse of her, but couldn't be sure.

Around midnight, the strobe lights suddenly ceased their dizzying swirl. Spot lights took over, aimed at the stage. A drum roll, and the curtains bulged and bumped and finally split open to reveal the first act stepping on stage. Her name was Miss Belle. Miss Belle was dressed like a black market Barbie Doll. She started to talk to the crowd. She was painfully nervous. It was obvious that she was overwhelmed by the numbers, but wanted desperately to perform her best for us. So we all felt sorry when something went wrong with her music. She was supposed to lip-sync to a number that the D.J. couldn't seem to find, although he was trying very hard to locate it.

She finally left the stage, and we gave her supportive applause as she climbed the steps to the sound booth to try to straighten things out herself. We waited quietly, kindly. At last, she suggested the next act go on, and she would come back. We applauded her again.

A couple of seconds later, new music blasted from the speakers and Miss Kitty came into view. She was tall, all in black, long-legged in fish-net stockings. Her height was accentuated by a plumy feather headdress. She looked a bit like a Vegas show girl on a budget. Another lip sync number. This time, the tape was fine, and the performer executed her act without a stumble. It wasn't a long performance, but interesting.

Then, the first act came back on stage: Miss Belle. She had apparently found her tape – or she had substituted something else. We couldn't tell and didn't need to know. I kept expecting her to take off her clothes in some sort of strip tease – but then realized that would have defeated the whole purpose. This was my first female impersonator revue. I was learning. When she ran off stage, we applauded her as much for her moxie as for her talent, I think.

Finally, the drum roll again – long and sustained. And out stepped La Femme Angelique herself. She sparkled from head to toe, both in costume and in personality. No bigger than a minute, she had a waist the size of a dime, and a full-length gown to accentuate it. It was emerald green, strapless, and slit up one side almost to her waist. Four-inch spike heels showed off her slender legs. She had a close-fitting cap of matching green sequins over bobbed black hair, sleek and shining in the spotlight. Her skin was the color of smooth cocoa. We were a good 15 or 20 feet from the stage, but her smile dazzled into even the deepest corners of the crowd. The applause and whistles went on and on. And she reveled in it. She held the microphone in slender, graceful hands with long blood-red-painted fingernails.

When she spoke, her voice was like smoke and mirrors. It sounded thick and husky, yet softly feminine – because it seemed to be coming from the lipsticked mouth of a lovely, smooth-cheeked woman. She charmed the crowd. She joked with us and laughed with us. She laughed a bit at us, too, but we didn't mind. She did it with such warmth and grace.

Out of the audience, different fans crept quietly on stage, moving hesitantly to her side, right in the middle of her act. They wanted their pictures taken with her. She never missed a beat, and smiled and hugged them as the cameras flashed and she kept up her singing or her banter. A few people shyly brought forward dollar bills – or possibly bills of greater denominations – and she said thanks with a throaty chuckle and tucked them enchantingly into her bodice.

She sang for herself – no lip-syncing for this star. She changed costumes two more times, and each ensemble was more lovely and exotic than the last, yet remarkably modest. Full-length gloves, a cut-away cape, long trains. Wigs and hairstyles and hair colors changed with each outfit. She did not look like a girl on a budget. She was thoroughly gracious and, somehow, a "real lady." La Femme Angelique was undeniably, albeit unaccountably, a class act.

During Miss Angelique's costume changes, other regular acts – of different colors, sizes and degrees of talent – took the stage. As the night progressed, the language and jokes and dancing degraded a bit and became rather rough. However, during her last number, the star explained that this "early" show was still considered the "G" rated version. So, if we were going to stay for the late show, she warned, we had better be prepared.

We clapped and whistled and called out for "more" with the rest of the crowd when she was done around 1:00 or 1:30 a.m., and we knew we shouldn't stay for what was to come. A large portion of the patrons decided the same.

We left La Femme Angelique, Miss Belle, Miss Kitty and the

other ladies in appreciative hands – returning the club to its rightful customers, and bid everybody good night.

Out in the fresh air, it all felt a bit unreal. I also felt unaccountably sticky. My hair and clothes reeked. My legs suddenly realized I had been standing for well over two hours.

We all told each other the parts we liked best in the show as we walked to our cars. Sally drove me to my back door, and I let myself in. The cats sniffed me from head to toe with great interest and more than a little disgust. I soaked for a long while in a very hot tub (the red hand stamp still refused to wash off) and I thought rather lovingly again about this remarkably diverse, always surprising town.

And I thought, too, about the unpredictable twists and courses of history. From the horrors of slavery, the courage of the Quakers and those who refused to be owned, the underground heroism of just 150 years ago – to the undeniable freedom of expression we had witnessed in Lucky's club this night by both black Americans and white, amidst an atmosphere of absolute racial and social harmony. And all of it had taken place – one extreme to the other – in one small Southern town called Selby.

I smiled as I slid down between two fresh, clean bed sheets and a couple of cats. I could still see colors strobing behind my shut eyelids and felt a slight numbness in my ears. And then I drifted into a deep and dream-filled sleep.

TWELVE

The next few weeks passed as full of memorable new experiences as the ones preceding it. I had already learned that there are several major planting seasons here and almost year-round budding. In the South, fall is every bit a new growth season as is early spring, late spring, and much of the summer.

In autumn, just as some of the long summer blossoms and scents are fading and drifting into sleep, others are waking and bringing new colors and fragrances to gardens all over town. As soon as some of the traditional annual flowers have barely reached beyond their peaks, a burst of rich velvet pansies is brought in to take their places.

Many plants that go dormant in winter up North are "evergreen" here. And some offer fresh new blooms that begin in the fall and extend well into winter. Seemingly overnight, bright berries of red, orange and white appear on lush deep green foliage – perhaps an anticipatory welcome for the birds that are beginning to arrive from more northern climates.

I had tried desperately to introduce some of this "new life" into my own front yard. With so much natural beauty surrounding me, in a town full of gardens and lawns that have been tended for decade upon decade with loving care and attention, I envisioned for myself a cool, green, shaded woodland full of trees and ivy and evergreen ferns, rich with fragrant wisteria and other flowering vines creeping over low, moss-covered garden walls. In reality, what I had – after the removal process of all the old and dying – were two rather nice winding brick walkways, set in the midst of a barren arena of scruffy grass patches, weeds, and scattered rocks.

For some unknown reason, the previous owner had removed all of the mature trees from the front of the property. So I had tried to plant new ones in their places. They looked woefully underdeveloped for the space. I had planted ivy that promptly withered and died. So did the wisteria. Earlier in the year, there had been a wonderful sale on roses at the local nursery, and I had impulsively bought half a dozen of them, planting them in front of the many low windows that grace the front of the house. Surprisingly, they didn't die. But they didn't exactly flourish. They bloomed well enough, on the ends of long, leggy, stick-like limbs with brown withery leaves. Against the otherwise red clay, rock and weed-filled backdrop, they lent a sort of haunted house look to the place.

Gardening, I must admit, has never been one of my strengths. But this had by now become a personal challenge – as well as a personal embarrassment.

To accommodate the grass that wouldn't grow, I had

tried covering the entire yard with pine straw. I had seen this done in some of the local wooded areas and found it charming. Without the wooded part of the scenario, however, pine straw tends to take on the appearance of a desert. The birdbath I added just looked pathetic. No matter what I tried, it kept getting worse. Even Sally could only utter "oh, dear," whenever she looked at it.

Mercifully, other matters won my attention away from this ongoing saga of frustration.

In autumn, in Selby, there is a noticeable increase in pace and activity. It is the beginning of the "In Season." Folks from up North have been wintering in Selby for generations, and it continues even today.

Stables become filled to capacity again. Art shows and music recitals and social activities build dramatically. The playhouse reopens with a new schedule. Some of the restaurants are available more days and longer hours. And there are horse shows and auctions, polo games and early morning track workouts. There are Saturday afternoon carriage rides, and tea parties, and debutante balls, and horses and hounds in the woods. It is perfectly lovely to be in Selby in Season.

Along with all of its uniqueness, its horses and history and the beauty of nature, Selby is also, in at least one way, a "typical" town of the South. And in the fall, in the South, there is Football.

In the South, football is a passion, rather than a pastime. Old rivalries date back to the very first game, the first victory, the first defeat. Perhaps it is the result of collective memory, but the South takes defeat personally, feels it deeply, and savors it for as long as it takes to reclaim glory. This is football played for honor.

This preoccupation permeates college ball. It encompasses pro-ball as well. But high school football reaches another level altogether. Here, emotions extend beyond the borders of a school campus or student body and engulf whole communities. For families who have graduated generation after generation from a single alma mater, the feelings and commitments rival familial pride and loyalty.

Not far from Selby there had been such a fierce rivalry between two neighboring town schools, that officials finally cancelled all future games against each other. One of the hardest to understand aspects of the intensity was the fact that most of the students were related to one another. Cousins, in laws, stepsons, half brothers. Families that would share Christmases and birthday parties and reunions and funerals, would set fire to each other's cars in the name of football.

Selby is not caught up in quite so spectacular an emotional fervor. Humor often prevails. But it is still football. And it is still the South.

Cautious of the heat and health, practice starts early in the year here. By mid-fall the teams are at their peaks. The Homecoming Game is a particular focus, and the entire town participates.

My next-door neighbor, Julia Barnes, invited me. Her youngest grandson was quarterback and playing his last season. Although Selby boasts two thriving high schools, one is a private preparatory school. This one, the public high school, is the oldest, with roots going back to the very beginning of the town. It is located not far from the center of town, and most students still walk to the campus. It was a fine late afternoon, so we decided to do the same.

Julia must be at least 80 years of age, perhaps older. But she looks absolutely ageless. Early in our friendship, she invited me into her home. We sat on the screened-in porch at the back of her immaculately kept house, sipping sweet tea and eating cookies. Julia is the epitome of a true Southern lady. A soft cultured voice with a silky smooth accent. Her back straight. Her legs crossed only at the ankles. Manicured hands. Every hair in place at all times. And a sense of humor that comes out of nowhere when you least expect it.

She told me how she had married young and buried her first husband – a hero in World War II. Her second husband is still living, but suffers from the advanced stages of Alzheimer's disease and is being cared for in a local nursing home. He won't eat unless Julia feeds him. So, like clockwork, she drives to and from the care facility twice a day, morning and evening. She never complains. She never misses a day. She remains a tirelessly devoted wife.

She showed me pictures of herself and her family when they were young. Julia was a storybook Southern beauty. With her golden hair, large blue eyes and a smile that could make men forget their names, she must have had her pick. She picked the most handsome man in town. He had movie-star looks. Tall, dark, with Gregory Peck-like features. And, judging from the photos, he obviously adored his bride. He was 21 when they married, she was barely 19. By the time she reached 21, she was the mother of a small child and widow of a war hero. Her second marriage to another exceptionally good-looking man produced two more sons. He had been a loving and loyal husband and father for over fifty years. And now, she was enduring yet another unspeakable heartache with pure Southern grace.

Julia's pride and joy are her grandchildren. So I felt privileged to be asked to join her and her family for this special occasion. But, I had to admit, I was equally intrigued with the idea of watching a real, live, Southern high school football game.

We got there early. So Julia suggested we go into the Field House. While she excused herself to visit the ladies' room, I took the opportunity to examine the trophy cases that lined the entrance walls. The photos and memorabilia were arranged approximately in chronological order, with different sports and other highlights intermixed.

There was a winning-game football from 1902, signed by all the team members. It was almost black with age, but the handwriting could still be made out. Next to it was a long, faded, framed photograph of a 1905 baseball team, with members wearing bulky woolen uniforms and leggings that looked exceptionally hot and uncomfortable. Tennis seemed to be a sport with early participation by both boys and girls. I couldn't see a date on the oldest photograph but, by the dress of the girls, it had to have been before the turn of the last century. It was accompanied by multiple silver trophies.

Within the 1920s materials, standing at the end of a long row of football players in an official team photograph, I spotted a young girl. She was tall and thin, hair in braids, and a smile as wide as her face. I suddenly remembered my mother telling me that back in the late 1920s and '30s, girls were often brought in as the extra point kicker – but usually for college teams. A kind of "fad" of the times. I wondered if Selby had been so forward-thinking as well.

There were over a hundred years' worth of memories

protected within these long, polished glass cases. There were well-worn bats and balls and rackets. There were loving cups and trophies of various sizes and metals. There were photographs of youth-fresh faces full of hope and anticipation and trust, many of whom were no longer of this earth, their lives lived, their promise fulfilled. I hoped they had realized their dreams. I knew that many of them had descendents who attended this school after them. Perhaps some would be playing tonight. Or at least cheering those who were.

Toward the end of the last case along the first wall, I stopped to look closer at the early 1940s-era artifacts: World War II. A time unique unto itself. A sad and somehow lonely time, caught somewhere between innocence and loss. Homecoming, 1942. No football team was pictured that year. But there was a Homecoming Queen. She was beautiful and radiant. And she was Julia.

Her full-length satin and chiffon gown was pale baby blue, which brought out the hue of her eyes. She held a large bouquet of lilies and roses, in arms that were gloved in creamy soft white leather. The gloves extended all the way from her slender finger tips to well beyond her elbows.

"I do believe I still have that dress, and the gloves, too ... somewhere," Julia's soft, gentle voice spoke over my shoulder.

"Those gloves had at least a dozen tiny pearl buttons at each wrist. The devil to get on. And they were ever so uncomfortable," she reminisced. "I remember, because it was unseasonably warm that night – the night of the homecoming dance. But Mama wouldn't let me take off my gloves," she said with a smile. "A lady never bares her hand in a gentleman's hand," she explained. "And a gentleman never touches his uncovered hand on a lady's back. He must use a crisp white handkerchief – placing it between his hand and the back of his dancing partner." She held out a Kleenex to demonstrate.

Still gazing at the photo, I could almost hear the muted echoes of a big band playing "I'll Be Seeing You" softly in the background from sixty-some years ago.

"You looked beautiful," I told her unnecessarily.

"It was a lovely night," she said simply, turning to leave.

I wanted to ask her more. I wanted to ask who her dance partner had been. Perhaps it had been her first husband. Perhaps that had been the night he had proposed. Perhaps he had left shortly after that night to join the armed forces overseas. I wanted to ask. I didn't. Julia would have told me, if she had wanted to.

We left the Field House to find our seats in the stadium.

The bleachers were filling up fast. Fortunately, Julia's granddaughter, Mariah, was saving places for us. Julia quickly found her; we waved, she waved, we made our way up the steep steps to the middle of the stands, and then excused and shuffled our way to our seats next to the young woman. Julia continued to amaze me with her agility.

I saw a few people I knew, but not many. Julia, on the other hand, seemed to be acquainted with just about everyone there. She introduced me to her granddaughter, who was a sophomore that year at a nearby college. Mariah was the daughter of Julia's youngest son and his wife, and sister of the star quarterback that we were there to cheer. Mariah's parents were not yet in the stands. Just then, the proud mom and dad came into view. People all around us whistled and called out greetings and questions about the shape of their son's arm and his general well-being that night.

"How's John Junior feeling tonight?"

"We gonna win this one?"

"Is your boy going to take us home?"

John Senior answered them with obvious pleasure and great Southern wit. His wife, Cherry, just smiled and waved to us. They climbed to their seats in front of us, kissing their mom as they sat down.

"Sorry we're late," Cherry stated. "John Junior forgot to bring the flag with him and we had to go back to get it."

I turned to Julia, who explained: "A flag is being presented to the school from the football team tonight in honor of Coach Dooley – Big Jake Dooley. He died in the train accident and chemical spill last February out near the Bricks plant. He was a volunteer with the Public Safety Officers."

I remembered hearing about the tragedy. Cherry turned around and added: "He was such a great, great man and a wonderful coach. John Junior just loved him like a second father. All the boys did. Our son had been playing for him since he was what, John, maybe 5 or 6 years old?" she asked, turning toward her husband.

He responded, "He started with Coach in Pee Wee football about the time he started first grade. Then, of course, Jake coached him again when J.J. started as a high school freshman. The loss of Coach Dooley shook the whole school – the whole community – but especially the team."

"So the team is presenting a flag to the school tonight in his memory," Cherry said. "It will be raised and lowered to half-mast for tonight's game. As team captain, John Junior is to make the presentation. But at this age, our son would forget his own name if it wasn't sewn in his underwear. So we had to go back and get it."

"Don't be so hard on the boy," John Senior defended. "He's

got a lot on his mind, that's all. Like winning this worldclass competition against Greenbriar High!" He raised his left hand high over his head and Mariah leaned forward and slapped it in unspoken agreement.

The band was playing loudly and rather well. The sun had been setting rapidly and it had gotten a little cool. The bleachers had filled almost completely. I smelled hot dogs and boiled peanuts, and listened to pieces of conversation and laughter floating all around me, and thought about Coach Dooley.

I truly believe the heaven that awaits us will be a beautiful place – beyond our simple comprehension of what peace and love and beauty can possibly be. And yet, when I experienced all that was creating that moment, and looked up at the millions of stars awakening overhead, and felt that strong presence of "hometown" wrapped warmly all around me, I felt sure that Coach would be missing us this night, too. Just as surely as he would be missed.

Just then, the band started playing what was obviously the school song, and just about everyone in the entire stands joined in singing. People rose to their feet with enthusiasm, and it ended with a huge rush of applause and cheers and whistles. The voice of the school principal came over the loudspeaker, and welcomed everyone, asking them to be seated for a special presentation. The crowd hushed themselves with remarkable speed.

The principal, Mr. Vonaugut, was standing at a microphone in the center of the field. The team had run out to stand next to him. He introduced Reverend Ridley Knox who gave a short and meaningful prayer. And then he nodded to a young man who stepped away from the line of his teammates.

"That's John Junior," Julia said in a low voice.

Principal Vonaugut introduced John Barnes, Jr., quarterback and captain of the varsity football team, and explained that J.J. was going to make the presentation and dedication on behalf of the team. At the same time, the school's R.O.T.C. color guard entered the field and took their place next to the team. One of the members, I noticed, was carrying a folded flag.

J.J. came forward to the microphone, his helmet tucked under his left arm. Without looking at any notes, and in a clear, strong, young voice, J.J. began: "I can barely remember my life without Coach Dooley in it. He wasn't just a presence in it, he was a very big part of it. He was one of the most important influences in it. He was one of the most important influences in the lives of most of us kids here tonight. I know I speak for the entire team when I say that Coach was always there for us, anytime, anywhere. And that included the time that some of us thought it would be a great idea to liberate the school mascot from Hillside – the ram. We got it into the back seat of my VW, but then we couldn't get it out. And then we got busted. And most of us were too scared to call our daddies. So we called Coach. In retrospect, it might have been easier to have faced the ram ..." Quiet laughter rippled through the stands.

J.J. continued: "Coach was there for us kids off the field as much as he was on it. He was there for Caleb Barnhard when Caleb broke his collarbone skiing and needed extra coaching to get fit enough to play again." He paused and a boy stepped forward from the team lineup standing quietly as J.J. resumed his remarks. "He was there for Antony Hollingsworth when he got his leg broken in the last game of the season.

Coach sat by Antony's bed all that night, and visited him every day in the hospital and at home, making sure he was going to be all right." A young man stood in the stands not far from us. "He was there for Sandy Taylor when he needed help getting a scholarship to be able to go to college." A young man stood up on the sidelines. "He was there for Lee Anna Leeds when she needed extra money to make it to the Olympic Trials running track." A young woman stood in the stands to our right. "He was there for Marcus Ransburg when Marcus' mama died." Another youth stepped forward from the team, his head bowed in silence.

J.J. continued, "Just about all of us have a story for when Coach was there for us. But, most importantly, last February, he was there for the workers at the Carolina Bricks plant. He gave us support and self-discipline, courage and love. But he gave them their lives." There was silence all around. "In honor of Coach Jake Dooley, the varsity football team presents this flag to Selby High School, and dedicates this homecoming game to his memory."

Accompanied by the haunting song of a lone bagpiper, the R.O.T.C. member holding the folded flag walked with precision to the base of the flag pole a few yards behind the field. He laid the gift in the outstretched hands of a two-member honor guard positioned there. They hooked it to the lines, raised it to the top of the mast, where it stayed for the count of ten swaying gently in the evening breeze, then they lowered it to half-mast and tied it off.

Applause started slowly and soon hit a fever pitch. Eyes that were blurred with tears watched the team jog off the field to the locker room and the R.O.T.C. return to the sidelines. All we could do was pat Cherry and John Senior heartily on the back. And share Kleenex and hugs.

Then the band broke into an upbeat number, and brought us back to the reason for the game. I prayed that Coach was watching.

THIRTEEN

By halftime, the score was a well-played 14 to 7, our favor. Throughout the game, we had been entertained by the school tradition that required every attending member of the senior class (players and band musicians excepted) to run to the home team goal post after each successful goal and perform as many pushups as total team points, and then run back to their seats. It was a unique showing of solidarity, with a subtle challenge to score even more.

It was also fun to see traditional cheerleaders again. Both boys and girls. Dressed appropriately, leading the crowd in light and sassy "call and response" – but without any over-the-top choreography. I was surprised that some of the cheers even dated back to my own high school days.

The halftime program was an additional bonus: the announcement and crowning of the Homecoming Queen and her Court. It was a lovely ceremony, after which the newly crowned queen – a friend of Julia's family – joined us in the stands to help cheer her home team to a resounding victory.

⁓

We were just descending the steep bleacher steps, discussing where to go to get a late supper, when Julia was hugged by a woman I hadn't seen before. It was apparent they were long-time friends.

Julia broke away from the greeting to introduce me to her goddaughter, Monnie Belle von Alden. "Monnie Belle, honey, may I present my neighbor and new friend Macy Harris," she said as the other woman took my hand in both of hers.

"It is a pleasure to meet you," she said warmly, distinctly emphasizing each word, infusing each syllable with sincerity, and looking directly into my eyes. I believed her. I thought I would probably always believe anything this woman ever said to me.

"Monnie is Head of School over at Selby Academy," Julia went on to explain. I knew that was the private boarding school in town. "She's been there for going on, what – 20 years or so?" she turned to Monnie.

"Twenty-two this fall, not counting the years I attended as a student, of course," Monnie smiled back.

As we finished the slow climb down, Monnie completed the full Southern introductory greeting by finding out where my "people" were from and what church I belonged to. She was just getting into which house I had bought (known by the original owners' names, rather than street numbers), when Julia's son announced that consensus had chosen "Southern

Barbecue" as the place to eat – as long as their Mama and I approved, of course. She did. I did. I had never been there, but had heard mouth-watering stories.

"Monnie, please do come with us," Julia invited.

"I am just so sorry, but I have to get back to the school tonight – late staff meeting," she replied. She turned to me: "But I know you'll enjoy it. It truly is the very best place for barbecue this side of heaven," she assured me. "Please come by the school for a tour, anytime," she invited. And I knew I would take her up on it as soon as possible. I had been intrigued with its compelling architecture and long history since the day I first passed its well-kept grounds and gated entrance shortly after moving to Selby.

"Perhaps tomorrow?" I called out after her.

"Come for tea," she called back.

I turned to Julia, "When exactly is tea?" I asked as we walked to the car.

The drive to "Southern Barbecue" made you feel you were soon going to cross a state line. "But worth the drive," I was assured several times. It was late when we arrived, but the parking lot was still almost full. We had combined our group of six into one SUV, (John Junior had joined us, but the homecoming queen had previous plans).

Entering the fabled eating place was a step back into a real Southern tradition. The smell of wondrous things happening on a slow-cooking grill filled the large single room. Standard wooden picnic tables were placed end-to-end in long narrow rows. You had to pick your side carefully; once you started down it, you were committed.

The tables were covered in slick red oilcloth. A loaf of "Wonderbread" was plopped in the center of each table, still in its universally recognizable wrapper. Salt and pepper in plastic shakers. Stacks of paper napkins. Extra hot sauce.

The food was served cafeteria style. Each bin of food looked better than the last. Pork, beef, chicken. Pulled, slow-cooked, baked, fried. And there was one entire bin of chicken parts called "pully bones." I discovered that this is a special cut off the breast of the chicken that includes the whole wishbone (i.e., the "pully bone"). Succulent, thick, pure white meat, this is a much sought-after piece and considered one of the prized cuts.

There were also large vats of green beans cooked to deep verdant limpness, mixed with ham bones and bacon and onions. Mashed potatoes with the skins included, corn on the cob dripping in butter, fried okra, batter-fried and boiled squash, plump pale butter beans, thick cream-colored buttermilk biscuits, Southern-style fat back. There was something called "barbecue hash," which was rather dark, almost muddy, and melted on your tongue in pure flavor. I didn't want to ask what it was exactly.

There was one whole corner of the room devoted to desserts alone. And one full wall held tray after tray of salad selections.

There is a long-held, ongoing Southern partisanship relative to the virtues and authenticity of tomato-based, mustard-based and vinegar-based barbecue styles. Personally, I am partial to tomato-based. But the question itself has resulted in expert and subtle improvements over the years that have done nothing but propel each style into the realm of ambrosia. Family recipes are as guarded as jewels, kept in locked boxes (if written down at all), and willed from one generation to the next. Deathbed pronouncements evoke promises of fidelity. If the pledge of secrecy should ever be broken, Grandma will surely haunt you personally, wherever your kitchen may be.

We ate until we could hardly breathe. We relived the game, play by play. We praised the Homecoming Queen selection. We remembered Coach.

"Didn't Coach have any family?" I asked.

Cherry answered, "Well, his mama and daddy passed a number of years back. But Big Jake did have an older brother, Charlie. Charlie was killed in Vietnam. It just about killed Jake, too, at the time, I remember."

"Big Jake wanted to join up and fight," John added. "But his folks convinced him to stay in school. He was pretty young anyway."

Cherry continued. "And he was married at one time, too. But it didn't last. Too many kids at that time got married just because it was the thing to do. And then found out it was a big mistake. At least they didn't have any children. I don't know where she wound up." I noticed "she" wasn't given a name.

"So Coach kind of adopted every kid who ever came his way," Julia added. "He was one of the kindest, most honorable and loyal men you'd ever want to meet," she added softly.

"So how did he get his name 'Big Jake'?" I asked.

John laughed and said, "Well, you never saw him, but he was one very large guy. Barrel chest, arms like tree trunks, hands like baseball mitts." He held out his arms as he described his lost friend to me. "He probably weighed at least

300 pounds, he was well over 6 feet, and still solid as a rock. I mean, he was just big."

"Amen to that," Cherry responded. "When he was playing football, the opposing team started sweating just looking at him." Everyone laughed.

"But he was also the guy who was first to offer his hand to help you up after he tackled you. Flattened you like a steam roller, you understand ... but then picked you up and put you back on your feet again," John added.

"He was just a classic 'gentle giant'," Mariah said. "He was just so kind and gentle and caring. Loved dogs and horses especially." Tears filled her eyes.

"Big Jake was as big in heart and spirit as he was in physical size," Julia summarized. "It's a real loss ... a real loss," she sighed.

"But it doesn't surprise me that he was first on the scene that terrible night of the train wreck," she added. "That was so like him – to be there on the spot whenever anybody was in need. It's why he served as a volunteer Public Safety Officer for so many years. He just had to be helping people. And he was absolutely one of the first on site that terrible night. He personally saved at least 11 people, they say."

"But wasn't that something nobody could figure out?" John Junior interrupted. "Why was Coach there so soon? It was like he was right there at the plant at the time of the wreck. He couldn't have heard the emergency sirens and gotten there so fast from his home."

"Nobody knows, Honey," Cherry said consolingly. "But he wouldn't have wanted it any other way. You know that. If he could help somebody – he wanted to be there. Nobody knows why – but he was there, and he saved all those lives because of it. Maybe it was all just part of God's plan."

John Junior nodded, but not particularly in agreement. And then, everyone ate in silence for awhile. Quiet, with their own personal memories.

Mariah broke the mood by bringing up the Homecoming Dance the next night, giving her brother a hard time about how he was going to look in his tux. She was pelted with a hush puppy from the sibling.

As soon as we were all sure we couldn't take even one more bite, we went over "just to look" at the desserts. There was the obligatory banana pudding, of course – a Southern staple and a must at any self-respecting barbecue. But there were also a variety of pies and cobblers – peach, cherry, apple, blueberry, banana cream, key lime. And cakes – layered, frosted, crumbed and drizzled in chocolate – served both warm and cold. There were cookies of every description. Fresh fruit. Jell-O – both regular and, inexplicably, sugar-free. And there was soft-serve ice cream in several different flavors with assorted sauces and other toppings.

We convinced each other we would watch our calories tomorrow.

When we left, the original founder and family matriarch of Southern Barbecue bid us good night personally. Probably in her 90s, she was seated near the door in a large, comfortable rocking chair.

She shook our hands and gave us red and white mints and asked us how we enjoyed our supper. Neatly dressed, perfectly coiffed, and utterly gracious, she then told God to Bless us and said she hoped we'd return soon. Somehow, I knew we would.

FOURTEEN

The next morning I called Monnie Belle von Alden as soon as I felt it was proper, to reconfirm my invitation to tea and a tour of the Academy. She assured me she was looking forward to it and had already invited a few other ladies in town to join us.

"Around 4 o'clock," she clarified the time. "But come early so I can show you our school." I mentally prepared to be there by at least 3:30 p.m.

I was bathed, dressed and ready by 3:00 o'clock. The drive was only about 5 minutes, so I took a walk around the yard behind my house and discovered several flowering camellia bushes just starting to bloom. I clipped some to take to my hostess, returned to the house, and wrapped the stems in a pale, gauzy ribbon I found in a drawer.

I could have walked to the campus, but it would have

taken a good bit longer. And I had on my dress-up shoes – worn mostly on Sundays, and not terribly comfortable.

As I turned my car through the impressive iron gates of Selby Academy, I entered an ambiance where time has held its breath for almost 100 years. The well-traveled gravel drive curves gently to the front entrance and adjacent parking. There are hedges of close-clipped and shaped shrubs. Stone benches with brass commemorative plaques. Old oaks with deep green ivy curling thickly around their trunks and limbs. It is a grand place, but not ostentatious. It was designed and built as a boarding school in the 1910s and retains its original functional style.

The main building is a three-story white clapboard structure. Large, round, white columns pose ceremoniously across the wide front porch, supporting a high and deep roof covered in sun-faded, patched black shingles. The wooden floor of the porch sags and is painted a glossy rich black, which matches the color of the operating wide-slatted shutters. Overhead, simple black-bladed fans hang on long mounts – silent on this comfortable sunny fall day.

Assorted wicker and wood furniture was positioned at opportune places across the porch, ready for a quick chat, a private moment with a book, a game of chess or cribbage. The chairs were angled and askew as if students had left them just moments ago, and would be returning at any minute. Or perhaps they had left them like this to play tennis in 1912. To listen to the radio in the '30s. To walk to the drugstore for a malt in the 1950s. To play soccer this afternoon. The atmosphere was that timeless.

Just then, young knees and elbows came crashing through the front doorway. A group of young girls dressed for sport.

Their giggles continued, but they stopped immediately upon seeing me standing there and all greeted me quite sweetly and sincerely.

"Oh, hello," one of the girls closest to me said as she came forward. "May I help you, Ma'am?" she smiled politely with clear young eyes dancing over a mouthful of braces.

"Yes," I replied, "you can, actually. I'm looking for Ms. von Alden."

"Yes, Ma'am. I'll be happy to take you to her, if you'll just follow me."

"I don't want to take you away from your game," I started to protest. But she assured me it was no bother.

"I'll catch y'all in a minute," she called to the other girls who scrambled and jumped off the porch.

"We'll be on the field," they called back. "Good-bye, Ma'am," they all said to me as they rushed off. It was a thorough delight to be treated with such genuine friendliness and hospitality by a group of young people I had never met.

Once inside, my eyes focused on a comfortable lobby area. Well-worn oriental rugs rested on hardwood floors. Straight-backed padded chairs were against the walls. A large, highly polished, pedestal table took the center of the room and supported a massive bowl of fresh-cut flowers. Their scent filled the space. A clock ticked, then chimed the half hour with a tone as familiar as my grandmother's dining room. Sun sifted in through sheer curtains that covered floor-length windows framed on either side by richly colored heavy draperies. French doors were flung open invitingly, allowing me a glimpse of a well-tended courtyard. Frame after frame of old black-and-white photographs covered wainscoted walls. A large block of brass plaques filled one section, floor to ceiling;

but I couldn't quite tell what they were commemorating.

A flight of wide, uncarpeted stairs climbed up the wall adjacent to the front door, and my young escort headed in that direction.

My immediate impression was one of peaceful silence on this Saturday afternoon. But then my ear realized the pleasing sounds of youth at play. Some of the voices were coming from down a long hallway to the right. Others seemed to float in from a distance. And then the unmistakable click of dog toenails approached us from around the corner, bearing into sight a large, perpetually gleeful golden retriever.

"Hey, Lucy," the girl greeted the dog with obvious enjoyment. "I hope you don't mind dogs," she said to me. "Lucy is supposed to be trained not to jump up on strangers, but sometimes she forgets."

From underneath great, wet dog kisses I managed to reassure her that I was quite a fan of dogs. And Lucy was doing her best to convey the message that she had been waiting just for me all day long.

"Lucy, please. Where are your manners," a voiced called down the staircase from one flight above us. I looked up into the smiling but slightly chagrined face of my hostess, Monnie Belle von Alden.

"Miss von Alden, this lady has come to see you," the girl said pleasantly as she looked up to the second-floor railing where the Head of School was leaning. "I was just showing her to your quarters."

"Thank you, Elizabeth. Please do bring her up," Monnie responded.

"Yes Ma'am," she smiled at me and started to lead the way up the stairs. Lucy raced passed us two steps at a time, then turned abruptly at the top to greet us all over again.

Monnie continued to talk, saying, "I hope you didn't have any trouble finding us, Miss Macy. You are right on time."

And then, before I had a chance to respond, she continued: "Elizabeth, dear, I am also expecting two more guests. Would you be so kind as to remain near the door and tell them to come on through. They'll know where to find us."

"Yes, Ma'am," young Elizabeth replied, without showing a twinge of regret from having to miss even more of her game with her friends.

"Thank you, Dear," Monnie said. "That's very good of you."

"Yes, thank you, Elizabeth," I added.

"You're welcome, Ma'am. Have a nice tea." She skipped down the stairs and out the front door.

"Are these for me?" Monnie asked as she carefully received the camellias I had clipped and carried to her. "Aren't they just the prettiest things? Why, you must have quite a green thumb," she enthused.

"Not exactly," I smiled. "I just haven't had time to kill them, yet."

Lucy, her tail and eyes happily flirting with us, led the way past a highly varnished heavy wooden door and into the parlor of Ms. von Alden's quarters. Sun burst through the open windows and filled the room. It was unpredictably light and airy, with cool linen slipcovers and pale woven throw rugs against deep mahogany floors and polished-brass accents.

In front of the main window, a small tea table was already set with a crisp white cloth and napkins. I counted five cups and saucers.

"What a lovely room," I told her. "It's so cheerful and bright."

She stepped into the kitchen to get a flower vase, but called back: "Yes, it's always been one of my favorite rooms in the whole school. It gets some of the best light. And I try to keep it un-intimidating for the students."

As she came back into the room with the flowers tucked into a handsome glass container, she continued: "Sometimes I think the children believe I must have cave paintings on my walls and was a bunkmate with Methuselah in my school days."

From down the hall to our immediate right, a familiar voice joined the conversation: "Well, you are older than dirt, my dear. After all, you do pre-date computers, and that's just plain ancient in anyone's eyes who wasn't born until Bill Gates was counting his first billion. And then there's the fact that you refuse to own a cell phone." The accent was deep-Southern-coated – the kind that has been carefully cultivated for tweaking a good friend or making a particularly barbed point. When the speaker came into view, I recognized Margaret Ann Lawton, whom I had first met at dinner in Jonathan's Gallery – the night I had seen René Robecheaux's ghost on top of the old post office. Our paths had crossed only a few times since. I was glad to see her.

"Margaret Ann, I believe you've already met Miss Macy Harris?" Monnie said as she motioned us to be seated.

"Yes, at one of Jonathan's supper parties," Margaret Ann confirmed with a smile.

"It's good to see you again," I responded as she gave me a quick, warm hug.

"So how are you settling in to Selby?" Margaret Ann inquired with sincere interest. "By reading your columns, I'd say quite well."

"I am finding it wonderful," I answered truthfully. "Except, perhaps, for a bit of landscaping frustration."

They listened sympathetically as I briefly outlined my woes. But I gladly abandoned the subject when Margaret Ann suggested that I must see the rose garden on the school grounds, which led to Monnie offering a full tour of the academy.

"Oh yes, please," I quickly accepted and stood up. "I've admired the property from the outside for months, and would sincerely love to see it all," I confessed.

Margaret Ann decided she would join us. And Lucy, of course, could not be left behind.

"Shall we start at the bottom and work our way up? Or the other way around?" Monnie asked.

"Oh, leave the ghost for last," Margaret Ann stated flatly. So we descended to the first floor.

"Ghost?" I prodded Margaret Ann on the stairs.

"In the attic," she smiled back.

But by then Monnie was starting with her narrative, and I didn't want to miss a word.

Selby Academy was established in 1910 as a result of an increasing number of Winter Colony families who wanted to provide a top-notch education for their children while away from their permanent homes in the East. It had to be a school that taught more than the basic reading, writing and arithmetic. Along with such instruction as the classics and composition, Latin and French, history and government, it needed to offer horsemanship and public speaking, debate and deportment, fencing and tennis, ballroom dancing and music, art and theater. And, at that time, that meant a private school.

It began as a day school, but quickly accommodated boarding students as well. It was unusual for the times, because it admitted girls as well as boys. Over the decades it has maintained its original high standards and dedication to producing well-rounded, well-educated young people – from Selby as well as from around the country. In fact, a good five percent of the current students even hail from homes outside of the U.S.

Although it is solid in stature and reputation, the Academy struggles economically. As Monnie explained it, "Old money tends to disappear after about the third generation. But not the image of it."

There was a time when the great families of Selby supported the school unquestioningly, with generous donations and funding for every need. More tennis courts. New polo grounds. Updated sleeping quarters. Complete libraries. Mostly without even being asked. Although, perhaps not without a bit of "showmanship," I suspected.

Today, however, the children coming here still appear to be coming from old names and, therefore, great wealth. "But frankly," Monnie confided, "more than half of our students receive some sort of financial aid. Tuition doesn't begin to cover our costs."

I thought about it. The economy is tighter. Education is increasingly more expensive. Family wealth is not as "disposable" as it once was. Sometimes family fortunes are even accountable to boards and investors, no longer available for individual discretion and decision.

Monnie sighed deeply. It was obviously an ongoing concern. But then she smiled, saying with a note of pride, "The students really want for very little, though. Somehow we keep going ... God and Great Aunts keep providing," she laughed. "Somehow, we keep our head above water, and we keep the children graduating into wonderful colleges all over the world. And most of Selby doesn't even suspect."

And this, too, is another eccentricity of the South, I have discovered. Perception is more important than reality when it comes to money – especially old family money. Pride is everything. No one must suspect that the coffers are empty. It is an attitude that has prevailed for centuries. And it is still a part of the culture today. A part that I can't help but admire, in a way. Yet, it makes me sad, as well.

As we talked, we had been walking. We had passed through the lobby and had entered a sizeable library. Floor to ceiling, row after row, it was one of the most impressive private collections I have ever encountered.

"Most of the books have come to us over the years from a number of families and donations from estates. But the library got its real boost from one of the oldest Winter Colony families in particular: The Faiths," Monnie said.

I recognized the name immediately, and looked at Margaret Ann who had helped tell me the family's story that night at dinner. She nodded that I was remembering correctly.

"The family had twin daughters that attended the Academy for a brief time," Monnie continued. "And it was at about that time that the mother, Lottie Louise Faith, began her donations. She continued her support for years, but usually gave to the school in the form of books and collections. Even when she donated cash, she would typically stipulate that the money be used for books."

"Rather out of character, I would have said," Margaret Ann observed dryly, obviously relating to the lady's reputation for having a somewhat less than scholarly personality.

"Anyway," Monnie continued, "the school would occasionally hear from one or the other of the twins, but nothing really after the mother's death in the late 1960s. Their father had died ages earlier. I suppose the girls are probably gone by now, too," she mused. The "girls," I noted mentally, would have been at least a generation older than we were.

I hated to leave the quiet, cozy, book-scented room, but Monnie was leading us out another door and into a long paneled hallway. It led to a dining room that was set with multiple round tables that would each probably seat eight or ten.

"We serve cafeteria style," Monnie explained, "except on Sundays at noon. Then it's family style. But we do try to lessen the institutional feel by providing smaller eating tables for small groups and quieter talking. The staff try to sit with the students as well, rather than all together."

She greeted a kitchen staff member who was starting to set up the room with fresh silverware and stacks of plates.

"On Sunday evenings, we keep the rather English habit of having a cold supper," she continued. "But on Saturday night, it's all-American: hamburgers, fries, pizza, ice cream ..."

"Even sodas," the kitchen helper added.

"Oh yes," Monnie rolled her eyes. "Even sodas. Over my personal better judgement and vote. But I was steamrollered by Olivia here and the kids."

Olivia laughed with obvious delight.

We were duly shown the kitchen – industrial strength, and cleaned to a polished gleam and bare wood beneath. Then the TV room, where only a small contingent was watching a soccer match on cable on this beautiful sunny afternoon. Lucy suddenly had a change of heart and loyalties and asked with pleading eyes if she could be excused to stay with the kids. Monnie gave her consent, and then led us onward into the old gymnasium, which doubled as a theater.

This room was a classic with its hardwood waxed floors, colored lines and boundaries embedded deeply beneath the sheen. Its high, vertical windows and light fixtures were still webbed with wire to avoid breaking from wayward balls. At one end of the room was the stage, hung with curtains that had to have dated back to its construction almost a century ago. Everything was apparently still in use and in relatively good repair. But it made me smile to think of all the hours and hours of Shakespeare and music recitals, "Our Towns" and "Oklahomas" that must have echoed against these walls over the years.

From here we went below ground to the natatorium and locker rooms. The ancient elevator creaked and groaned alarmingly, but Monnie didn't seem to notice.

The smell of poorly ventilated chlorine was powerfully evident even before the doors clanged open again. Green and black tile covered the floors, walls and ceilings in practical protection against perpetual humidity. We walked through a low passageway into the pool room and found two boys watching with stop watches as another two lapped the pool. It must have been state-of-the-art at the time. Built-in bleachers, carved marble ornaments, a dozen different shades of green, all contributed to a lovely – but historic – picture.

"Hello, boys," Monnie called out.

"Hello, Miss von Alden" they called back, and then quickly returned their eyes to their teammates in the pool.

"We have a very competitive swim team this year," she said

with some pride.

"You ought to see the swim trophies Miss Monnie herself brought home in her day," Margaret Ann added.

"Oh, a long time ago," Monnie said with humility.

"Yes, it was," Margaret Ann answered straight faced. "But you were brilliant, my dear."

"She was a national competitor and won just about everything she entered," Margaret Ann bragged to me.

As I expressed how impressed I was, we glanced into locker rooms that matched the beautifully outdated natatorium, and then we retraced our steps toward the elevator. With longing, I eyed the wide, rubber-matted stairway as we passed it, but Monnie didn't hesitate to load us back into the cramped, decrepit, very scary electric lift again.

Eventually, it moaned and cranked its way safely back to the ground floor and I released my breath.

We then walked through the French doors onto a beautiful open courtyard. Monnie took us past fragrant gardens still lush with late-blooming roses and scented herbs and other attractive plantings. And she pointed toward clay tennis courts and busy soccer fields and well-tended riding stables beyond. I asked to come back for a special tour of just the grounds and stables, and was granted my wish "anytime."

A short covered walkway led us to the classrooms building. Two floors of traditional and vaguely familiar architecture. Classrooms on either side of long central hallways. Hallways lined with lockers and drinking fountains and pictures of former student body officers and service groups. I am a devoted fan of old black-and-white movies, and this building would have served as a film set for many of them. It was wonderfully timeless and woefully outdated. It was patched and re-patched and held together with ingenuity and determination. There were obvious roof leaks in practically every room. There were long cracks across old slate blackboards. And, as far as I could tell, there was only one room that accommodated computers. I could see that what Monnie had said about finances was achingly true.

As we stepped back through the French doors into the lobby of the first building, we were joined from the front entrance by two other women, led obligingly by young Elizabeth.

A flurry of greetings and introductions presented me to Hattie Montgomery and Michael Weems. I wasn't sure I had heard correctly when the name "Michael" was pronounced for this lovely 70-something woman. But, in response to my raised eyebrows, she said with a smile and practiced words, "Yes, it's 'Michael.' I also have an Aunt Steve and an Uncle Harriet. It's an old family custom of disregarding current-day society in favor of honoring our British ancestry. The name Michael dates back to King James the first, House of Stuart. First-born ... boy or girl."

Monnie explained that we were just in the middle of our tour for my benefit, and all of them decided they would tag along as we finished.

We walked back up the staircase toward Monnie's quarters. But, when we reached the landing, she turned us to the left and through a pair of wide, heavily draped French doors. We entered a long passageway with tall, individually transomed and painted wooden doors on either side. This was the girl's dormitory wing – or sleeping quarters, as Monnie called them. I counted 8 doors on each side.

She stopped about halfway down, at one of the open doors,

popped her head around the corner and asked, "Would it be all right if we show a visitor your room, Sally Jean?"

"Yes, Ma'am," a sweet voice replied. "If you don't mind the mess."

Sally Jean was about 16, tall, lanky, wearing comfortable looking sweatpants and T-shirt. She was standing self-consciously, with book and pencil in hand. We had obviously interrupted her study.

The room was absolutely charming. Much more spacious than I had envisioned. Each room was designed to accommodate from two to four girls. They averaged two students per room currently, Monnie said.

It was an old-fashioned, very feminine room. Lots of pink and pale green and roses. Light, airy curtains fluttered over an open window, with slatted blinds pulled all the way up. Books overflowed the built-in cases and individual desks. Stuffed animals were piled invitingly on soft, narrow beds. Laundry waited to be done in a heap in one corner. Birthday cards were stuck on a cork board, while a bright red Mylar balloon was tied to the headboard of one of the beds and drifted goofily in the breeze.

I noticed a laptop computer sitting on one of the desks, but no table-top models. Monnie explained that they couldn't afford the wiring necessary to accommodate computers in the sleeping rooms yet. They were all confined to one computer lab in the classroom building. Some of the students, however, did have their own laptops. But the internet was only available in that one classroom. Which, Monnie admitted, did have some advantages.

"But it's first on our list after the roof repairs, isn't it Sally Jean?" she smiled as she looked at the student.

"Yes, Ma'am," Sally Jean smiled back.

We thanked the young girl as we all paraded through her sanctuary back into the hallway.

At both ends of the central passageway, and on each side, there are swinging wooden doors, each with a cutout window at eye's height. Each of these four doors leads to a communal bathroom. Each bathroom contains a set of privately enclosed toilets, showers, and deep, footed tubs. Grouped-together sinks and mirrors are circled in the center of the black-and-white tiled room.

A mirror-image to this wing exists on the opposite side of the building – the boy's sleeping quarters. There, we found décor that reflected an almost "craftsman" period appearance. Lots of oak, with stained glass and iron accents. It was cozy but sturdy, so old-fashioned it was back in style. While the girls' wing received the morning sun, the boys' quarters was bathed in a late afternoon glow.

It was then that Monnie took us to the foot of the narrow, dark stairway leading to the third-floor.

"This next floor has been pressed into dormitory use only when we have been filled to capacity – with over a hundred students. Mostly, it's just utilized for storage," Monnie told us.

"It's actually never been needed under me, but I understand it was frequently filled in the early days of the school," she continued. "And it's the wife of the first Head of School who haunts it now. Well, she's been sighted often enough – and heard by almost everyone. So I suppose we can say she is an actual 'presence'," Monnie said as she started up the winding staircase. The lighting was terribly inadequate, I observed silently.

"Have you seen her yourself?" I had to ask.

"Oh, yes. And I hear her quite regularly," she responded as if she were talking about an intrusive squirrel.

"They say she comes back to check on her boys," Margaret Ann contributed.

"That's what she was doing the night she fell," Hattie chimed in.

"Yes, this floor was quite full of students in those days. And she was making a night check, as she did quite often," Monnie continued. "She must have tripped in the low light and she fell down the stairs. Her neck was broken, poor thing. Of course, the students were devastated. And the school was closed for the rest of the semester."

"She was actually a friend of my grandmother's," Michael said. "A dear thing and terribly missed. The children were all very fond of her. And her husband never really recovered from the loss. I believe he left the school the next year or so."

At that moment, however, the main space of the third floor contained nothing more exciting than dust-covered boxes and old filing cabinets. Although a few old leather-bound trunks and broken pieces of antique furniture also leaned invitingly in shadows. I could see a stack of old framed photographs. Several rust-ridden trophies. Even some vintage sports equipment. I could spend a few happy hours exploring up here, I thought.

"We're hoping we might find a famous old painting in the bottom of a trunk or taped to the back of a bureau one of these days," Monnie said. "That would certainly solve our economic woes, now, wouldn't it?"

Single file, we traipsed our way down the steps again and Monnie shut the connecting door with a solid pull on the handle and click of the latch. And then we returned across the landing to Monnie's personal quarters – where tea and small finger sandwiches and attractively frosted petit fours had magically appeared on the tea cart.

FIFTEEN

Over the course of the next hour, I discovered that small
finger sandwiches – the preferred main course for afternoon tea
in the South – while dainty and lady-like in and of themselves,
may be piled on the plate as high as you wish. Hattie must
have helped herself to more than a dozen the first time they
were passed. The other ladies were almost as unrestrained. I
felt a little silly for only taking two. So I made up for it on the
next round.

The sandwiches were constructed with slim columns
of white bread, the crusts carefully cut off. There were two
different kinds. One contained thinly sliced chilled cucumber
on buttered bread, sprinkled with ground pepper; the other
was chicken salad with mayonnaise and wafer-thin almond
slices. Both were absolutely delicious.

The tea was hot, sweet and strong, and we were offered

sugar, lemon or cream. I was probably the only one of the five who didn't add at least one of the choices. There were also stalks of celery and young carrots and assorted cubes of cheese. And it was all followed by an array of heavily frosted petit fours and chocolate-dipped candies.

Aside from the charming refreshments, I was completely captivated by the conversation. It was thoroughly unique. It was perfectly Selby.

Margaret Ann began by asking Hattie how her sister was doing. She is a patient at a local nursing home and, sadly, suffers from dementia.

"Leticia doesn't seem to know me most of the time, I'm afraid," Hattie reported. "But she seems very happy. She's quite convinced that she's living in Scotland in a castle with her first husband, Albert. 'Bertie's gone fishing again,' she tells me. And then she orders the menu she wants prepared for the evening meal. I believe I'm the housekeeper."

"Oh dear," Monnie sympathized.

"I think it's a hoot," Margaret Ann responded.

"Did she ever really live in a castle in Scotland with her first husband?" Michael wanted to know.

"Not that we're aware of," Hattie replied. "But Grandfather used to talk about Scotland a great deal when we were children, and he gave us many picture books with great estates and castles in them. I'm guessing that's what she's remembering. I'm just glad she's at least happy in her delusions."

Monnie then told us of an aunt she'd had who had suffered from frightening visions as she got older. And Michael contributed another such story.

"Well, I'm never going to face that problem," Margaret

Ann declared. "I have it all worked out with Brooks – it's all documented and legally sound," she continued, and I remembered that her husband, Brooks, was a local attorney.

"If ever I get to that state, he's going to take me to India. I will be aided with drugs to die on my own terms. Then, my body will be cremated and my ashes will be sprinkled on the Ganges River."

"Oh, that river is so filthy," Michael commented with a look of distaste. "But I approve of the idea."

"Yes, as do I," Monnie agreed. "A very sensible thing to do. And very like you, Dear."

We all nodded and murmured our general consent.

"But I just have one question, Dear," Monnie continued with sincerity. "You love Selby and the South so deeply. It's where you were born and where you've lived all of your life. And we have the beautiful, beautiful, Savannah River right on the edge of our own state. Why would you travel all that distance – to India – to have your ashes scattered on that filthy river? Why not stay right here where you love it so, and be sprinkled across the Savannah River?"

We all looked expectantly at Margaret Ann.

"Because, Monnie dear," she replied with her deepest accent. "I simply hate India. And I wouldn't mind leaving there."

Everyone laughed with delight. And then Hattie snorted, and that sent everyone into a gale of laughter. And I began to appreciate that I was in the midst of a gathering of perfect Southern ladies. I have found that it is always most evident in a very particular sort of off-center sense of logic and humor – along with the ability to tell a good story. And this group seemed to be one of the finest examples I had come across yet.

Preferred means of death soon segued into a discussion of cemeteries. We were reviewing individual local family crypts, and Monnie declared her favorite was the one housing the remains of the Laroque family in the Episcopal churchyard. And then, of course, as a newcomer, I had to be told the fascinating Laroque family history – with special attention afforded Mr. Henry Laroque, II.

The family had come up from the Low Country in the early part of the 1800s, and had been among the first to settle in Selby. It was an extended family, including two brothers – Henry "the first," and James, their wives, children, and entire households. They were a family of some means, with modest fortunes already realized from cotton and wheat crops. And they quickly established two of the largest plantations and first brick-built mansions in the county – on the far northwest side of where the town of Selby was slowly growing.

They had been born into the Quaker faith. In fact, they had been very generous in building a new Quaker meeting house near their plantations. But they were also slave owners. And it was this issue that split them from their home church and moved the entire family to join the recently built Baptist Church in downtown Selby. But this, too, proved to be a lifestyle problem for James, who had discovered dancing and absolutely loved it. So the Episcopal Church soon found them all seated attentively in their congregation. This one apparently suited their needs.

In the beautiful old Episcopal cemetery that I had admired so much during the "Ghost Tour" a few months earlier, I remembered seeing several impressive, large crypts. Life-sized, mournful statues of weeping angels watch over massive above-ground tombs made from intricately carved marble or sandstone. Many are further guarded by graceful ironwork and brass, now weathering to a crusty deep red or a powdery blue-green that leave remnants on your fingers when you touch them. Most of the structures are nearly black with mold, or moss-covered to a dark slippery green. Nature's decay only adds to their mysterious beauty, somehow.

Monnie described the burial site belonging to the family Laroque, and I recalled it immediately. Positioned squarely on top is a seated angel, her hand outstretched to gently cup the chin of a dog. It is so poignant and had deeply touched my heart. I could not have forgotten it.

"Of course, I remember it vividly," I claimed.

"Well, it's absolutely my favorite in the entire town," Monnie declared.

The others agreed that it is charming and well worth visiting.

"So how many Laroques are actually … um … in there?" I asked, not sure if I was over-stepping the boundaries of good manners.

But Monnie never hesitated, and began to count them off on her fingers: "Well, there are both the brothers, and they each had two wives – not at the same time, of course. And Henry, 'the first,' had two daughters and one little boy, I believe."

"You make them sound like royalty," Margaret Ann interrupted, "calling them Henry 'the first' and Henry 'the second' like that."

"Well, Henry – the second – was the son of Mr. James, the brother, and I was just clarifying that for Macy, that's all," Monnie defended. "And James had just that one son … Henry *the second*," she added with emphasis.

Counting them up I said, "So that means there are 10 ... well ... 'enclosed'?" I asked, and then thought to myself, "Why they must be stacked right on top of each other."

As if she had read my mind, Monnie answered: "Actually, some of them are buried underground, beneath the crypt itself. The others are laid to rest within its walls. But there are only nine. Because Mr. Henry – *the second* – refused to be buried there," she answered. "He was a very unusual child."

"Perhaps he was just claustrophobic," Margaret Ann offered.

"No. He was unusual," Hattie agreed.

"Brilliant people often are," Michael added. "And he was nothing if not brilliant!"

"Yes," Monnie said. "He was born to the second wife of James Laroque around 1835 or so. And he was a remarkable child. He went entirely through school before he was 14, I believe – including receiving a degree in chemistry from Yale University. Then he came back here and returned to the family plantation."

"But he never did take to farming," Michael picked up the story. "He was always frail and sickly, never a strong boy. He always preferred to just stay inside and tinker with his inventions and other things."

Hattie said, "His father even built him a laboratory of sorts on the grounds of the estate. And he produced some most remarkable things in his short lifetime. Many of them helped with the cotton and wheat farming immensely."

"But then he died before he was even 30," Monnie said.

"He was actually only about 25, I think," Hattie added.

"And yet he invented or developed a number of wonderful things. And not just for the agricultural industry. He also invented some sort of process that helped purify medicines. And wasn't there a sort of hearing aid prototype or something like that? Hattie said as she looked at the others. "And then, of course, there was his work in astronomy."

"I don't really remember everything he did," Michael said. "But I do know he was greatly respected by everyone in Selby, and made quite a name for himself in the world of science for his work. And he was so very, very young. It was just such a tragedy when he died. There's no telling what he might have accomplished if he had lived longer."

"And when he did pass away – it was from a weak heart, I think they said – but he had left a will with all of his inventions carefully documented. Book after book of them," Monnie continued. "He left them all to the science department at Yale. Didn't ask for anything for them. Just wanted the world to benefit from his small contributions, he said."

"And then, he asked not to be buried in the family crypt," Hattie returned to this part of the story. "He said he wanted to be buried in that pretty little valley next to the old Quaker meeting house near the plantation. By this time, the Quakers were all leaving Selby, of course, because of the slavery. But that's where he wanted to be. Next to an old pine tree, I seem to remember."

"And then everything out that way was all burned out by the Yankees," Michael added with disdain as she straightened her back.

"How lonely," I thought out loud. "Out there all by himself."

"Not so much any more," Monnie explained. "After World War ... *II*," she looked over at Margaret Ann, "the Carolina Bricks factory was built out that way. And then quite a few homes went in. And the school. So he's not terribly 'lonely' any more," she smiled.

"His marker is still there, though," Hattie replied. "I went to see it awhile back. And, do you know ... there were fresh flowers on it," she exclaimed. "Like someone had just picked them."

"But there are no more of his family left, are there?" Margaret Ann asked.

"I didn't think so," Monnie replied. "I thought the family died out a long time ago."

"How odd," Michael said. "But I'm glad he's got somebody who still remembers him."

And I marveled that, for the past 30 minutes or so, five women who had never known Henry Laroque, II, and were no relation to him whatsoever, were also still fondly remembering him. He had been buried more than 70 years before any of us had even been born. And yet these wonderful ladies had been talking about him as if he were a favorite nephew. But this is the way it is in Selby. History is family. History is simply family being remembered.

SIXTEEN

Toward the end of November, the days were still marvelously sunny and warm, but the nights began to take on an autumnal crispness. Soon, it was Thanksgiving – my first in Selby. It turned out to be one of the most enjoyable days, and perhaps one of the most spiritual, that I had yet experienced in Selby.

It started when Brooks and Margaret Ann Lawton called me the night before and asked if I wanted to attend the "Blessing of the Hounds" in Selby Woods. I had read about it in the papers. And had heard it talked about a bit. And I sensed it would be something I would enjoy immensely.

On Thanksgiving morning, I walked to the edge of Selby Woods. Brooks was waiting. I thanked him sincerely for thinking of me.

As we began walking into the woods, Brooks explained

that Margaret Ann was not with him because she was heavily involved with the event itself. She was the current Master of the Selby Hounds – the local Hunt Club – and they are the group that is responsible for the Blessing each year. It is their inaugural event of the season.

Although Brooks is also very active in the group, he had taken a bad spill about a year ago, and was still not recovered sufficiently in one leg to ride – at least not equal to the demands of the hunt. It also accounted for the slight limp I had noticed on the first night I met him and Margaret Ann. Today, he even used an attractive walking stick to steady himself on the uneven grounds of the woods.

Selby is rightfully proud of its Hunt Club history. They were one of the first in the entire country to become exclusively a humane "drag." No live fox is ever involved. No one is hurt, or frightened, or even "worried."

It was a perfectly glorious weather day. As we walked, we were surrounded with warm, soft sun filtering through towering pines and leaves that were still clinging to ancient oaks and maples and other trees too numerous to name. Sometimes, a breeze would shake the boughs and a flurry of golden-brown and deep reds would cover us. The ground had the perfect crunch of autumn underfoot. But there were also unexpected greens from grass and lush ferns and vines that grabbed playfully at our passing boots.

Brooks nodded and returned greetings to a number of people who called out to him as we walked. Occasionally, he would pause to introduce me and exchange a few words. Everyone was extremely gracious to me – for which I am quite convinced I had my escort to thank. Although some of them said they recognized me, and mentioned my newspaper column or book, I believe it is more likely that anyone who is a friend of the Lawtons is probably automatically accepted into Selby horse society.

A familiar voice came up behind us: "Hello, you two," Jonathan Hancock said. "Isn't it a perfect day for the Blessing?" he went on.

We both turned around and I was glad to see my new friend. "Where's Claire?" I asked. It was one of the few times I had seen him without her.

"Oh, this is the one event when dogs are not invited into the woods," he explained. "It would be too distracting for the hounds, I'm afraid."

Jonathan quickly fell into step with Brooks and me, and then he brought his head up and said: "Listen..."

The bay of the hounds echoed around us long before we could see them. But as we turned the next bend, there they were – in specially made long-bed trailers, with open mesh sides so they could smell, hear and see everything. Brooks explained that they were called "hounds," never "dogs." He said they included a range of ages and experience levels. And that this was the first hunt for many of them. They had been bred for this, trained for this. Indeed, there was no mistaking their excitement and anticipation.

"And look who we have here, then," Brooks said as he walked toward a woman high atop a magnificent horse. It was Margaret Ann. She looked splendid in her hunt clothes; her boots gleamed black against the sides of her highly groomed chestnut mount. Her breeches were a soft fawn color. She wore a scarlet red coat – but the color is always referred to as "pinks," Jonathan leaned down to tell me. Beneath her coat was a white shirt and patterned tie. Her hair was pulled back, smooth against her temples and tucked under a classic black "flocked" riding helmet – a protective safety cap with a velvet-like covering stretched over it.

We visited for a few minutes, but then she needed to be attentive to her duties, so we walked beyond the gathering into the very heart of the woods. Many people were already present there and continued to approach from seemingly every direction.

We came to a set of massive old brick and mortar "gates" at one end of a natural arena where the event would take place. Brooks explained that this is where the Blessing and other events occur annually.

Jonathan then told me, "The gates were created to commemorate the family that originally owned Selby woods almost a century ago. At that time, they owned over 8,000 acres. Aren't they marvelous?" he said quietly as we both turned to view our splendid surroundings.

"They donated more than 2,000 acres to the town of Selby, to be held in trust, in perpetuity," he concluded.

From understated brass plaques on either side of the entrance, I read silently the gratitude expressed from the town in loving terms to these generous ancestral benefactors.

More people came up to talk to Brooks and Jonathan, interrupting their historical narratives. But it gave me a chance to thoroughly take in my surroundings. The clearing was almost a natural amphitheater, with softly sloping hills encircling it so everyone could have a good view. Spectators gathered in casual groups along the banks, forming a gentle circle that was just outside of the gates, an unspoken yet somehow defined distance from the horses and hounds.

Within the circle there were a few selected individuals.

Some were seated on horses, some on blankets covering large fallen tree limbs or low gnarled stumps. There were also a few old-fashioned dark wooden folding chairs available for them. Other members were simply standing quietly, or leaning with elegance against great old trunks of trees. It was obvious that these were the "honored" guests.

As a full subscribing member of the Hunt, and husband of Margaret Ann the current Master of the Hounds, Brooks was welcome – even expected – to sit within the circle. But neither Jonathan nor I would have been allowed as non-members, and Brooks' strong and gracious Southern manners prevented him from diplomatically even bringing it up. However, Jonathan told him he would be more than happy to substitute as my "host" in his absence, offering him an opportunity to join his fellow members for a better view. Brooks simply waved it off as of no consequence, claiming he'd much rather have the company of his "two dear friends."

As we waited, Brooks continued to explain the various traditions of the Hunt. "I heard John telling you that the red hunting jackets are called 'pinks'," he said. "And, that's traditionally spelled 'p-i-n-q-u-e-s' – most likely because the original tailor who made the first British hunt coats was named 'Mr. Pinque'.

"So they might just as likely have been called 'Wilsons' or 'Smiths' or 'Teds' or 'Bobs', for that matter," Jonathan joked.

Brooks went on to explain that there is a whole clothing etiquette involved. For instance, different hunt clubs may choose to wear coats of different colors – they don't always have to be scarlet. Young riders under the age of 18 must be attired a certain way – sometimes it even depends on the time of year. Club staff members wear different colors yet again. And the collar design and buttons worn are of deep significance and privilege. It was a bit more than I could understand all at once.

Jonathan then picked up the narrative: "For weeks prior to this first hunt of the season, countless hours are spent in clearing and preparing the trails, making them as safe as possible for all the participants – riders, horses and hounds," he said. "And, it's done almost entirely by really dedicated volunteers. It's been done that way for decades."

"Exactly," Brooks commented, and then added, "Then today, way before dawn, the scent was laid down or 'dragged' through the woods."

"That's the trail that the hounds will track or 'chase,' followed closely by the riders," Jonathan explained.

"You might also find this interesting," Brooks added, "because of the often difficult terrain involved, fox hunting was actually the forerunner of such equestrian sports as steeplechase and dressage."

My lesson in fox hunting came to a halt just then, because with a bit of a stir, the priest who was performing the ceremonies arrived. He was from St. Thomas, the local Anglican Church.

Jonathan spoke quietly to me saying, "St. Thomas has been performing the annual Blessing ritual in Selby since its beginning – and this particular priest has been doing it for over 20 years."

The distinguished-looking clergyman was tall and moved gracefully, and was dressed ceremoniously in long white robes, sashes and a black shoulder cape, with a high, intricately shaped black hat crowning his head. He made a striking contrast against the natural setting.

In a sort of massed parade, the hounds were then ushered into the circle at a trot. The rest of the horses were brought forward as well.

The crowd of watchers was large and respectful. Hundreds of people had gathered. All ages, all backgrounds, all levels of familiarity with the occasion. From horseback, Margaret Ann graciously welcomed everyone and gave a brief history of the event. For the benefit of new audience members, she carefully reviewed some of the nuances of the Hunt in general and the Blessing in particular.

Then, she invited the children in attendance to come quietly forward to pet and greet the hounds.

"It's important," she noted, "to encourage a new generation – of people as well as animals – to learn and to experience this … to build early memories … and to carry forward with the tradition after us – after we are gone."

Suddenly, one of the young hounds decided he couldn't wait for the call. His first actual hunt. He broke away from the pack and dashed at full speed into the woods. A few on foot and horseback went after him and succeeded in coaxing him back for a bit. But then he felt compelled to be on his way again. The general consensus was "never mind, let him be." After all, he knew these woods well, and they would catch up with him soon enough. He would be Blessed in absentia.

There was a traditional celebratory toast of whiskey by Margaret Ann, and then the priest stepped forward to do his part – to perform the brief but touching ceremony.

The Blessing itself was very old. Its lovely words echoed from years long past. It asked for safety for animals as well as humans. It quoted scripture. Its language was lyrical and from ages past. It carried history in its words.

In contrast, the prayer was relatively recent – it had been written just two years earlier. And it had been crafted especially for this place, this event and this time. It was incredibly beautiful and moving.

A soft breeze rustled leaves; sunlight slid down on golden streamers. Everyone paused with heads bowed. The hounds, hushed. The horses, silent. God felt near.

When the Blessing was concluded, the horn was sounded, and the hunt was on. And there was no mad dash as portrayed in the movies. It was a quietly controlled, happy sending off into the woods. Away they went, through light and shadows, across gentle streams and valleys and hills, after the scent. A morning well spent with horses and hounds, nature and man. New memories born out of an old tradition.

And all too soon, it seemed, Jonathan gently took my arm and we joined the rest of the spectators moving out from the tranquil beauty of these amazing woods. Walking quietly, in close camaraderie, to go our individual ways.

Brooks, Jonathan and I began to take our leave from one another at the entrance of the woods, just where we had begun, and I thanked them both warmly for the wonderful morning experience that had left my heart filled with love and peace. Brooks asked about my plans for Thanksgiving dinner.

"Actually, I've decided to take part in that 'One Table' event," I responded. "The one downtown in The Alley, where the whole town is invited. I think it really sounds like fun – and kind of what this day is all about," I said.

Jonathan said he thought it sounded like a wonderful

idea. Although he and his dad had plans for eating together at his father's home, he had heard wonderful things about the planning of this year's somewhat new effort. "I'm quite jealous – you'll have to tell me all about it," he told me.

Brooks added that he thought he and Margaret Ann might stop over later, but that they were going to eat their meal at the Selby Hotel, as this had been a long-standing tradition for them.

I hugged them both sincerely, sent my love to Margaret Ann, and Brooks turned and re-entered the woods to wait for his wife, who would be finishing the hunt in a little less than an hour. Jonathan headed off in another direction, and I swung the opposite way to walk the few blocks over to The Alley – the little district that housed a hidden row of restaurants and other stores, tucked behind the main streets of downtown.

As Jonathan had said, "One Table" was relatively new to Selby. It had grown out of the practice of offering complete Thanksgiving dinners in the town community center throughout the day for all Public Safety Officers who had to be on duty. One man – Freddy Paul, himself a Public Safety employee – had conceived of the idea of serving those who serve. He personally arranged every detail, and even cooked the turkey himself. One year, someone asked if they could please join the group, as they had nowhere else special to go. "Of course," Freddy agreed immediately. And it started him thinking. Perhaps there were others in Selby who had "nowhere else special to go" on Thanksgiving Day. He decided he would offer everyone – regardless of economic need or personal wealth – "somewhere special" to be.

Word spread rapidly, and volunteers came looking for him.

Soon, it had grown into an event that no one room or facility could easily contain. So, long tables were put outside, end-to-end, down the center of The Alley. And, at the place where a smaller brick alley intersects the main one, more tables were fitted. It created a symbolic cross – perfect for this day of giving thanks, and also as a very old and traditional sign for "hospitality." Everyone who is able is invited to bring a side dish. But nothing is required or expected. No money is collected. Private donations flourish, local restaurants volunteer goods and kitchens, florists provide centerpieces. The weather seemingly always obliges, too. And this year was no exception.

I began smelling the unmistakable aroma of turkey and dressing before I even turned the first corner. And then I could see why. On a large patio next to one of the restaurants, there were three huge grills, two deep-fryers, and one smoker. Each was working to capacity, manned by obviously hot but smiling cooks covered in formerly white aprons. Freddy was one of them.

Behind this cooking area, were tables crammed to capacity with different kinds of prepared foods covered with foil and plastic wrap. There were barrels of ice, where gallon after gallon of sweet tea waited. And beyond it all, there was a steady line of people, arriving with hands and grocery sacks filled with lovingly prepared side dishes and desserts and other contributions. This was just the "staging area."

When I turned to my right, I entered The Alley itself. Here, at each end of the "cross," were multiple tables for people to walk down cafeteria-style on either side. Paper plates, napkins and plastic-ware got us started. And then volunteers, who were corralled between the serving tables, helped us choose our personal feast.

No two dishes were exactly alike, because so many hands had prepared them in so many kitchens all over town from so many favorite family recipes. Choosing was especially hard. But after a morning in the open fresh air and a good long walk, I dug into everything that was presented to me first. And it was all fabulous. Selby is simply filled with remarkably good cooks, I have decided.

I was just beginning to look for an open spot in which to sit when I heard my name called out. It was Rosemary and her family. They waved me over, and I made my way to their side of the table. Greetings and hugs all around.

As I sat down, I noticed that directly across from me was a family about to say grace. "Do you think I could be included in that?" I asked. They stretched out their hands to enfold mine. It sounded like an old family blessing. Everyone recited it in unison.

All around us, people were coming and going at different times, so thanks was being given and blessings were being sought almost continuously throughout the afternoon. How wonderfully fitting for this particular day, I thought.

At that moment, music began to come from a small stage that had been put together in a nearby alcove. It was gospel music. And it was excellent. It filled the air with love and faith and welcoming warmth.

Rosemary leaned over to me then, shouting a bit to be heard over the music, and said: "Happy Thanksgiving to you, my friend. I think we will be going along now – I think they can use the space, and since we're actually done eating, we should probably go and make room for others."

I nodded my understanding, hugged them all again,

and they were on their way. Rosemary danced happily to the music as they disappeared into the crowd. And I was soon surrounded by new folks to meet and wish Happy Thanksgiving to. The two women who sat to one side of me I learned resided in a homeless shelter. The man down a bit from them was the owner of one of the town's men's clothing stores. There was a family who had recently moved here from Florida, escaping the hurricanes from the year before. There was a young man who had lived here all his life. A couple from New York was in Selby for the horse season. Another had retired here a year ago; their grandchildren were with them. There were two Public Safety Officers on their dinner break.

I also saw a few more people I knew – Brooks and Margaret Ann, who stopped by for the music; the Mayor, who actually remembered me; the Cinkowski family; Ridley Knox and others from my church. A wonderfully eclectic and harmonious group.

Eventually, I made my way over to where the music was originating. There were extra chairs and a small set of bleachers set up just for enjoying the entertainment. Throughout the afternoon, a variety of gospel groups took turns, each playing and singing their hearts out for us. We all clapped and sang along, too.

Then, one group of five women got up to perform. They specialized in close harmony, a cappella. They began with an incredible rendition of "The Star Spangled Banner." People rose to their feet, hands over hearts. It brought tears to most eyes, my own included.

It was time to make my way home then, I decided. This had been a long and perfect day. I wanted to write about it. I wanted to try to capture its meaning and essence. To tell how it had epitomized what Thanksgiving Day was supposed to be. Sharing together. Serving each other. Celebrating our oneness. Recognizing our freedoms.

With my heart filled to overflowing, the setting sun still warm on my shoulders, and a breeze softly at my back, I walked home and wrote my column. And I thanked God for so blessing this amazing town of Selby.

SEVENTEEN

People in the South go to church. It's simply a part of the culture. In Selby, very little else is even open before 1:30 p.m. on Sunday – according to custom as well as by law. First, you attend services, followed by a leisurely Sunday dinner with family or friends. Both rituals seem to be equally sacred.

An early story from the history of my own church – the First Presbyterian Church of Selby – relates how a new minister repeatedly preached longer and longer sermons. The habit particularly upset one of the original members, an Elder of the church. This Elder was of the strong opinion that the Sunday mid-day meal should not be kept waiting – and he made his feelings on the subject quite well known to the preacher and others in the congregation. One Sunday, after more than two long hours, just as the new Reverend was working up to a wonderfully impassioned point (and with no sign of winding down anytime soon), the offended gentleman stood up, motioned for his family to follow him, and they all paraded down the aisle to the door. The pastor, caught thoroughly by surprise, hurled a pointed comment to the departing group. The exact words have been lost over time, but it caused the retreating patriarch to return a stern look of his own – but then he bowed his head graciously and maintained his dignity and the social custom of self-controlled courtesy as he continued out the door. Approximately an hour and a half later, the minister was still going strong. The doors of the church were suddenly thrown open wide, and the entire family returned down the aisle and retook their original seats. They had enjoyed their family Sunday dinner, but still respected their Southern dedication to good manners and faithful church attendance. The pastor got the point.

This, and equally quixotic stories, were related to me one very unusual night by one of the church's assistant ministers: Reverend Ridley Knox. In addition to being First Presbyterian's minister of pastoral care, he is also a chaplain at the local hospital. And he often works late into the evening, catching up with notes of condolence and other paperwork. It amazes me that he is so consistently upbeat and cheerful and full of fun, when his professional duties deal with such sadness and heartbreak. I asked him about it once. He answered: "The Lord just didn't give me any better sense, I guess," and then smiled broadly.

The night in reference was early December. I had been asked to fill in for one of the church "hosts" who was unable to honor his duties that evening. There are 30 such hosts, and each is assigned a particular night of the month for which he is responsible for welcoming guests, answering the phone, and then securing the church for the night. He is to arrive at 6:00 p.m. and leave after conducting a final "walk-through and lock down" around 10:00 p.m.

The church is old and sprawling, having grown over time and space. The central structure dates back to pre-Civil War. It is claimed that a cannon ball missed the still functioning bell tower by a matter of inches. Even today, its bells call out at exactly 11:00 a.m. every Sunday morning, and then again as we leave at noon to join the rest of the community. Its spire rises tall and straight and can be seen for blocks.

The majority of Selby's churches are still located within the downtown area. Insightful early town planners allotted a full block to each of the then existing congregations. So it has given them the opportunity for growth over the decades since.

On this church, wings have been added that stretch out in either direction from the core building and then angle toward the back of the property. In one of these additions, there's a large open space with a kitchen at one end that hosts the Wednesday night church suppers and other special group gatherings. Sunday School classes are taught in rooms that line the other wing. There's a basement that houses the local Boy Scout troop. There's a tiny chapel just behind the sanctuary. And there's a small tidy cemetery just outside its doors, along with a columbarium where urns and ashes have been lovingly held since the early 1950s.

When I lived in Indiana, I belonged to the Methodists. But when I first moved to Selby, I took the opportunity to visit a few different denominations. While the Methodists will bear-hug you the minute you walk through the door, Presbyterians sit quietly next to you for a bit first. But if you sit patiently, they'll come up to you soon enough. And it's a genuine, warm hospitality.

On my first Sunday visiting, I sat in the middle section of the sanctuary about one-third of the way back. The senior minister, Dr. Hunter Bell, was preaching. I noticed his stole was a little cock-eyed and his shoes were well worn. He had a deep humility about him – the way he held his shoulders and hands. He was kind. Then he welcomed all visitors and he seemed to smile right at me. And he delivered a wonderfully thoughtful sermon without looking at a single note. His priorities touched me. And I was pretty sure I had found my new church. An excellent choir and seeing a few faces I already knew further convinced me.

By December, I felt confident enough to agree to perform the "church host" duties. But it was only then that I learned there are 63 doors to the church, and more than 75 light switches. And, in a power failure, it becomes very, very dark, and ever so creaky.

The weather had blustered most of the day. It was uncharacteristic for December in Selby. But there it was. Straight out of the north. Chilly and damp. Blowing and gusting. Whipping power lines and tree limbs and traffic lights with abandon.

I was making my final rounds of the church early – about 9:45 p.m. – when, suddenly, a loud, close "boom" – and all went absolutely pitch black. A transformer, surely. Everyone who had been there earlier attending meetings was already gone, of course. And I knew only vaguely that I was near the chapel. I felt my way along the wall. Not even any "emergency lights" had switched on – at least none that I could see from where I was. After what seemed like a mile, I finally touched a door handle that I believed opened into the chapel. I remembered there were some permanent candles in there on the small altar. I didn't think God would mind this utilitarian use of them in an emergency. Another couple of miles, and I had felt my way to the front of the room and tripped over the small steps approaching the altar, landing on my knees and elbows.

"Ow."

"Are you O.K.?" a voice called from around a corner. I must have jumped to my feet. I didn't remember getting up, but I was suddenly standing – on very shaky legs.

"Yikes! You scared me to death," I complained to the voice. "I didn't think there was anyone else still here."

"Oh, sorry. Just searching out some matches for candles," the disembodied voice replied. And then I recognized it as belonging to Rev. Ridley Knox.

A quick scratching sound, the smell of sulfur, and the soft warm glow of a lit candle came around the corner, followed by the shadowy outline of Ridley himself.

"Oh, terrific," I said with sincere enthusiasm. "It is so dark."

"And just a tad scary?" he asked. I couldn't see his face properly, but was sure it contained a huge smile at my expense.

"Little bit."

He lit a second candle, handed it to me, and then started lighting every taper around the room. I followed suit on the opposite side.

The space soon filled with yellow warmth, and things didn't feel half so threatening anymore. Of course, having company didn't hurt, either.

Outside, however, the wind was pounding the building,

and rain began striking the roof and windows with needle-like stings – loud and insistent.

"I think you had better wait this out in here," he said unnecessarily.

"I wasn't thinking of going quite yet," I answered. "And besides, I haven't finished with my lock-up."

"Well, obviously, that can wait, too."

He asked cordially, "Want to take some candles back to the office or wait in here?"

"I think here. It's kind of cozy now, isn't it?" I decided.

"It's one of my favorite places in the whole church," he said quietly looking around him.

"It really is quite lovely and peaceful in here – especially by candlelight," I agreed.

"Then pull up a pew, my dear ... and I'll regale you with fascinating stories about Old First Pres ... or old Selby ... or whatever you'd like to hear."

"Oh, yes please!" I had heard about his deep knowledge of people and places in Selby, and loved listening to the old family tales that were still so new to me.

He began with Miss Onna Ferguson Babcock. One of the oldest living first ladies in Selby. "Her people came from New York originally – railroad money. Her parents and grandparents started coming here as some of the first Winter Colony families in the early 1900s. She was born around 1912 or so. She used to be one heck of a tennis player. Could beat the pants off of everyone – even the fellas. She had her heart broken by one suitor, no one really knows that whole story but Miss Onna. But she married the brother of one of her best friends and it was a happy enough union. Only one child, who died young – around the age of five. And then her husband was killed in a riding accident. She bore both tragedies like the true lady she is. And she's absolutely one of the most generous, loving people you'd ever want to meet. During World War II, she opened her very home – it's one of those big old original mansions, on the corner of Magnolia and Main Street – well, she opened it for recovering wounded soldiers. A lot of the hospitals just didn't have room back then. And Selby still had such a reputation for its recuperative powers. She practically turned the whole house into a sort of rehabilitation facility. Used her own money for nurses and food and clothing and blankets and such. Word got around that it was a blessing to be wounded if you wound up at Miss Onna's. She'd pamper you 'til you never wanted to leave. She had plenty of proposals of marriage then, too. But she turned them all down. She still opens the house anytime there's a tragedy nearby – hurricane victims, floods, the ice storm that hit a couple of years back, the train derailment last year. Miss Onna and her nurse companion – Millie, her name is – will take you in and treat you like personal family friends. She is truly one of Selby's real treasures."

"I'd love to have the privilege of meeting her sometime," I said as he paused. "She seems like she's part of the reason why Selby is Selby – that culture of genuine caring and hospitality."

"She one of a kind. It will be a sad day for Selby when we lose her. But for now – she's healthy and doing great, God Bless her."

"So, who are some of the other personalities of Old Selby that I should know about?" I prompted.

"Well, speaking of Southern manners reminds me of one old story about this church membership," he smiled. He then went on to relay the tale of the long-winded preacher and Sunday dinner.

"I'm glad we have Hunter Bell preaching today," I remarked. "He's right on the dot every Sunday."

"He does have a rare talent," Ridley replied.

Then he scrunched down in his pew a bit more for comfort, tipped his head back and said, "Let's see ... have you heard about Old Fergus Campbell the horseman?"

"I believe I would have remembered that name," I replied.

"O.K. ... now Fergus was from an even earlier family – up from Savannah in the days before the 'Unpleasantness.' A tremendously dedicated horseman he was. He had a way about him that was truly amazing. It was like he was the original 'Horse Whisperer' – the creatures just took to him and trusted him, and he was dedicated to them in return. When word reached Selby that the Union troops were on their way, Old Fergus went from house to house and farm to farm and gathered together all the horses he could find. He took them deep into Selby Woods and hid them. No one – not even today – knows where he kept them. But he kept them silent, and safe, well fed and watered. And he returned every single one of them completely unharmed to their owners after the threat was passed."

"Yea, Fergus!" I commented with enthusiasm.

I had to ask: "What about the role the Presbyterians played in the Underground Railroad?"

"There was definite participation by many of our early leaders. But there was one woman who was absolutely passionate about it. Her name was Anna Lucille Robecheaux."

I recognized the name immediately. "Any relation to the postmaster René Robecheaux – from the early 1900s?"

"Yes, as a matter of fact," he responded with a bit of surprise. "Anna Lucille was René's grandmother. But how did you know about René Robecheaux?"

I told him briefly about my conversations with K.C. Korngold and my encounter on my first stormy night in Selby. Ridley is quite familiar with both K.C. and the post office ghost story – and was impressed that I had been so lucky as to have sighted the apparition myself.

He then resumed his story about René's grandmother. "Well, Anna Lucille was a strong woman – a woman of principle. And she was completely committed to the abolishment of slavery. If she'd lived about a hundred years later, she would have been leading the marches and making the speeches for equal rights. But in her day, about all she could do was work underground. Actually, I mean that literally. She was deeply engaged in the fight to educate African Americans – both slave and freed. But it was against the law – and against local popular opinion as well – to teach reading and writing to Blacks. So she had to be quiet about it."

He paused for a minute and said, "Actually, not everything she did was so 'quiet.' You're familiar with our balcony in the sanctuary, right?"

I nodded.

"Well, back in those days, the balcony wasn't just the place that held the choir and the organ like it is now. Back then, it's where the Black members of the church used to sit during services. The Presbyterians – and a lot of the other churches in the area at that time – welcomed people of all colors into membership. But there was still a significant 'separation' in practice – kind of a 'separate but not particularly equal' approach, I guess you could call it. The Black membership would sit in the balcony during the White members' service, and then they would come down into the main part of the sanctuary after all the White's had left, and have a bit more of their own service with their own pastor and all."

"How odd," I had to comment.

"I guess that's what Miss Anna Lucille thought, too," Ridley continued. "Because she made a point of sitting up in the balcony during services. Usually her husband and children joined her, too. I understand no one commented about it. They just sort of accepted it – but nobody joined them in their cause, either, I'm sorry to say."

He went back to his original train of thought, "Well, that was about the most overt action she took. But underground – which is where I was actually going with this story, I think – she did a lot more. Literally, in the basement of the church, she used to teach reading and writing to the Black community. It was at night, and they only had candles to see by." He looked around the room and said, "Maybe it looked a lot like this does right now."

We both were silent for a moment as we considered that scene so many years ago that took place just under our feet, just a few yards away from where we were sitting tonight.

"And quite a few times – quite a lot of times, actually – a student would come to Miss Anna Lucille for a lesson, and never go back to their plantation. Somehow, they would be spirited away into the night, only to surface weeks or months later up North or out West. On those nights, it was said that Miss Robecheaux would come to her class with an extra full parcel. Along with the books and pencils and writing tablets, would be bread and clothing and a few extra dollars. Miss

Anna Lucille put her money where her heart was."

"Sounds like Miss Anna Lucille was your kind of woman," I smiled.

"That she was … that she was," he mused. "You know, she really did put it all on the line for her ideals. If she'd been caught, they wouldn't have gone easy on her just because she was a woman. And, believe me, there were a few close calls."

"Like what?" I asked, fascinated.

"Well, like one night when she was teaching, and her young son – that would have been René's father – ran in all excited and out of breath with the message that one of the town's residents – a dyed-in-the wool slavery supporter – had heard rumors about Miss Anna Lucille's 'school' and he and his cronies were coming to close it down. Quick as lightning, she got the students out a back door and into the cover of night. Then she and her son gathered up all the books and papers and things, she heaped them on the ground, threw her long skirt and petticoats over them and quickly knelt down on top of them. She grabbed her son, threw him down on his back in front of her, covered him with her shawl, and told him to shut his eyes and lay still as death!

"At that exact moment, the door to the basement burst open, and the raiding party swooped down on them. Miss Anna Lucille assumed a prayerful pose there on her knees, leaning over her prostrate young son. The boy's cheeks were flushed and he was damp with sweat due to the exertion of running and panic he must have been feeling. His labored breathing also lent a ring of truth to her story that she had brought her son to the church to pray over his sick body. 'His fever just came on him so suddenly,' she claimed. But she just knew the Lord would cure him if she brought him to this place of worship and lit candles and prayed all night for him.

"The men were apparently convinced – and probably more than a little put off by the thought of exposure to an unknown fever. Especially when they asked her why she was doing her praying in the cellar, and she said: 'So as not to spread the fever to the rest of the congregation.' So with that, they promptly fell all over each other to leave them alone."

I had to laugh in appreciation for her quick wit.

Ridley continued with her story. "Other times, if suspicions were high, she would cease classes for awhile and hide the books and materials down an old cistern on the outskirts of town. Actually, it's the same place the church secreted the silver and other valuables when the Union soldiers invaded the town a few years later."

"Is the cistern still there? Can people still see it?" I asked with interest.

"Afraid not. It was closed up and covered over around 1910, when the town got a central public water system. Unfortunately, a lot of the old springs and wells were lost then, with the rest being closed up soon after World War II. The 'natural healing waters' turned out to be just mineral-rich well water. And developments in city sanitation issues over the years eventually shut them all down."

"But cool history about Miss Robecheaux," I said with genuine enthusiasm.

"Yes, Ma'am. She was a very cool lady. Unfortunately," he laughed, "that gene pool kind of dried up as well … eventually disappearing altogether."

"What do you mean?"

"Well, her oldest son – aside from that theatrical night of stunned bravery – never distinguished himself particularly after that. His son, René, was the town's post master for a number of years, but then he may or may not have had an illicit affair with one of the Winter Colony widows, and died 'under mysterious circumstances,' as they say. And two generations after that was the last of the line: Dennis Robecheaux – now there was one sad, unfortunate boy."

"How do you mean?" I asked.

"He was born to older parents and an only child. So maybe that accounted for some of his loneliness. My daddy actually taught him in Confirmation classes, and I knew him through church all of his life. He was always so quiet and timid. I don't think his father treated him very well. The father himself was a bit of a strange duck.

"Anyway – Dennis was kind of a loner. He was befriended by just a couple of the boys: Big Jake Dooley – who was a sucker for anyone in need and the down-trodden – and, oddly, Brooks Lawton. Brooks was a bit older, but a real leader. All the kids looked up to him. And he seemed to take pity on Dennis. Big Jake just loved everybody.

"Then, sometime maybe in the early '60s, when the boys were all teens, something happened to Dennis. He started to be even more withdrawn, kind of nervous all the time. And he began to drink a lot. The few friends he had drifted away. His parents were gone not long after. Later, after seminary, I tried to help – but failed miserably. Big Jake kept in touch. So did Brooks a bit. Several of the downtown merchants tried to help, too."

"How?" I wondered out loud.

"They'd feed him, give him clothes, and an occasional job. He used to get sloshed every Saturday night. But then one or the other would dry him out on Sunday, and put him to work washing dishes or sweeping up. Jonathan Hancock used to let him live over his stables. Dennis paid a sort of rent by mucking out stalls," he said.

Then he smiled and looked up with a cocked head at me and said: "He's a good man, is Jonathan Hancock, even if I can't get him to services."

"Yes, a good man," I smiled back.

"Then, last January, there was the train derailment and chemical spill over near the Bricks plant."

"I know."

"Dennis was killed in it."

"How?" I asked in astonishment.

"Don't know, really. He was there, it was the middle of the night. He saved a dog, actually. But he died five days later. He's buried here in the churchyard," he motioned to the cemetery just outside the chapel doors. "I conducted the funeral myself. Not many came," he concluded with sincere regret.

"How sad and lonely," I said.

"And mysterious, really," he added. "We're not sure why he was over that way. None of the taverns he frequented are out there, he didn't have any jobs in the area, and he didn't have any friends. And, now that I think about it, he had the strangest things to say in the hospital just as he was dying."

With heart-stopping surprise, the electricity shot back on again just at that moment. Lights so bright they hurt our eyes suddenly broke the spirit of "story time around the campfire."

"Whoa!" I exclaimed with a jump.

"Lord, have mercy!" Ridley said as he put his hand over his heart.

We stood up, noticeably stiff from the hard pews, and

began blowing out candles around the room.

"Would you like some help finishing up the 'lock down'?" Ridley offered.

"Oh, yes, that would be nice," I responded gratefully.

"You go east, I'll go west, and I'll meet you around back by the big doors," he suggested.

The wind had ceased almost completely, and the rain had let up significantly, so the chore didn't take long at all.

When we met up at the doors as planned, I gave Ridley a big hug for his wonderful stories and companionship and able assistance, and we wished each other a safe good night.

On the drive home, I encountered almost no other cars. But I had to dodge downed trees and huge limbs, wind-tossed trash cans and lawn chairs, loose papers and plastic sacks and potted plants. Some obstacles made me zig-zag my way down side streets and alleys, so it took quite a time to reach the safety of my house. Thankfully, nothing appeared to be amiss in my own yard – although it would have been hard to notice and there really wasn't much to mess with. Inside, I could tell by some of my clocks that the power had been out for a time there, as well. And the cats seemed exceptionally grateful to be reunited with me.

The storm was deemed important enough to be given a name. And it would take weeks for the cleanup to be completed around town. It would take even longer to fully realize the significance of the stories with which Ridley had entertained me that night.

EIGHTEEN

A couple of weeks after the storm, when everything had
been cleaned up and returned to normal, I was sitting outside
downtown enjoying a leisurely lunch at one of the sidewalk
tables in front of the hotel dining room. The warm sun on
my face was still a surprise that made me smile. It was
approaching Christmas – and I was eating lunch at an outdoor
table. It was wonderful.

"This Indiana girl is never going back North," I promised to
myself, rather more out loud than I had intended.

"Glad to hear it. So how's today's lunch?" a familiar voice
asked at my shoulder.

"Fabulous," I mumbled around my excellent sandwich, half
turned, and gave a 'thumbs up' with my one free hand to a
smiling Jonathan.

He pulled out an empty chair opposite me and asked if he

could join me for a few minutes. "Oh, please do," I responded as well as I could, considering my full mouth.

Jonathan smiled broadly at me, refusing to look politely away as I continued to try to keep my dignity. Finally, he said, "Well, you've certainly got a ring-side seat – it ought to be starting any time now," he looked southward down the street that was just a few feet in front of us.

He was referring to the town's annual Christmas parade that was to come down Main Street in about 15 minutes. It was the reason why I had delayed having lunch until after 1:30 p.m. I was combining two pleasures into one.

I had yet to see a Selby parade – but this one promised to be quite an event. It is a very egalitarian affair. Everyone who wants to be in it can be. They just have to sign up and show up. It's amazing that there is anyone left in town to watch. But several hundred of us had come to see our neighbors and friends, our dentists and Sunday School teachers, school bands and Boy Scouts and other people's grandchildren, march down the street to happy applause.

"Oh, good, it hasn't started yet." Breathless, Cris Demerist ran up and grabbed a third chair at my table.

"What can I get you, Cris?" Jonathan asked her.

"Ooo, some of their lovely peach-flavored sweet tea would be great," Cris answered. It was one of the Hotel's specialties.

"No lunch?" Jonathan asked as he was about to find our waitress.

"No. I already ate. Just the tea will be wonderful."

As Jonathan disappeared inside for the tea, we began to hear parade music from down the street and around the corner. The children that had gathered to sit on the curb in front of us jumped up and down with youth-filled excitement, leaning and peeking as far as they could around the crowd of legs that surrounded them.

"This is the first Selby Christmas Parade for both of you, isn't it?" Jonathan commented as the waitress who had followed him out placed the tea in a tall glass in front of Cris.

"The very first," I smiled with genuine joy. I absolutely love parades. Small town parades in particular. And now, I was quite sure, Selby parades the best of all.

The obligatory opening banner came first. It was carried by two young girls in short skirts and calf-high boots wearing Santa hats. And it pronounced this to be the 53rd annual Selby Christmas Parade and wished us all a Merry Christmas.

A couple of floats were next. And then the first band. It was the Selby High School marching band. In a sea of school colors, bright brass instruments gleamed in the sun. Traditional band hats had been replaced for this special occasion with more Santa caps – some clinging precariously over an ear or drooping slowly down a sweaty forehead. One of the tuba players was wearing jaunty reindeer antlers. In typical high school age-related growth spurts, they were a mixed group of heights and sizes. But, despite their youth and bits of discomfort, they played wonderfully well.

Selby Academy had a float with its band riding on top, along with a number of other students who were waving and tossing candy into the crowds. All of them were wearing their traditional deep green school blazers, the school crest displayed on their pockets. Miss von Alden was among them, too, and I shouted and waved as she recognized me.

Ed and Ruth Ann Cinkowski rode in an open antique car with a banner representing the newspaper. Good coverage of the parade would surely follow.

The Mayor and his wife were in a modern convertible car, waving and pointing to people who called out their names. Other local and state officials and dignitaries were similarly transported.

The entire force of mounted Public Safety Officers were present – their horses wearing matching reindeer antlers.

Even a contingent of clowns came by in tiny cars with honking horns leaving multi-colored confetti in their wake.

Santa himself appeared in one of the town's many splendid, privately owned, horse-drawn carriages. A driver and four, with a footman at the back for good measure. Old Saint Nick was wonderfully jovial – almost regal looking – and had lots of candy canes to disperse. He looked a great deal like Freddie Paul.

For the next hour and a half, we waved and clapped and were serenaded with carols and wished Happy Holidays from a vast array of marchers and floats, performers and fancy cars. There were more horseback riders and more bands, scout troops and local retailers, scientists of tomorrow and future farmers, and an abundance of pretty girls wearing crowns. There were pet dogs wearing hats, and horses pulling carriages, one giant rabbit, and a great deal of pretend reindeer. Cris, Jonathan and I laughed out loud and caught candy with the best of them and had a perfectly wonderful afternoon.

At the end of the line, Jonathan excused himself, saying he had to meet a potential buyer. When Cris and I went to pay our bill, we discovered our gentleman friend had already taken care of it. So we walked with the majority of folks up the street to be served cookies and lemonade and sweet tea on the lawn of the First Presbyterian Church. There, we also found a traditional crèche – almost life-sized. And a sort of "petting zoo" of assorted Christmas-appropriate animals: sheep and goats, a small donkey, and even one young – very friendly – camel. We stopped to pet them and watched the youngsters giggle with delight as the creatures were equally curious about them and playfully nibbled on their shirts and shoelaces.

We were told that the animals were "extras" to be appearing in the annual Christmas pageant, staged by the children of the church, which would be taking place momentarily. Cris and I looked at each other and immediately agreed that we just had to stay for this.

"I guess I had forgotten that the pageant was this Saturday," I confessed. Even though this was my church, I had somehow not remembered the date for the event. So I was glad we were already there.

"You know, maybe I ought to get back to the gallery. We've got this special hanging ..." Cris started to express concern.

"No, no. Don't leave. Don't you remember how great these things used to be?" I cajoled her. "You've just got to stay."

"O.K.," she agreed without any real fight. "You're right. It's once a year."

"And there are live animals!" I reminded her with a wave of my arm.

"And there are live animals!" she exclaimed back with a laugh.

"And there is Sally!" I continued as my neighbor Sally Houseman came out of the crowd.

"Hello," Sally smiled. "Perfect timing. I just dropped off some cookies. Are you staying for the pageant?"

"Absolutely," we answered. "Come on."

We were welcomed with the rest of the crowd into the

main dining room of the church and started looking for empty folding chairs. But all of them were apparently filled, so we stood in the back of the room with a number of other audience members, moms and dads and grandpas and aunts. Cameras seemed to outnumber actual participants.

The backdrop was truly well done. Painted skillfully on long sheets of paper draped over room dividers, which created a gently angled central scene of a stables. There were real bales of hay, and a small wooden bench where we believed Mary would probably be seated eventually. Off to one side was a large "throne." The other side featured a background of open hills and trees and meadows.

Cris asked in a low voice: "What's the throne for?"

I responded that I really had no clue.

With that, music came blaring out of speakers, but was quickly toned down to a more appropriate level. And it was quite lovely.

A young narrator came forward and was handed a microphone. She was dressed as an angel – all gossamer white and sparkles, with feathered wings and a golden strand of ribbon encircling her head like a halo. The costume was truly magnificent, and she was delightful.

The angel narrator did a lovely job describing the story as Mary and Joseph entered. Together, they were leading the donkey we had visited outside. They all took their places in the stables area. The donkey was behaving beautifully, despite the linoleum floor and flashing cameras and crowds of squirming families. A real pageant pro.

"Where's the Baby Jesus?" I whispered to both of my friends.

"Don't know. I can't see him," Cris replied.

"Nope, not from this side either," Sally shook her head. "Maybe he hasn't been born yet," she suggested.

Mary's baby brother, however, had spotted his sister and squealed with delight: "Hey, Ashlan ... hi! Ashlan ... HEY! That's Ashlan, mommy!" He called and called despite his mother's attempts to quiet him. So Mary stole a quick look up and sent a small wave in his direction.

The shepherds then came in and took their places in front of the painted backdrop of the hills and meadows. They were accompanied by most of the goats and sheep that we had also seen outside. This did not go quite as well.

One of the goats was startled at the sight of a large, live audience and rather slippery floor, and did what startled goats will do. And then it began head-butting the shepherds, who promptly got the giggles.

As the rest of the angels were cued for their entrance, a mother tried to sneak forward from backstage to remedy the goat deposits on the floor, but they just kept rolling off the piece of paper with which she was trying to scoop them and she finally gave up. So the angels came bravely ahead – all beautifully dressed in long gowns and feathered wings and sparkling halos, each valiantly lifting her skirt as she tiptoed through the goat poo.

The head-butting goat and a couple of the sheep got a little rowdy at this point, nearly wiping out the backdrop. So they were escorted rather unceremoniously off stage by the same dedicated mother who had unsuccessfully tried to scoop.

As the story unfolded, King Herod took his place on the throne.

"Ah – the throne," both Cris and I turned to each other.

The three wisemen came to visit him, bringing with them

their young, amorous camel with the penchant for kissing and nibbling the actors' hair. This caused the King to stand up on his throne out of desperation – to avoid these unwanted advances and deliver his lines unhampered.

Throughout the performance, the sound system was rather sporadic. The room was overly warm. Some actors' lines were forgotten completely, while goats were continuing to ad-lib, and baby brothers and sisters in the audience kept talking at all the wrong times.

The audience was pretty much doubled over with weakly suppressed laughter by then. But the children pressed on undeterred. And through it all, because of it all, it was one of the most beautifully presented Christmas pageants I have ever attended.

The children were truly amazing. They portrayed this timeless story with utter innocence and passion and joy. They filled the room with peace and love. They reminded us of the true meaning of the season. We all laughed and cried and hugged each other. And we left the church with the spirit of Christmas firmly planted in our hearts.

As we wiped our eyes, my companions and I wished each other a Merry Christmas. Then, Sally and I parted from Cris and walked home together.

That night, I wrote my Christmas column for the paper. It began with the words: "Christmas arrived in Selby this day. It came in with a parade and was told in the voices of children."

NINETEEN

My first Christmas season in Selby presented me with a very difficult personal decision. I am blessed with a wonderful family – both of my parents, two sisters, their families. But we are all scattered about the country. I am the only unmarried person in my generation. So, for most holidays, I typically travel to be with at least some of my relatives. In my entire adult life, I had never celebrated Christmas in my own home. My first Christmas in Selby, however, I decided to stay here. And my family was graciously understanding and lovingly supportive.

I had already made a number of good friends here, and there were days and weeks of holiday events and activities to experience. After the highly memorable parade and church pageant, there was an almost constant flow of concerts and art shows and parties and open houses. There was a walk of lights that turned the local downtown public gardens into absolute magic. There were carriage rides and strolling carolers. There were bake sales and garlands to hang. Holiday house walks and hikes through the woods. A sing-along "Messiah" at one church. Candlelight services at another.

And there was the Christmas Eve party hosted by Jonathan Hancock.

This Christmas Eve tradition has been celebrated by Jonathan for as long as he's lived in Selby – almost 30 years. The guest list changes occasionally. But not much. The location, however, varies greatly and is typically quite unusual and unexpected. When I received my invitation, I was thrilled. I stuck it up on the door of one of my kitchen cabinets and smiled at it for the two weeks leading up to the event.

The evening was to start at the gallery with cocktails, and would involve a rather large number of guests. Then, around 7:30 p.m. or so, those who were also joining the dinner party – a much more intimate number – would leave and move to the next location. This year, it was to be held in a large open field at the edge of town. On a farm owned by someone Jonathan knew, apparently. "Dress appropriately," the invitation had advised. But I wasn't sure what was "appropriate" when a party began with wine and hors d'oeurvres in an art gallery, and segued into a formal dinner in an open field.

Finally, the day arrived. Each guest had been asked to bring something to the menu: a bottle of wine plus a side dish or dessert of our choice. I chose cheesecakes because I knew of a local bakery where I could buy some absolutely delicious ones already made. My cooking skills rank right up there with my gardening abilities.

As instructed, I brought all of my food contributions over

to Jonathan's house earlier in the day. It was the first time I had actually been to his home – he seemed to virtually live at his gallery.

The house was reminiscent of a Frank Lloyd Wright prairie style. Low roof lines intersecting at interesting angles. Windows with six square panes above, and a single large pane below. A wide porch sheltered the entire front of the house. A painted wooden swing hung at one end. There were well-sculpted evergreens potted on either side of the wide, oversized front door.

I rang the bell and heard Claire announce my presence at the same time.

Immediately, the door swung in on an interesting pole-type hinge. Jonathan had on a jacket, and Claire was next to him. They were just on their way out it appeared.

"How delightful," he said, giving me a swift hug and taking "my" cheesecakes and the wine from my arms. "Let me just pop these into the refrigerator." He started to the back of the house. "Come on in, please," he called over his shoulder.

Claire was letting me know that she thought I was every bit as "delightful" as the cheesecakes – greeting me with old-friends familiarity and enthusiasm. I appreciated the fact that Jonathan never "apologized" for Claire's attention. I think if you're going to have dogs in your life, you should of course train them, but then accept their presence and personalities as you would any other member of your household. After all, would you apologize for your husband shaking a visitor's hand? Or your wife smiling and saying "hello"? Dogs simply do these very polite things in their own dog-culture way.

Once inside the entry hall, I was surrounded with a very welcoming, comfortable, sense of style. It was also somehow extremely masculine. No woman has ever lived here, I thought to myself.

The floor was slate. The walls were plaster, painted a warm red and filled with framed prints of dogs and horses, steeplechase and flat racing. With just a quick glance, I could tell they were valuable originals. They always are in the South – and definitely would be in Jonathan's home. The rug was a well-worn oriental, deep reds and blues. Peeking into the next room, I could see at least one wall covered with simply framed black and white photos. I would want to get a closer look at them, sometime, I knew.

But at that moment, Jonathan reappeared in the entryway and grabbed my arm turning me toward the front door again.

"Claire and I were just on our way over to my dad's," he said. "Please come with us. I'd love for you to meet him – and vice versa. It's just across the street and down a ways."

"That would be very nice," I responded. I had heard a bit about Mr. Hancock, Senior – John Marshall Hancock (called Mr. Marshall or Marsh by most). He is around 90 years old, well respected, but also known as a bit of an "eccentric." I was a little vague on the details about that. But I reasoned that at 90-something, one had earned the right to be a bit off-center.

Marsh Hancock had grown up in Selby, and then a career in the Navy had taken him all over the world until his retirement about 30 years before. This was also about the time that Jonathan had moved here and opened his art gallery downtown. Jonathan had lost his mother many decades earlier, and Mr. Marsh never remarried.

"We both claim credit for making the decision to live here first – and then talking the other one into it," Jonathan said as we strolled down the quiet street. "But Dad usually wins, pointing out that he was born here, after all."

We arrived within a few minutes – Claire a bit before us – and I looked up at one of Selby's grand old homes. It was brick, covered with stucco; although whole chunks of the overcoating were missing, exposing the brick underneath in an appealing storybook fashion. One side of the house was completely engulfed in climbing ivy. An old-fashioned "drive through" split the house into uneven halves. The main entrance was in the larger portion to the left. French doors stood open farther along at the front of the building, letting fresh December air into the downstairs.

Thick with mature trees, the front yard was so shaded, there was not much opportunity for a garden. A wide gravel drive circled in front, so there was even less ground for possible plantings. But huge pots had been placed at both sides of the ground-level entry, and holly bushes were flourishing there. There were pansy faces smiling at their feet like baby chicks peering out from under their mother's feathered skirts.

Down the two sides of the property and across the back was a tall "Old Selby" brick and stucco wall that could still be seen behind great drapes of vines – some of which were green, others just clinging woody fingers interlocked into massive woven robes.

We crunched up the driveway to the front entrance, and Jonathan unlatched the door, swinging it wide for me to enter. Claire went clamoring in. I notice Jonathan ducked a bit, as the door was unusually short.

"Hello, Dad?" Jonathan called out. "Mrs. Ferguson?" That's dad's housekeeper, Jonathan explained to me in an aside. "Anybody home?"

"Woo-hoo...in the kitchen," a woman's voice sang out.

"I've brought a guest with me," Jonathan called back.

"Be right out," a man's voice answered.

"I'll go see if I can hurry him along," Jonathan said as he left me in the dark entryway.

As I stood there, my eyes slowly became accustomed to the dim light, and my gaze traveled throughout the rooms to my left and right.

There were no actual cobwebs, but it bordered on what I can only describe as decaying opulence. The rugs were very large orientals, but so worn that the warp threads were all that were left in some places. Colors were almost indiscernible. Most of the furniture was draped in sheets, as if the residents were going to be – or had been – absent for a long, long time.

Great, tiered crystal chandeliers hung from the center of both room's tall ceilings. A breeze from the open French door sent them quivering and tinkling like windchimes. But there was no glowing light, no reflection, no sparkle from either of them.

Gossamer window coverings billowed from the same open doors.

Built-in bookcases overflowed with old leather volumes and aging papers and folders of brown newspaper clippings. More books were piled on the floor next to chairs or on tables tied together with string.

A small ball came thumping eerily down the stairs in front of me, followed closely by a small orange kitten that took one look at me and scurried with feigned emergency back up the stairs.

The grandfather clock to my right suddenly wheezed and clunked and then chimed the hour: it rang out seven times, although it was fourteen minutes to one, according to my watch. It then picked up its hesitant ticking again, like the labored uneven breathing of an old man dying.

"Rather Miss Haversham-ish, isn't it?" Jonathan said with a smile as he came back around the corner. I knew he was referring to what just happened to be one of my favorite characters from a treasured book of my youth: Dickens' *"Great Expectations."* Ironically, it was exactly what I had been thinking at the moment.

"But somehow it just works for you, right Dad?" he turned to the gentleman just a step behind him. "The clock just struck seven – so what time is it?" he asked him jokingly.

"About a quarter to one, smarty pants," the older man said. "And there's no molding wedding cake anywhere to be found."

"Now, who is this pretty young thing?" the father then asked, extending his hand to me.

"Dad, I would like to present Miss Macy Harris to you,' Jonathan said with easy formality. "Macy, this is my father, Mr. John Marshall Hancock."

Mr. Marshall took my hand in both of his. They were warm and dry and remarkably strong. "It is my pleasure, Miss Macy," he said with a smile and clear blue eyes looking deeply into mine. "My pleasure," he repeated for emphasis.

I could see where Jonathan got his manners, charm and incredible eyes – pale blue but framed in dark, black lashes. Mr. Marsh also definitely liked the ladies. Jonathan had a bit of that same reputation, I had heard.

We went into the living room, removed a couple of sheets, and sat on soft leather chairs. Mrs. Ferguson brought us sweet tea and homemade Scotchbread cookies. And we passed a very pleasant hour, as I learned more about these two distinguished gentlemen.

The love between them was obvious. But their upbringings kept them a bit formal with each other. I gained extended respect for Jonathan as I realized he never explained or apologized for his father's eccentricities any more than he did for Claire's enthusiasm. The house was like it was because that's the way his father liked it. He never chose to say why. He just did. Marsh Hancock also frequently spoke to people who weren't there. "I just talk to some of the angels," he said simply. "I can't help it if other people don't see them. But they're here with us, you know." I believed him.

By the time we left, I had fallen head-over-heels for Mr. John Marshall Hancock, as most of the town has. A charming gentleman with a marvelously quick wit and a terrific sense of humor and wondrous stories to tell about life on the sea. A man who loved horses and dogs and kittens. A man who somehow lived right where he belonged – on the pages of a classic tale. A man who could talk to angels.

I had dressed for the evening in a warm sweater and flannel slacks. Lightweight gloves covered my hands. I wound a scarf around my neck remembering that much of this party was going to be outdoors. There was just enough nip in the air to know it was truly a winter's eve. And yet it was still warm enough to appreciate being outside. The night sky was rich with silver stars across a black velvet backdrop. The moon was almost full and deeply haloed.

As I walked up the flight of stairs to the gallery, I could

hear laughter and holiday music pouring down. I entered
to warm greetings from those that I knew, as well as from
many I had never met before. There were plenty of hugs and
firm handshakes all around. Jonathan was the perfect host,
introducing us to each other, making sure we had something
to drink, assuring that no one was left out of the conversations
and laughter.

Drew Henderson – Jonathan's oldest friend in town – was
once again unofficial bartender. He pressed a glass of deep
red wine into my hand and kissed me gently on the cheek just
as Margaret Ann and Brooks Lawton called me over to them
and introduced me to Holly Hamilton, a woman who's name I
recognized immediately as an outstanding local photographer.

"Oh, I love your work," I told her with enthusiasm. "Your
images of horses are absolutely beautiful – and so insightful."

Over the years, Holly has captured a great many of the
local Selby horses on film, as well as hundreds of others
throughout her frequent trips to Europe. Her study of the
Gypsies and their horses and dogs in Spain will take your
breath away. These shots in particular, which I had seen
during a show featuring her work at the Art Museum – as well
as some hanging at Jonathan's gallery – kept me intrigued for
hours and made me create untold stories in my head. When I
told her this, she responded with a laugh and a hug and said
that she had been longing to meet me, too. She had been
following my columns. And she had envisioned that perhaps
we could collaborate on some projects together.

Suddenly, we were old souls. We knew we would be
partnering together on as-yet-undefined efforts, and both of us
couldn't be happier about it. It was as if we had been brought
together for a purpose. This night was, indeed, the beginning

of a most interesting, intriguing, and endearing friendship.

Holly and I chatted together for several minutes before she was begged to come meet someone new. Then Jonathan, Margaret Ann and Brooks all made sure I had met or was reacquainted with everyone else who was there.

At about 8:00 p.m., it was time for the "non-dinner guests" to leave. Only in a very few places can this type of social behavior be accepted. Selby is one of them. But everyone simply kisses and hugs their host, and leaves as asked. The rest of us – the chosen few – then go on to the keynote event. I suspect we all experience the same rather bizarre mixture of feelings at this clearing of the room – a bit of humble embarrassment, tempered privately with an equal bit of a thrill for being so honored.

Jonathan ushered us all down the back stairs, and there in the alley were waiting a number of horse-drawn carriages and a few extra mounts.

"I've taken the liberty of assigning you to a transportation mode," he announced. He then handed us off into carriages or horseback. Two of the couples were driving in a car. But the rest of us pulled lap blankets over us and shared body warmth and got thoroughly into the spirit of the night.

Jonathan and Margaret Ann rode horseback. Drew drove a carriage that included me and two others. And one more carriage of four brought the rest of the party. A total of 14 left for a greatly anticipated experience.

We didn't have long to wait or far to go. Selby opens its arms into wonderful farms in every direction at the outskirts of town. I believe we went north, but wasn't sure. Soon, however, someone pointed with excitement: "I see it there – look on the left – just look!"

There before us, in the middle of an open field, were what looked like a thousand candles and oil lamps giving off an almost celestial glow. Some were hanging in low-branched trees. Others were on poles or placed on the ground. Their brilliance rivaled the very sky, which looked like a reflection – two great pools of stars above and below.

Stepping out of the carriages, we walked toward a circle of flickering light that enclosed a long banquet table. The table was clothed in tartan plaid. Place settings of heavy silver and china were laid for 14 guests and sparkled in reflected light. At the center and each end of the table, massive, tall silver candelabras were ablaze with wax candles.

Along each side of the table, in place of traditional dining chairs, were large, oblong, unadorned bales of hay.

The horses were unhitched and allowed to graze in the field surrounding us. We soon discovered there were cows nearby as well, their curious lowing added a wonderful touch. A few small goats wandered up to see what was happening in their field, too. Claire and three other dogs had been invited and were full of spirit, but behaving beautifully.

More wine was served and we all found places around the table. Our host called for our attention, and gave a wonderful toast that was actually more of a blessing in anticipation of dinner.

"Thank you for being here, my friends," he started. "Most of you know that I hold this annual dinner because I lost both my mother and my brother around the holidays many years ago. Up until about five years ago, Dad used to be an integral part of this event. But tonight, he again sends us his love, and wishes us well ... but prefers to remember in his own way, surrounded by candles in church. Here – also surrounded by candles, and in a different kind of church – let's all raise our glasses to those who are with us … and to those who will be remembered. Happy Christmas one and all."

"Merry Christmas," we said in unison in soft voices.

"Here, here," someone said.

"God Bless."

"To absent friends."

Jonathan was silent for a moment, and then said with a clear voice, "Everyone bring your plates and come help yourselves."

The dinner was served buffet-style. The centerpiece was a marvelously prepared beef tenderloin, grilled outside. It was accompanied by the side dishes supplied by the guests and transported here by a small staff Jonathan had hired to help with the preparations. The sides including twice-stuffed baked potatoes, a potato casserole, a rice dish, several vegetable selections, a number of salads, and a wide array of desserts. We all complimented each other on our contributions and culinary skills. And most of us confessed if they were store-bought and not created from scratch. There was no holding back on seconds this night. Appetites were as upbeat as the atmosphere. The crisp weather helped, as did the outstanding aromas and general camaraderie.

One of the more interesting aspects of the evening was when the horses decided to creep up casually behind us, reach out and nibble on our baled-hay seating. Some of the more robust grazers reduced the platforms throughout the evening significantly. And dinner guests slowly sank down with the dwindling hay.

Throughout the meal, laughter was almost constant, due in no small part to one of the couples present – a retired corporate president and his wife. She was his "straight man" and he told hilarious stories about their dogs and other house pets. Most of the beloved animals apparently adored the wife, but hated him with a passion or considered him nonexistent. And he kept firing off one great, perfectly timed tale after another.

Then, we all began sharing important Christmases in our lives. The retired executive and his wife, Rich and Susan Easterly, of course recalled a brilliantly funny story involving the animals.

Jonathan talked about how he and his dad had started the Christmas Eve dinner tradition the first year after moving to Selby, and how it had been held that inaugural time in the attic of the house where his father now resides. "Carrying all the stuff up and down three flights of stairs makes me incredibly aware of the fact that it was some 30 years ago," Jonathan laughed.

Margaret Ann and Brooks remembered a treasured Christmastime spent in Wales, experiencing centuries-old traditions.

Holly Hamilton and her husband Tom became engaged on Christmas Eve twelve years earlier, and Tom related how he couldn't find the ring for a panic-filled several minutes.

Monnie Belle von Alden was a guest, as was her long-time friend Dr. Frank Dupree, a prominent local physician – an ear, nose, and throat specialist. Monnie remembered her first Christmas as Head of School and how the students had all made small gifts and paintings and cards welcoming her, which they brought to her door singing carols. She couldn't finish telling about it with dry eyes. In turn, "Doc" Dupree recalled a childhood Christmas spent with his grandmother in one of Selby's oldest Winter Colony homes. It was heated by an early form of hot water pumped through the floors, but was also assisted by fireplaces in just about every room. The young boy begged his grandmother to not allow any fires on Christmas Eve – giving Santa his pick of chimneys, and then worried that his stocking might be hung on the wrong one. So he and "Gran" dutifully hung a stocking on each of the mantles throughout the house – a total of 16. And, low and behold! on Christmas morning, a special treat was found in every single one of them. The following year, his mother quickly put an end to the multiple stockings idea, assuring him that Santa would find it just fine.

Cris Demerist, also a new guest to the occasion, told us about her first Christmas as a young mother with the second one on the way. Her husband had gotten snowbound out of town on business, but had somehow managed to get through and back home late on Christmas Eve.

Chance and Elizabeth Montigue offered a tale from their early marriage. It was a time when they could barely afford gifts for each other and made their own decorations for the tree. That year, Christmas Eve was particularly memorable, because one of their horses developed colic in the middle of the night. This can be a particularly frightening condition, they explained, because it almost always comes on at night, and it can be fatal. The vet came and went, and then they spent most of the rest of that night walking the animal, making sure he was going to be O.K. They passed the time talking quietly together, planning their future and what they envisioned for their stable. As if on cue, just then, a horse wandered up right behind Chance and gave an approving "whinny" that made us all break into laughter again.

I was next, and said I thought this night would be one of my most memorable. But I also recalled a time the family Christmas tree fell over on top of me.

The last to contribute a story was Drew. With typical humility and grace, Drew claimed he had no stories to offer that would be nearly as charming or as memorable as those that we had all shared. But with a little prompting, he did remember a Christmas gift that he thought might be of interest to us.

"I was still living in Charleston," he began. "But I had some great friends already living up here in Selby. In fact, they were refurbishing one of the old Winter Colony homes at the time. Up in the attic of the house, they uncovered a wonderful old writing desk that dates back to the early or mid 1800s. And, knowing my absolute passion for that period furniture, they graciously gave it to me as a Christmas gift that year."

We all expressed our pleasure for him. But suspected that it wasn't yet the core of the story.

"My friends even allowed me the honor of cleaning it up – fearing they might inadvertently destroy some valuable aspect of it – which I greatly and sincerely appreciated. But when I was working with one of the drawers, it became severely stuck half-way out. I gently continued to work it and finally got it pulled loose. And then I found jammed into one of the corners, practically glued to the bottom with age, was an old letter. It was brown with the years, and filthy, and was coming apart at the creases. But it had been written on what had once been a very fine writing paper and the ink was still quite legible – due to the fact that it had been kept in the dark all those years."

By this time, we were all sitting forward waiting for where

the story was going.

In his fine, soft, Southern voice, Drew continued: "The letter itself was not nearly as old as the desk – no valuable note from Robert E. Lee to his troops or anything such as that," he smiled. "It was, in fact, dated July 29, 1916." He leaned back slightly, taking a sip of wine, and then quoted the contents by memory: " 'My dearest R' – no name, just the initial R," he said as an aside. "'With the enclosed, I must also return your heart.' And it was signed, 'Your friend always,' and the initials 'L.L.' – very short, very sweet, very mysterious," he concluded almost in a whisper and with another smile.

"A 90-year-old 'Dear John' letter," Margaret Ann responded immediately.

"Oh, I think it's terribly sad," I said, "and romantic."

"Who are 'R' and 'L.L.'?" Cris wanted to know.

Drew answered, "Well, I do believe I know the answer to that."

"Well ... who were they?" Jonathan pushed.

Smiling widely, Drew responded: "René Robecheaux and Lottie Louise Faith."

Just about everyone at the table knew who these two names belonged to in the history of Selby, and Drew quickly filled in the details. He had traced the desk to the one used by René in the old post office. It had been the Robecheauxs' personal property and returned to the family after his death. Eventually, it had been auctioned off and purchased by the original owners of the home Drew's friends were refurbishing. After having established that fact, it was easy enough to identify the writer as probably being Lottie Louise – based on common gossip handed down through the years.

"Well, Drew, now why haven't you shared this with anyone

before?" Margaret Ann wanted to know. "It's a part of our local history and certainly confirms the suspicions over the years about René and Miss Lottie Louise."

"Somehow, it didn't seem to be the proper thing for a gentleman to do," was Drew's answer.

"Besides, it doesn't really matter, does it?" Brooks asked. "It doesn't change anything, and both of the families have now died out."

We all nodded in agreement, and then decided that Drew's Christmas story was one of the best after all.

"But what was 'enclosed'?" I wondered out loud. "What item was she returning 'with his heart'?"

"That, I do not know," Drew confessed. "There was no hint of it – no envelope or box of any kind, not even a left-over imprint on the page, I'm afraid."

By the time we had all finished dessert and after-dinner drinks, we had been entertained by more and more stories until someone noticed the candles were slowly going out and decided we needed to all go home. But it was just a few minutes away from Christmas morning, someone else observed. So we counted down the minutes, and all hugged and wished each other the best of the season.

I snuggled back into the corner of a slow-moving carriage, which would take me right to my door. Covered with a warm woolen blanket, and drowsy with food and wine, I looked up into the clearness of the sky again. Among the thousands and thousands of stars that filled the heavens that night out in the open fields, I privately looked for "The star." I knew it was two thousand years after the fact. But, in a way, it was also as recent as this night itself.

Candles and oil lamps and open night air. Food and wine

and people gathered together who knew each other well with others they had never met. Horses, cows, goats and hay. Those folks probably shared the food each brought, too. They must have talked about things great and small. They must have hugged and held hands. They must have petted the noses of horses and the heads of goats and held a dog or two on their laps. I can imagine they even laughed together. And gossiped a bit. And they remembered. They held that special night in their hearts forever.

And so, it was a perfect night. A seamless blend of secular and spiritual. My first Christmas Eve in Selby.

TWENTY

I spent Christmas morning in front of a wonderful, crackling fire opening gifts with the cats and eating scrumptious croissants that Jonathan and Marsh had sent over. The Ridley Knox family had kindly included me for the afternoon at their home. And, that evening, I invited Sally, Jonathan and Marsh over for a light chili supper.

"Mr. Marsh doesn't eat at other people's houses, I'm afraid," I was told politely by Mrs. Ferguson. But both Sally and Jonathan accepted.

I started the basics, and then Sally and Jonathan – excellent cooks each – gladly jumped in, adding ingredients here and there, which made it all amazingly better before it reached the table. A small salad, a bottle of wine, and a fun evening with some of my first dinner guests.

By the time I talked to my family by phone that night, I was happily exhausted, and glad I had nothing planned for the next few days.

The following week, the morning of New Year's Eve, I was even more thankful that I had nothing much on my calendar. I awoke with the worst sore throat and deep cough I think I have ever experienced. I had to cancel plans for the evening. But I couldn't even get out of bed.

For the next several days, Sally kept popping in to check on me and feed the cats, Jonathan called frequently, and Marsh and Mrs. Ferguson sent over chicken soup and homemade bread. But by the fifth day, when it had progressed into tremendous sinus problems, plus one eye had swollen shut – Jonathan insisted that I make an appointment with "Doc" Dupree, the E-N-T he had introduced me to at his Christmas Eve party.

"He is one of the best," Sally assured me with knowledge. "But he's very hard to get in to see. I know people – let me call for you," she offered.

"Thanks," I croaked weakly. "Help." My voice hurt to speak. My head pounded. My ears were ringing. My eyes were sticky. My skin was a funny ashy-gray. Even my hair felt sickly.

I began coughing and sneezing all at once in a sort of juicy explosion, and flopped back down on my pillows.

"I'll call now," Sally said as she left the room.

Within 20 minutes, she had an appointment for me later that afternoon. I loved Sally with all my might right then. She was brilliant. The best human being ever.

As the time for the appointment drew near, I tried to pull myself together, but nothing would cooperate and I really didn't much care. Old sweater, sweat pants, mismatched socks, scarf, Kleenex, cough drops. As I was driving to the doctor's office, I realized that I didn't have much depth perception with only one functioning eye. Again, didn't much care. I sort of parked in the gravel drive and shuffled inside.

The office was actually in Doc's home – an old-fashioned concept still alive in Selby. But once I entered, I couldn't really tell if his office was in his home or he lived in his office. It seemed to be an odd mix of both.

The front door opened into a small, formal entry hall with a coat rack, a couple of straight-backed chairs, and a table containing magazines. The living room was to the left through an arched double doorway. This seemed to be the waiting room. There were only three adults and two children present, counting me. But we had our choice of a large sofa, a smaller love seat, and assorted living room chairs on which to wait. At the far end of the room was an old upright piano, complete with an antique swivel stool. The front end of the room was lined with library shelves filled with books. There was a fireplace opposite the doorway; a well-painted portrait of a lovely young woman hung over it, reflecting an era of maybe 60 or 70 years ago.

One of the youngsters waiting was sitting on the floor playing with some toys. The other was kneeling next to an old-fashioned hassock, coloring in a book spread across its padded top. A woman, who appeared to be their mother, was seated at one end of the sofa. A second woman was in a winged side chair. Feeling completely germ-ridden, I took an overstuffed arm chair that was the farthest away from them that I could find.

The woman in the wingback chair looked up and smiled. "You need to sign in," she said.

I coughed back, excused myself, and asked her to repeat

what she had said to get through my stuffy ears.

"You have to sign in," she said a little louder – this time, pointing toward the table in the entry hall.

I looked around and saw a small black guest book on the table. But, upon closer examination, I found that it did, indeed, serve as a sign-in book for patients.

"Thanks," I told her hoarsely.

"First time here?" she asked.

I nodded.

"Allergies or sinus infection?"

"I don't know," I answered flatly. "But I'm going to have to get better to die."

She nodded back sympathetically. "Probably both."

I would have answered her again, but just then a long-haired yellow Tom cat leaped onto the arm of the chair I was occupying.

"Well, hello," I half whispered to him.

The woman asked, "Are you allergic to cats?"

"Oh, no ... two of my own," I responded.

"Good," she said. "Doc has quite a few cats that wander in and out." A black and white short-hair came around the corner at that moment to prove the point, and my yellow visitor jumped down to meet it.

"But he specializes in treating allergies, right?" I asked.

"Oh, yes. And he's very good," she answered, apparently not seeing anything out of the ordinary for an allergy doctor to have cats walking around the patient waiting room, sleeping on chairs and sitting on laps.

The other clients waiting this day obviously accepted the fact as well. The children even stopped playing to pet the animals.

On the opposite side of the entry hall, sliding wooden doors rumbled apart and a nurse stepped through calling: "Miss Barclay?" It was pronounced in the Southern manner as two distinct syllables – "Bar-Clay." And, regardless of the woman's marital status, in the South, she is always "Miss."

"Bubba ... Travis. ... come on boys," the mother on the sofa called gently. "You put those toys up now, just like you found them," she admonished with obvious practice.

"Yes, Ma'am," they answered in unison, as they began clearing their spaces, the older boy instinctively helping the younger one.

By the runny nose and dark circles under his eyes, I could guess that it was Bubba who was the patient in the family, on this particular visit anyway. As he passed by me, we coughed at each other in a sort of mutual sufferer's greeting.

They all disappeared with the nurse as she closed the heavy oak pocket doors behind them.

My remaining companion said, "It won't be a long wait. Doc is very good about that. He doesn't see many patients any more, so sometimes it's hard to get in. But it also means he doesn't stack us all up out here waiting, either." She paused and then explained: "I'm just here for an allergy shot. The nurse will be able to give it to me. So you'll be next with Doc."

"Thanks," I sort of whispered to her, as my voice had gotten stuck somewhere deep in my chest at that point. She graciously went back to reading her magazine and left me to my misery.

As the "new patient," I seemed to be the most interesting to the cats. My incessant coughing and sneezing, and reeking of menthol and eucalyptus, didn't bother them in the least. I soon had two of them perched on the arms of my chair – one on either side of me – and another one inspecting the contents of my purse, carefully pulling out used tissues and lining them up at my feet. Then I felt something licking the back of my head and hoped desperately that it was a fourth cat.

The doors softly grumbled open on the other side of the entry hall again, and the nurse asked for Miss Hairs, which was apparently me, as my companion had departed after receiving her shot several minutes earlier. Bubba and family were just leaving as well.

"Well now, Miss Macy, you're looking pretty poorly. Let's see what we can do to help you get better," the nurse said with great comfort.

"Yes, please," I answered in the best voice I could manage.

She sat me down at a corner of the dining room table to take my temperature, blood pressure and pulse. There was a small desk in the bay window at the front end of the room, and a few old metal filing cabinets along the walls. But there was also a breakfront filled with china, a sideboard with candlesticks and a silver tea set, and assorted family photos and paintings on the walls. The wallpaper was probably from the early '30s, but the furniture was much older – lovely antiques, really. In the center of the dining table, in place of the expected bowl of fruit or flowers, was a tray with a collection of cotton swabs, tongue depressors, and thermometers soaking in a jar of alcohol – all carefully placed on a lace table runner.

During the preliminaries, Doc appeared in a doorway at the back of the room. He stopped when he saw me, did a bit of a double-take, and said: "Oh, Sweet Jesus! You look awful, Macy. I almost didn't recognize you."

"That's just Doc's smooth bedside manner talking," the

nurse said quietly to me. "But don't let all that medical jargon scare you. You're going to be just fine."

A small wave and a "Hey" was all I could muster.

As soon as the nurse was done, she took me into an exam room. Obviously a converted bedroom, but outfitted with all the necessary tables, chairs, lights and other medical paraphernalia. Many of the pieces, though, were right out of the 1940s and '50s – classic design, hospital green, enameled steel. I loved this place, I decided.

Over the next 20 minutes or so, I could tell Doc was, indeed, a very good doctor. And extremely compassionate. He diagnosed a severe upper respiratory infection, compounded by – and probably brought on because of – untreated allergies. He didn't seem to think it was necessary to identify which particular allergens were to blame. He simply began treating them symptomatically – along with a strong dose of antibiotics to combat the infection. He also reaffirmed Sally's and Mrs. Ferguson's treatment already in force of as much hot tea and chicken soup as I could hold.

During the exam, he conveyed the information that allergies are very prevalent in the midlands of South Carolina. And newcomers – Northerners especially – are particularly susceptible to them. Molds, pollens, even stray winds from across the Atlantic Ocean, can become caught and cradled between the mountains and the sea and attack unaccustomed, un-acclimated, human airways, he explained. And surprisingly, January and February are typical months in which to begin showing symptoms.

I was his last patient for the day, and he didn't seem to be in a hurry to get me out of there. So we continued to visit a bit. He told me to follow him from the exam room into his office.

Another converted bedroom. This one was lined with books, and a very small antiquated oak desk was perched right in the middle of the room, with a consultation rocking chair opposite it.

"That desk got me all through school," he said. He must have noticed me staring at it. "And the rocker was my mother's."

"They're very nice," I replied, as I slid rather gratefully into Mother's rocker.

I was beginning to want very much to get back to my bed and lie down again. But he was sorting through drawers and cabinets to find free samples of all the drugs he had prescribed for me, so I felt compelled to wait. We began talking about Jonathan's Christmas Eve party and how much fun it had been. It was Doc's fifth or sixth year to be invited, he said. Then, of course, we had to further dissect the story Drew had shared that evening about Lottie Louise Faith and René Robecheaux and the mysterious note in the desk drawer.

"I did a little digging myself when I got home," Doc said. "Drew said the date on that letter was July 29, 1916. And I confirmed that that was the very night René died – the night he slipped off the post office roof in the storm."

"Really?" I responded, as he caught my renewed attention. "Any connection, do you think?"

"You'd have to think so," he said.

He continued to talk as he pulled a rumpled plastic grocery sack out from under a stack of books and started filling it with small sample bottles and packets. "I only wish I had paid more attention to the stories my dad used to tell me about the Faiths."

"Were your families friends?" I asked.

"Well, they were neighbors. The Faiths lived next door to Gran – the house Dad grew up in. He used to be a regular playmate of Lottie Louise's twin daughters back when they were all about five or six – actually, up until they were, oh, maybe, 11 or 12 or so. That's when the girls went to Selby Academy, and my dad went away to boarding school up North."

The sack was getting pretty full as he absently kept putting more and more into it, and I wondered how long he thought I was going to be sick. But I hated to interrupt his reminiscing.

"They sort of lost touch then," he said. "If I remember correctly, I believe I heard they all moved to California ... or maybe it was New Mexico ... or Maryland – but I don't remember when that was."

"So your dad used to have stories about them, did he?" I prompted him again.

"Oh, yes. He used to talk about the house and all its wonderful 'modern' conveniences. They had a central vacuum cleaner built into the walls, I remember. And an elevator. They also had an incredible playroom at the top of the house above the servants' quarters. The girls had a huge miniature circus layout up there. Actually, I think that's in the Selby town museum now. And he said you could see for blocks and blocks from the windows it was so high up."

He handed me the full sack. It must have weighed five pounds. And then he continued: "Dad also said they used to ride ponies all around the estate. The girls had a pony cart, too. Dad loved to drive that."

"Did he ever mention seeing the famous Faith ruby – the Carolina Star?" I had to ask.

"Oh, sure. Lottie Louise used to leave it all over the house. And the girls would wear it to play dress up. Used to fight over it a great deal, too."

He stopped abruptly then, as another thought came to him: "Dad also said that at one point he remembered the girls fighting over who would wear it, and the next time he saw them, they had a second ruby. How odd – I haven't thought about that in years," he concluded.

Even in my foggy, stuffed-up brain, I realized this was something of real interest. Something I would like to hear more about when I was back among the living.

As Doc kindly escorted me to the front door, he took me through the kitchen. Along with the microwave and toaster, there sat a sterilizer and bottles of alcohol and other medical supplies. Next to the bread were gauze and bandages. I eyed the refrigerator, but didn't really want to know.

Through a half-open door, I could see another bedroom that appeared to be an actual bedroom, with pajamas and robe laid at the foot of the bed. It must be where he sleeps, I decided.

A dedicated man. A very dedicated man, was all I could think.

God Bless Doc. By the next morning, the iron-fist grip of the respiratory infection had loosened and I was already feeling better. Within a week, I was just about myself again.

I had intended to look deeper into the story of the second Lottie Louise ruby. But something else soon claimed my attention that put all other thoughts and concerns out of my mind for the time being.

TWENTY-ONE

Christmas sales of my book had been brisk. In order to keep the demand up, my agent had accepted a number of post-holiday speaking engagements for me, followed by book signings. I had just completed a couple of days in Georgia on such assignments and was driving home to Selby.

It was early February. I couldn't believe the natural beauty that was already reawakening from a brief winter season's nap. I doubted that I would ever become accustomed to or unimpressed with these early-breaking Southern springs.

The sun sparkled invitingly through tall, long-needled pines. The air was warm and sweet. I had crossed the Savannah River bridge and entered South Carolina, when I decided on impulse to travel the rest of the way home via back roads. I took the first turn off of the main highway and headed down a steep slope through a wooded valley. In less than a mile, I had left the traffic behind. In fact, there wasn't much civilization of any kind around I noticed. I slowed my speed to be able to more thoroughly enjoy my surroundings, and something caught my eye at the edge of the road immediately ahead of me.

Two puppies. Tiny, reddish-brown, obviously lost or abandoned – but keeping close together. One significantly larger than the other.

I pulled quickly to the opposite side of the road and turned off the motor. No traffic in either direction. No houses in sight, either. Only a sadly forgotten barn collapsing a few yards back.

"Hello, babies," I called softly as I knelt down. "Come here, sweeties ... come on," I coaxed.

One of the pups came walking shyly, hesitantly, over to me – the smaller of the two. But the larger one followed as soon as I picked her companion up. I scooped them both into the back seat of the car and got in beside them.

Both were little girls. No collars or tags. Not more than a few weeks old, I guessed. The larger one was probably older I thought, but not by much.

"Where did you come from?" I cooed at them and stroked their soft heads. "And what are you doing out here on the road?"

The little one was short-haired, with a coat as smooth as velvet. She had a tiny round face, with large black eyes set behind a black button nose. She trembled slightly as I held her, but made no attempt to wiggle away from me. The bigger girl was long-haired, fluffy as a dandelion puff, and a gorgeous red. She had feet already half as big as she was. "You're going to be a big girl, aren't you?" I told her as I hugged her close to me. She gave a shy little lick to my chin and nudged me with her nose. Soft brown eyes blinked at me.

"Oh, dear," I thought. "Have I just adopted two dogs – one of whom is going to be rather large when she grows up?"

Then, on second thought: "Or maybe I'm stealing somebody's pets."

But after looking as far as I could see in all directions – and when a few cars had sped past me – and as I envisioned frightening consequences for these two little creatures if I left them behind – I decided I would just take them with me in order to keep them safe. Just until I could find where they belonged, I rationalized. Yes, just until I could find them good homes.

Sally was thrilled.

"Oh, how adorable. What are you going to name them?" she wanted to know.

I protested that they were not mine to keep. I was only making sure they were safe until I could get them adopted or returned. I was only bathing them because they were so road dirty. I was only feeding them because, of course, they had to be fed. And the fact that they had already bonded with the cats meant nothing. The blankets and toys were just some that I had found in a box, I told her. They were left from when my beloved dog Pookey had passed away a few years ago – my very best friend for well over a dozen years, and whose loss my heart stilled mourned.

Sally joined me on the floor, hugged each of them and tickled them on their tummies and behind their ears.

"So what are their names?" she asked again with a sly smile and tremendous insight.

I sighed and said that the bigger of the two – the redhead – had actually told me her name was Sophie. The smaller one hadn't yet disclosed her name. A few days later, however, she somehow let me know that it was Maggie.

Sally had recommended a good veterinarian for the cats when I first moved to town. I called him first thing the next morning to get the puppies checked over and to begin their shots.

Dr. Vincent Edgar – known by everyone as "Dr. Vin" – has a wonderful practice that he brings right to your door. A terrifically skilled vet, he has a mobile unit that is outfitted with all the latest equipment. He can do exams, immunizations, x-rays, even most surgeries, all within the large white van – right in your own driveway. My cats adored not having to ride in the car and then wait in frightening rooms filled with other animals, just to be poked with sharp instruments and prodded in private places, and then returned to the car for another disagreeable ride home. I loved it for them. For me, there was no stress, crates, or trying to get a cranky and nervous cat to put on a harness and leash.

The puppies benefited from the at-home practice as well. Dr. Vin pronounced them to be relatively healthy, albeit a bit undernourished. He also said they were actually the same age – about 8 weeks old. He even believed them to be from the same litter. As different as they were in appearance, he said they shared many similar traits. The fact that I had found them together when they were still so young, and that they were so bonded, made him willing to put money on the opinion that they were littermates.

I scoured the local and surrounding area newspapers every day to see if anyone had put a "lost puppies" ad in any of them. I also tried rather halfheartedly to find "the twins" a home – someone who would take them as a pair. But none of the papers alluded to anything close. And, although everyone thought they were perfectly delightful, I had no willing takers. Well, at least none that I approved of.

Days turned into weeks. And, slowly, I began to realize that I wasn't going to be able to let them go.

Right from the start, I seemed to bond more closely with Maggie. She was so tiny, so vulnerable – never quite as strong as Sophie, not quite as robust. Oh, she could hold her own in a good rough and tumble game with her sister. But she tired more quickly. And then she would come to me, begging to be held and cuddled.

Sophie could barely sit still long enough for a good snuggle. And she was more independent than Maggie. Extremely outgoing, yet with a pronounced submissive personality. Her inbred "follower" instincts, along with her natural canine social skills, caused her to avoid making direct eye contact with me. I knew that it was her way – a dog's way – of being polite and non-aggressive. She was simply trying to say, "You're in charge. I won't challenge you or get in your way." But it somehow significantly impeded our ability to communicate.

Maggie, on the other hand, was the definite leader of the two, in spite of her small size. Instinctively, she was the "alpha." She would look long and hard and deeply into my eyes, reading my face, "talking" to me with her expressions.

They both adored the cats. Sparkey in particular was a delight to them. Whenever Sparkey came into view, Maggie's tail wagged her entire behind and she wiggled with joy to lick his ears and whiskers. He graciously complied, tolerating her infant enthusiasm with considerable grace.

"So, do you think you might keep just Maggie?" Sally asked one day as we were watching the puppies play in the yard.

"I don't know." I exhaled deeply. "It would be easier. Mags is not going to be nearly as big, and she's so quiet. I knew I wanted to get another dog someday … someday. But not quite yet – and not quite so big – and definitely not two of them."

"You just can't separate them, Macy – look at them," she said unnecessarily. "They are so sweet together. They are so close to each other. It would break their hearts to be separated."

"I know."

It wasn't the only time we had that conversation. Practically verbatim.

It was almost imperceptible at first, but Maggie began to grow progressively weaker. Before too much longer, I knew. Maggie was seriously ill. Dr. Vin agreed, but was at a loss as to the cause.

Over the course of the next two weeks, she became more and more fragile. She ate less and less. I tried baby food, soup, anything to get nourishment into her. Then, she couldn't eat at all. Finally, she couldn't even drink water.

Throughout those last few days, Dr. Vin was at my house daily – sometimes more than once a day. His compassion brought him over some evenings as well, stopping by after his final appointment for the day. As a last desperate measure, he even tried surgery on Maggie's small belly – at midnight on a Friday night. But nothing seemed to help.

I kept Maggie close to me all through her final days and nights. Sophie – as well as Sparkey and Katie – seemed to know there was something seriously wrong with their friend, their sister.

Sophie would play outside for short periods of time. But then she would come rushing back in, breathless, to check on her "Mags." At first, she tried to urge Maggie to play with her – pushing her with her nose and nipping her on her ears. Eventually, she got too rough, and I had to keep them separated.

I put up a wooden baby gate at the door to the TV room to give Maggie a protected, private "sick room." Sophie would come to the gate, put her paws up as high as she could reach, and peek through the opening at her buddy. She would also throw special "prizes" over the top for Maggie. A favorite toy. A stick. Once a broken-off flower. She would drop them gently, carefully, just inside Maggie's room.

Maggie's last day began with a rainy morning. It was a day when I had to go out of town – a commitment I couldn't break. I had been up all night holding Maggie near my heart. But I knew it would be soon. We couldn't let her suffer anymore.

Dr. Vin came in to check on her after I had gone. He called me on my cell phone. I asked him to please wait until I could get back, please wait until I could hold her in my arms – so she wouldn't be afraid.

"Maggie can't wait," he said.

Maggie left my life as quickly as she entered it. And I am better for having loved her. But I never expected to love something so little, so much, in such a short time.

For the few weeks in which I knew her, Maggie became my hero. She was gentle and generous, patient and utterly courageous, and grateful for every kindness.

I can still feel her silky hair underneath my hand, her

soft puppy breath against my cheek. I can see her ears that flopped and her eyes that were too wise. I will remember Maggie's eyes.

That night, Sophie was terribly anxious. She kept searching the house, searching the yard, searching for her sister – her tiny soul mate. How could I help her understand? How could I help her grieve? I walked with her, talked to her, tried to hold her. But she would pull away, and go running room to room again; inside, then out.

Around midnight, I lifted Sophie into bed with me and held her close as we tried to fall asleep in each other's arms – as we both mourned. But neither of us could find peace. So, at around 2:00 a.m., I got up and went out to my office at the other end of the house. Sophie followed and, uncharacteristically, settled next to me on my chair as I wrote my column for that week. I titled it: "In memory of Maggie." I told about her brief little life, about the joy she had brought, and about loving her. And I wrote about Sophie, too – finding them together, learning about them, caring for them. I concluded the piece by saying simply: "Five weeks and three days ago, God blessed me with two precious creatures to love. This morning, He called Maggie home."

TWENTY-TWO

The horses were loading into the starting gate with difficulty. To be more precise, only one was proving rebellious. The others had gone in without hesitation. But one colt was having none of it. And, of course, they all had to wait while this youngster showed his displeasure. Jockeys and track workers were speaking calmly to the four mounts already enclosed, stroking their necks, keeping them focused. Other personnel were working with experienced efforts to get the final horse to enter through the metal frames and into his narrow, gated slot. His rider was wisely waiting off to the side a bit – wary of flying legs and a bucking neck.

At last, gripping an ear of the young racehorse, men on both sides of him locked arms behind his rump, and pushed, guided and cajoled him into place. The rider was swiftly up, feet in place, reins in hand. The bell sounded almost immediately, the front of the gate released them, and the loud speaker system announced, "And... they're ... off."

Little compares to the thrill of experiencing thoroughbred horses leaving a starting gate and thundering down an open track. Especially when you're right on the fence. Depending on how far down the track you are, you typically see them first – silent, a burst of flurried, blurred colors and determined motion. Then the sound of great, striking, hooves pounding against the ground reaches you. You hear the heavy, deep breath of these giant animals as they get nearer and nearer. Sometimes, you catch the jockeys' calls and whistles. The sheer power and speed and muscle and heart take your breath away as they pass you like a soaring wind toward the finish line. Then, it's the crowd noise that slowly begins to fill your ears. And the announcer's voice – practiced, controlled, but still exuding excitement. Of course, in reality, the cheers and calling and announcer have been constant throughout the race. But, I have found, if you listen properly, you only hear the horses.

While we were all watching the load-in at the starting gate for this particular race, I was leaning against the outside rail next to Chance Montigue. We were about an eighth of a mile down – about halfway between the gate and the finish line for this event.

"Your two are behaving nicely," I commented. Chance had two horses in this race, both loaded calmly and were waiting with patience as the renegade was refusing.

"It's an integral part of our training program," he said, and then continued: "That colt's going to leave his race at the gate, I'm afraid."

"Mmm," I agreed. I had not a fraction of the thoroughbred

experience Chance had, but I'd seen it happen many times myself. It's rather like an athlete that works out too vigorously just before a game. With a horse, however, it's mostly nerves and over-excitement. But the result is the same: There's simply nothing left for the actual performance.

The more acquainted with the entire experience of racing that a horse can be, the better it can perform. That's what the "Selby Trials" are all about. For more than a century, Selby has provided the stage, backdrop, props and extras for young thoroughbreds in training – those that are still learning the craft of what was once called "flat racing."

Every year, one entire beautiful early spring day is devoted to creating a "typical" race track experience for the horses. They're walked into a paddock encircled by strangers. They're among horses they've never seen before. They're loaded into a starting gate – although they've all been schooled in it before that day, it remains a relatively new and strange experience. They're running against horses they've not trained with. And throughout it all, there are crowds of people looking at them; people who are wearing bright colors and constantly moving and calling out to one another. There is a loud speaker – a loud human voice, sometimes saying their names. There is music and excitement and odd smells. And there are numerous other new sensations – new aspects to the sport in which they are just beginning to participate and understand.

Most of the town of Selby and surrounding areas come out for this important local event that is held at a permanently maintained training track near downtown. Here, the horses do not race for us. We are there for them. It's a fabulous tradition.

The racing was just starting. It was early afternoon.

But the humans had begun arriving around mid-morning. Tailgating and other forms of picnics had been going on ever since. Picnics here are complete with fine-linen tablecloths, crystal vases of fresh-cut flowers, and catered dishes from old family recipes.

The only prefabricated seating is a small spectator grand stand on the infield at the finish line. This is strictly reserved for horse owners, trainers, and their guests. The rest of us have the full use of the grassy infield or along the rail, encompassing the homestretch from the final turn to the finish line – an area that is soon dotted with carefully aligned pickup trucks, SUVs, cars, card tables, lawn chairs and blankets.

The dress code includes a bit of just about everything. Ladies in broad-brimmed straw hats suitable for the Kentucky Derby. Men in sport coats and expensive shirts worn over faded blue jeans and work boots. There are polo shirts and tank tops and baseball caps. There are young boys in bare feet and rolled up pants, and little girls in sundresses and sandals.

Between races, children play catch and take short naps in the shade. The sound system this day was playing classic Beatles music – which, somehow, seemed perfectly appropriate. And the rest of us simply ate our picnics and talked to one another, walked over to see the horses in the paddock preparing for the next race, and placed one-dollar bets back and forth.

The jockeys all visited with each other and shook hands before the call "riders up" told them it was time to mount their horses and move to the starting gate.

Chance appeared incredibly calm and was gracious and warm to all the well-wishers who called out to him and stopped to shake his hand. But he kept moving. Didn't sit in the bleachers. Didn't stay in any one place very long. I tagged along with him for as long as I felt I could and not be intrusive, although he would never have said so.

In this race, the two horses from Chance's stables placed one and two. Third wasn't even close. The slow-loading colt finished last by several lengths. Chance was pleased with his stables' showing, but not surprised. He makes a point of not only knowing his own horses, but the competition's, as well. His winner was named Clever Turn.

"Nice race, Chance."

"Terrific showing."

"You've got another good one."

"Very clever," one friend teased.

He acknowledged the remarks with humility, nods and smiles, and then went to stand in the winner's circle to collect the trophy with the partners who co-owned Clever Turn. Counting Chance, there were three of them.

Chance routinely retains just five percent of each horse he buys and trains, and he sells the rest in shares. Although he had exceptional faith and hope for Clever Turn, he ethically would not own more than the typical five percent. The remaining shares had been bought at 45 and 50 percent, respectively. It was rumored that Clever Turn could possibly be a serious contender for the Kentucky Derby in one more year. When asked, Chance would smile and say, "Let's see how he does in the Trials first." Now that we knew, we would all be following this horse's career very closely.

I had been watching Chance earlier, in the paddock, as the horses were brought in just prior to that race. He had looked his animals over closely, especially in their eyes. He had run his hands over their necks and noses and down their legs. Then he had turned and spoken quietly to each of his riders. They listened intently. The jockey for Clever Turn was a young woman. She was small, wiry, and had hands that would match any man's. Her hair was tied in a long braid that fell down the middle of her back below her helmet.

I couldn't hear what Chance said to her except the last bit, when he cupped his hands in front of her, she placed her left foot into the cradle, and he lifted her into the saddle at the command for the riders to be in place: "You know what to do," he had said with simple confidence. "Now, have a safe trip."

He then turned and said, "Safe trip," to the jockey already up on his second horse as well.

"Yes, Sir," they had both responded.

Chance had walked away and out of the paddock with his customary folded arms across his chest and a slight stoop to his shoulders. It's a posture that he maintains almost constantly during a race and many other "public" moments. It makes him incredibly hard to read, and I suspect he knows that.

After that race, while I was watching Chance and Elizabeth and the others in the Winner's Circle, a familiar voice said behind me: "So, do you want to ride in the carriage parade?"

It was Jonathan. I turned to greet him, but he was walking quickly away, calling over his shoulder: "C'mon! If you want to ride, you've got to come along now."

So I followed him as quickly as I could. With Jonathan, you can never be sure of exactly what he has in mind. But it's always quite fun. Often rather different. Definitely worth the effort.

"Wait, please," I called out, stopping to empty my shoe of a load of red dirt.

"You shouldn't have worn those shoes," he reprimanded, but at least he slowed down and took my arm to steady me.

"Apparently not," I responded, hopping on one foot.

"Did you bring a hat?" he inquired as he kept me walking.

"Do I need one?"

"We'll find something for you to wear."

We were leaving the training track property at this point, and crossing a dirt road into a wide drive that circled across the front of the Chance Montigue stables. There, aligned in a very neat and proper order, were half-a-dozen or more horse-drawn carriages. All styles – from grand and stately four-horse types to single pony-drawn carts.

The horses were groomed spotless and gleamed in the sunlight. Their tack was brilliant brass and silver and hand-rubbed leather. The carriages were lovingly restored originals. Paint and trim immaculate, polished to a deep glow of pride and respect and affection. The riders were dressed to match the era of their carriages: broad-brimmed hats, morning coats, long flowing skirts, spit-and-polished boots.

Across the drive, Drew called out to us from a one-horse, two-passenger carriage toward the end of the line. The carriage was a quiet black with deep mahogany trim. Two large wooden-spoked wheels supported a low-backed leather-padded bench seat. It was small and neat; it reminded me of something a doctor would have driven to make house calls in the 1800s.

The lovely carriage-trained horse was named Trevor, and was posturing with pride and enthusiasm, certain that no horse there that day was nearly so handsome as he. He may have been right.

"Hurry," Jonathan encouraged with a grin, "they're about ready to start."

"Here." Drew tossed me a sort of scarf/shawl as I climbed up beside him. "And put this over your lap and cover up those shoes," he instructed shaking out a lightweight lap blanket.

"Wait a minute." Jonathan reached down and pulled a bonnet out of a pile of goods a few feet away. "Put this on, too."

"The dress code is rather strict," Drew explained, "so we bring extra things." Then I noticed that he was wearing an old-fashioned suit, tie and cap that looked historical and quite spiffy.

The other carriages were beginning to pull forward.

"These, too," Jonathan said, as he gave me a pair of gloves to pull on.

"Buddy, Hamlet ... up!" Drew commanded, and two terriers appeared out of nowhere – one a white Westie, the other a black Scottish Terrier. With practiced paws they found their way to the seat. Buddy, the Westie squeezed and snuggled his way in between us, his tail hanging over the back of the seat just so. Hamlet bounded into my lap, planted a kiss on my chin, and looked up at me as if to say, "Well, hold on to me, please. That is, after all, the main reason you are here."

A flip of the reins, the click of Drew's tongue, and we were moving.

Jonathan waved and laughed as I grabbed the edge of my seat in one hand, and Hamlet in the other.

The parade of carriages headed out the drive and across the street and onto the training track. One by one, the announcer introduced the carriage owners, drivers and passengers. Each was greeted with warm applause and support. Special friends called out along the way.

When it was Drew's turn, he was introduced along with Buddy and Hamlet, and they were applauded by the crowd. I was a "mystery" woman to the announcer, however – a last-minute rider. But as we were traveling down the track along the rail, whistles and yells were coming from a few yards away: There was Jonathan again, with Marsh and Mrs. Ferguson. Cris was greeting us with enthusiasm, along with Brooks and Margaret Ann Lawton. Farther down were Sally and her ex-in-laws Barbara and Patty. There were Monnie Belle ... and Julia ... and Doc – all dressed to the teeth. Rosemary and Tim and their children were peeking over and under the rail as we passed. I recognized Ridley Knox and several others from church. Even Chance and Elizabeth Montigue waved and gave us broad smiles. Indeed, it seemed as if everyone in town – at least everyone I knew – was there watching this happy annual event.

The parade consisted of one trip around the entire track. At the end, we exited the same way we had come onto it, and returned to the staging area across the road in front of the stables.

It had been great fun and I was a bit out of breath. Hanging on was more a part of the ride than I had realized – clutching Hamlet, my hat, my lap robe, and my seat.

"That was wonderful!" I enthused to Drew as I began to relax my muscles. "Thanks so much for including me."

"You're very welcome," he replied. "But I must confess, it was Jonathan's idea. He thought you might enjoy it."

Buddy and Hamlet leaped to the ground and sat patiently in the shade of the carriage while I "disrobed" from my special attire.

"Oh, wait!" a voice called. "Just one more shot."

It was Holly Hamilton, my new photographer friend and collaborator. She had apparently been getting a variety of candid photos of the entire parade and was wanting just another close-up of Drew's.

He posed obligingly with Buddy and Hamlet, and then headed back to his stables.

Holly and I both waved goodbye to them all as they drove off, and I called out my sincere thanks once again. "Hang on, Hamlet," I added as they disappeared around the bend.

"Have you been capturing the whole day?" I asked Holly, nodding to her camera as we returned to the track.

"Oh, yeah," she answered. "This is one of the most wonderful events to shoot. I just love it. It's never the same two years in a row."

"How about you?" she asked in return. "Are you gathering inspiration for yet another fabulous column?"

"I don't know about the 'fabulous' part, but yes, I'm pretty sure a column will be forthcoming."

Typically, when I am considering a column, I need to concentrate and observe and sort of "process" the entire experience alone. Being with someone and talking and discussing it tends to be a distraction. Somehow, that human interaction causes me to lose the personal, emotional response to it – unless, of course, the people themselves and the conversation are an integral part of the experience. I expected that it was somewhat the same for Holly and her photography.

Although we stayed together for much of the rest of the afternoon, we talked little. Between two of the races, she led me to the edge of the track near the finish line.

"Come with me," she said simply.

With a signal that I never saw, the track officials who were guarding the ropes keeping attendees off the track, suddenly lifted the barriers. People from both sides scrambled to cross it – from the outside over to the infield, and vice versa. It reminded me of a bunch of cats caught on the wrong side of a door: terribly anxious to get to the other side ... and then, once there, not sure why.

It did give a whole new perspective to the race, however. And, by walking across the infield to the far side, we were able to stand within feet of the starting gate for this longest of races. Far from the crowd, it was an intimate glimpse into the raw emotions and hushed excitement of the horses and riders and track personnel at the very start of a race. The terrible shrill of the starting bell. The heart-beat-skipping moment when the gates part and the riders say "go" with their heels and hands. That moment in time when thought must turn instantly into action. Don't waver, don't bump, don't fall, don't lose precious seconds. Run. Run now. Run with all your might and heart. Run.

I don't remember who won that particular race.

Holly then led me to another little-known spot in the infield. A hundred yards or so behind the private spectator grandstands was a small stand of trees. They were old and gnarled, oaks and cypress. Nestled at the base of what appeared to be one of the oldest of the trees was a smooth, dark, marble headstone. I read the carved message slowly, its crispness faded over the decades of exposure to the elements: "Beau Geste, 1902-1924, A Selby thoroughbred champion. He won as many hearts as races."

"Oh, how lovely," I said. "How perfect that he is buried here where he was so loved. And memorialized for generations who never knew him."

"I thought you'd appreciate it," Holly said smiling.

"And here's another – although it's just a memorial, not an actual grave marker," she pointed to a flat ground-level stone a few yards away.

It read: "Jimmy John Jackson, 1895 – 1983, Groom to 22 stakes winners, friend to all."

"These are amazing," I said to Holly. "This is so full of history and sentiment … I just don't know what to say."

"Oh, there's an even better one over at the Steeplechase track," she indicated pointing south of the field in which we were standing. "I'll have to take you over there sometime."

"No, no … you can't do that," I laughed. "You've got to tell me what it is now. You can't just leave me wondering."

"Well, it's reportedly an actual grave site, just off the Steeplechase track near one of the jumps. And it's for a guy named Harley T. McPherson who died about 20 years ago. It says something like: 'His last fall' or maybe 'He lies where he last fell' or something like that."

I gave her a quizzical look and she continued.

"Apparently, Harley was notorious for his serious narcolepsy. He used to fall asleep literally standing up – or even on a horse. No kidding! He would just drop off and fall over – sometimes right in the middle of a conversation. And people would just step over him or let him sleep or sit him back upright. And then he'd come around again and pick up right where he left off. There are some real stories about good old Harley. So one time he dropped off watching a Steeplechase event, and finally someone noticed that he didn't come around again. And so that's where they buried him."

I laughed out loud, but was fascinated.

Looking at my face, Holly said: "Honest. I'm not making this up. Tell you what, I'll take you to dinner next Saturday night at a place owned by his niece and her husband. This place is a real experience anyway in and of itself. You'll like it."

"You're on," I answered without hesitation.

It was just before the last race of the day, so we crossed over the track again while we could, in order to watch the last event on the rail near the finish line. Another entry from Chance's stables won – this one a filly. It was close, but she led all the way from the gate and never faltered.

Chance had had a good day, his horses placing first – and often second as well – in every race he had entered. Of course, all of the participating horses could be considered "winners" that day – now all one step closer to actual track experience and possible championships.

I said goodbye to Holly and looked for Jonathan to thank, but couldn't find him. So I just watched as people packed up and cleared up their places. It was amazing how everyone tried their best to not leave any trash or sign of disrespect for the property. I didn't want to leave, somehow, so I simply stayed around. I chatted with a couple of mounted Public Safety Officers. I watched the track crew disassemble or return equipment to barns. It felt a little like taking down Christmas decorations. A tractor pulled a rake-like bed behind it, smoothing the track, erasing all signs of our having been there.

The sun was setting, a golden liquid fire, when I walked home, the last to leave.

TWENTY-THREE

Holly was as good as her word, and she and Tom picked me up at 7:00 p.m. the next Saturday night for dinner. I had been told very little about the place to which we were headed, except its name – "Cabbages and Kings" – and that it was owned and operated by a couple of "old hippies." In the car, both Holly and Tom elaborated a bit.

"Sylvia and Wayne St. Martin are fabulous," Tom began. "And they run a pretty good restaurant," he added almost as an afterthought.

"Now, when we get there, Sylvia will probably wave us in with a wand," Holly said.

"A wand?" I repeated.

"A wand," they said in unison.

"Why?" I naturally asked.

"Don't know, really. Never actually asked."

"It's pink. Plastic. It glows," Holly offered, as if this would make it easier to understand.

"And she'll probably be wearing a rhinestone tiara when she does it," Tom added.

"The restaurant is a big, ancient white clapboard house out on the old highway," Holly then went on to say. "Wayne and Sylvia live on the top floor. The ground floor is devoted to the restaurant, and they've kept most of the original rooms – so it feels relatively intimate. There's a great old kitchen in the back."

She continued, "On the second floor is where they host larger private parties – like family reunions and wedding receptions. There was an original ballroom up there, and they have opened up some of the rest of the space as well."

"It sounds grand," I observed.

"Well..." they looked at each other. "Once was, and could be, perhaps. But it's rather run down now."

"So Holly loves it," Tom grinned. "But to be honest, I don't know how they keep it going. They do a pretty good business on weekends – Sunday brunch is wonderful! But the rest of the week, there aren't many patrons, I'm afraid."

"Yes, I do love it in all its decay and former glory," Holly said with an artist's dedication to all things visually intriguing. "But I wish more people would remember to eat there. I think that's the only problem – out of sight, out of mind."

Most of the popular eating establishments in Selby are, indeed, downtown. There are quite a few of them, and we pass by them daily in our everyday business. It is funny how easy it is to slip into the small town mentality of not expecting to "travel" very far to meet one's needs. And, although "Cabbages and Kings" is a mere 10-minute drive away, it is not a place one sees regularly as a reminder of its existence.

We pulled into the gravel parking lot and our headlights swept across a prominent old painted-wood sign welcoming us to "Cabbages and Kings, Wayne and Sylvia St. Martin, proprietors." More accurately, it said: "Cabbages and King" – the final "s" lost to years of weather and wear. The same apparent fate had been realized by the proprietors' last name, which now appeared to be "S Martin." There had been some sort of painted image as well, but neglect and evening darkness prevented me from properly seeing what it was.

Although this was Saturday night, there was plenty of parking still available. Soft outdoor lighting gave a warm, dignified glow to the old structure, kindly absorbing any more signs of obvious decay. From inside, old-fashioned chandelier lights and flickering table candles beckoned invitingly. In addition to bits of laughter and conversation that floated through the open windows, all the night sounds of a Southern springtime filled our ears, reminders that we were in the country. The heady scent of wisteria and roses wrapped around us, and competed with the succulent aroma of a wood-fired barbecue.

"I am hungry," Tom stated on behalf of us all as we carefully wound our way up the packed-dirt and cobblestone walkway.

We climbed thick, solid stone steps to the wide, wood-planked front porch. It creaked and groaned, announcing our arrival.

The generously sized front door swung wide before we could even reach for the handle. Sylvia – chef's coat, tiara, wand, and all – greeted us with passionate hospitality.

"Welcome, welcome, welcome," she recited as the wand

waved ceremoniously over our heads. "Welcome to 'Cabbages and Kings,' where great food and wine is exceeded only by excellent conversation."

"Ah, ha," the connection hit me. " 'The time has come,' the Walrus said, 'To talk of many things...,' " I recited from Lewis Carroll's The Walrus and the Carpenter.

" 'Of shoes and ships and sealing wax, of cabbages and kings – and why the sea is boiling hot, and whether pigs have wings'," Sylvia and I finished in unison.

"I like her," Sylvia said in a loud stage whisper to Holly. "She can stay."

Then, with a quick twist of her wrist and wave of the wand, she led us to our table: "This way, my lovelies, this way please."

We were paraded to a well-positioned, white-linen-covered corner table near a very large old marble fireplace. The precious stone of the fireplace front was split in several places, pits and crevices black with age. The huge mirror above it was missing most of its silver backing, creating numerous large blank spaces and an intriguing tarnished crackle across it massive face. Its frame was antique gold, carved, and gorgeous.

"What wine will it be to start the meal?" Sylvia asked.

"Why don't you choose something for us," Tom answered. "Red or white."

"White, I think..." Tom looked at us both and Holly nodded in agreement.

"Just water for me tonight," I said.

"Water for me as well," Tom said. "I'm the designated driver tonight," he explained in a light manner.

"Well, then," Holly said, "I'll have mine and perhaps theirs as well."

To which Sylvia responded directly to Holly: "Of course, you realize that St. Martin is the patron saint of drunkards, innkeepers, and geese. So, you just feel free to get as drunk as you please, act like a goose, and we'll put you up for the night."

"Thank you," Holly answered resolutely and with a straight face, as Tom and I roared.

Beverages were served, our orders were taken, and we broke into a loaf of wonderful homemade Irish soda bread. Munching away, I began to look at all the old photos covering the walls. Even in the soft candlelight, I could tell they were from all eras of Selby's impressive history – from the second half of the 19th century, through the heyday of the Winter Colony, to the 1950s, and as recent as a few years ago.

There was only one other table of patrons in the room with us, so I asked Holly and Tom if they would mind if I wandered and took a closer look at some of these fascinating glimpses into the past.

"Oh, please. This is one of the reasons we brought you here," Holly said. "In fact, let me see if I can find one of old Harley McPherson – Sylvia's uncle – the narcoleptic."

She rose from the table with me and started peering at the framed photos on the wall nearest us. There were debutante balls and people on horseback, garden parties and political rallies, and numerous graduation classes, polo matches and picnics.

"Here you go," she motioned to me to come to her. "This is him ... this is Harley ... I think."

"Who are you looking at? Uncle Harley?" Sylvia had returned bringing our salads. "Do you want to hear about

'Uncle H.' and his 'affliction,' as my grandma used to call it?"

"I was telling Macy about his grave at the Steeplechase track, and she got kind of interested," Holly explained simply.

"Well, he was a real hoot," Sylvia said, putting our salads down and coming to stand between us.

"Yes, that's him," she confirmed, "the one in the middle."

I looked closer at the black and white photo. It must have been taken in the 1920s or '30s. Three people were on horseback, dressed in fashionable riding clothes. A fourth individual – a man – was on foot, standing to one side and behind them. He held a good amount of what looked like hunting or camping gear.

Uncle Harley's riding companions were a man and a woman. The man was grinning widely. Handsome, with the look of inbred casual confidence that so often comes with extreme wealth. The woman was a real beauty; strong and glowing – evident even in shades of faded sepia. She looked familiar.

"He's hunting in that shot, with some of his old friends," Sylvia continued. "That's Ashton Montgomery," she pointed to the man, "and that's Lottie Louise Faith," her finger tapped the woman rider. "The man in the background was probably somebody's servant. There were likely others nearby. Groups of 10 or 12 usually hunted in Selby Woods when it was four times its current size. It was originally well over 8,000 acres, you know."

The man in the middle, "Uncle Harley," looked to be in his early to mid-20s, not terribly bright, but very affable. He, too, was smiling broadly. A shotgun lay casually across his lap.

"With Uncle Harley, it was always a bit of a scare to go hunting. You never knew when he was going to go 'lights out',"

Sylvia said frankly. "He'd be riding along, maybe even have a quarry in his sights, and you'd hear a wild shot, a loud 'thud,' and there he'd be at the foot of his horse, sound asleep. Folks used to try to keep him in front of them whenever he had a loaded gun. But, bless him, Harley did enjoy his hunting."

"Good Lord, people let him have a loaded gun?" I asked incredulous.

"Oh, sure," she responded. "But, like I said, you tried to keep him out front."

"Didn't he hurt himself when he fell like that?" Tom wanted to know.

"Not so much as you'd think," Sylvia responded. "I guess your muscles are pretty relaxed when you're asleep like that. Of course, there was that one time, when he went head first down an old well. He broke a shoulder that time, I think. It took quite a crew to get him out, too – with pulleys and ropes and all. He was only about 10 or 12 years old. But grandmother used to talk about it. She said if it hadn't been for the local postmaster – a guy named René Robecheaux – Uncle H. might have died down there. But the man went down into the well himself and pulled Uncle Harley out."

"Wait a minute," Sylvia then said, hustling over to another wall. "Here it is – here's the newspaper clipping about it." She lifted a large plain black framed unit from its place and brought it to our table. A well-formed outline of faded wallpaper clearly marked where it had been hanging undisturbed for years. We all resumed our seats as she said: "Go ahead and eat your salads, I'll read it to you, if you'd like."

"Oh, yes, please," I said. Holly and Tom quickly agreed.

She tipped the framed newspaper cutting toward the light and read out loud, beginning with the headline: "Boy Saved from Certain Death by Hero Postmaster."

"I just love the prose they used in newspapers back then," she grinned in an aside to us.

She then resumed reading: "In a feat of engineering genius and heroic strength, young Harley McPherson, age 10, was pulled from an abyss of death yesterday by Selby's postmaster and life-long resident, René Robecheaux, along with other men of the town. The young McPherson is the son of Mr. and Mrs. Robert McPherson, and resides with his family on Mulberry Street, and attends the Selby Academy day school where he will be in the 5th grade this coming fall term. The boy suffers from a tragic illness that causes him to suddenly and without warning enter an unconscious state. He slips into this deep 'sleep' many times throughout the day, but regains consciousness again within a few minutes. Doctors do not know the cause of this strange malady, and there is no known treatment.

"Yesterday morning, at approximately 10:00 o'clock, the young McPherson was playing with friends near the remains of the old Quaker Meeting House at the edge of the Woods. His father says he has been warned repeatedly of the dangers of the abandoned place, but that Harley is a boy of strong will and no good sense. The children were dropping stones into the unused cistern on the property when Harley had one of his sleeping 'fits.' The children said he tumbled forward into the well and disappeared. With great alacrity and fear, the children ran calling for help. The public alarm was struck minutes later, and volunteers responded to the call with quickness and sense of purpose, René Robecheaux among them.

"Mr. Robecheaux, known and respected well by most

readers of this newspaper, resides with his wife on Holly Avenue. He has served faithfully as postmaster for Selby for many years and performs his duties without complaint or fault.

"Immediately grasping the seriousness and need of the situation at hand, Mr. Robecheaux directed the volunteers to construct a pulley system of ropes and human bodies to raise the fallen child. They did not know if he was still alive, but prayed for the optimum outcome. Mr. Robecheaux then volunteered without regard for his own safety to enter the deep, black hole to rescue the boy. He was tied to the ropes and lowered down; foot by foot, he crept closer to the bottom. When he finally signaled with a series of sharp tugs on the rope, the other men began the painstaking process of pulling them both back to the safety of the surface. When they both emerged, Mr. Robecheaux called out the wonderful message: 'The boy is alive.' Cheers went up as the happy cry was repeated by all: 'The boy is alive.' Doctor Phillips treated the child at his home and said he is resting comfortably. He has a broken shoulder, but should recover fully, we are told.

"Our congratulations to the McPherson family for this joyous outcome averting tragedy, and our salute to the bravery of René Robecheaux, Selby's own hero of the day."

"Ta-da!" Sylvia sang at the end. "Biggest news story of the year probably for our little community. And I understand good old René then headed up the town's efforts to cover over or fill in that old cistern right after that."

"I thought that was done all over town around 1910 when the city went to a central water system," I said, remembering one of the stories Ridley Knox had told me during the thunderstorm at the church.

"You know some weird stuff," Holly said to me.

"Well, this would have been right around then," Sylvia confirmed. "Uncle Harley was born in 1901, I think, and it said he was 10 when this happened."

By then, we had finished our salads. A man, also garbed in a chef's coat – but clearly having come from the kitchen – came around the corner with his arms loaded with dinner plates. He was followed closely by a young waiter I had seen serving the other table of patrons in our room.

"I thought I'd find you out here gossiping," the chef said with feigned disgust. "I've been slaving over a hot grill all night, and now I have to serve the food as well." He placed the steaming plates in front of us, somehow knowing exactly who had ordered what.

"My fabulous and talented husband Wayne, ladies and gentlemen," Sylvia announced with obvious love. "Thank you, dear," she told him sincerely. She then introduced me to him and we all complimented him on his skills at the grill.

"We've been talking about Uncle Harley," Sylvia went on to explain to Wayne as she re-hung the framed newspaper account.

"Ah, the famous fall into the abyss of Hell and lived to tell about it!" Wayne teased. "Well, please enjoy your suppers and please excuse me. Somebody has to work around here," he said as he bowed out of the room.

He then called around the corner to Sylvia: "Syl, table seven is leaving – got a bill?"

"Oh, yes, where's my wand." And she left the room on his heels.

"Great dinner story," Holly commented.

"Makes everything we have to talk about rather mundane

now," I said.

"So ... saved any children from certain death lately?" Tom asked us as he began eating.

———

We continued enjoying our marvelous meal and exceptional conversation and were delighted to see Chance and Elizabeth Montigue, Cris Demerist, and a couple of others we knew coming and leaving throughout the evening as well. Everyone stopped to chat with the familiarity and friendship appropriate to a small town.

Sylvia popped in to check on us several times, and then somehow convinced us to have dessert. While we were waiting for its delivery, we all walked around the perimeter of the room again, looking at the old photos and other framed memorabilia. Images and artifacts also extended down the hall and into the other rooms, and I followed them with interest, trying to be as inconspicuous as possible.

I found one particularly compelling photo of Lottie Louise dressed for the hunt – and wearing what looked very much like the Faith Ruby around her neck. But then I found another shot of her at some sort of party, with a gem at her throat that must have been the fabled ruby. The stone's settings were quite different in the two photos, and I commented on this to Holly and Tom. Holly looked at the images in question with me and said we should ask Sylvia about it.

When our hostess next entered the room – bringing three chocolate concoctions that brought us back to our seats immediately – we introduced the subject of the ruby settings to her attention.

"Well, during the 1910s and '20s," she began, "it was the fashion to update your jewelry with new settings per the style of the day. So Lottie Louise probably had that done frequently. Fortunately, she was wise enough to always keep the stone intact," Sylvia observed. "I mean, she was nutty enough to have cut it into pieces at some point – but never did, that I'm aware of."

"Does the Carolina Star still exist?" I wondered to my companions, but none of them seemed to know.

"Oh – and you might find this bit of trivia interesting," Sylvia added while she filled our coffee cups. "The French had discovered a way to make synthetic rubies about that same time – maybe 1910 or 1915 or so, I think. They weren't particularly good quality or of significant size, but it caught on in Europe and then in America. So pretty soon, lots of women of wealth had them as 'novelty jewels' – they even got almost as expensive as the real thing then, too."

"Didn't that hurt the value of real rubies?" I asked.

"Not really. The craze didn't last long. And, like I said, their size and quality were not particularly good – almost anyone could tell a real gem from a synthetic. Mostly, they were used for industrial purposes, more than jewelry. The folks it really hurt were the ruby mine owners in North Carolina. Most of their stones were small, industrial quality, so the synthetic process put the majority of them right out of business. In fact, it kicked the stuffings out of my own grandparents' bank account. They had big holdings in some of those mines. Uncle Harley eventually even had to quit school – he had just started at Yale."

"I'm so sorry," I said with sympathy.

"Oh, that's too bad," Holly said at the same time.

"Yes," Sylvia laughed. "But for those darned French, I might have been a ruby heiress."

"How true," Tom added. "The Faith Ruby – the Carolina Star – would have been but a mere bauble next to the famous 'McPherson Rock,' I'm sure."

"And I would have missed all this love and magic!" Sylvia sang as she waved her glowing, pink, plastic wand over us again.

At the end of the evening, we were "wanded" out the door again, after having been hugged and kissed on both cheeks and made to promise solemnly that we would return very soon. We pledged we would. Wayne even joined us from the kitchen, and handed each of us a small brown paper sack of warm, fresh Irish soda bread to take home.

Sophie, Katie and Sparkey greeted me at my door and sniffed me approvingly from hand to hand. As I got ready for bed, I told them all about Sylvia, Wayne, Harley McPherson, heroic René Robecheaux, and French synthetic rubies. They were utterly fascinated.

In just a few more months, I would remember some of these stories again. This time, with even greater understanding.

TWENTY-FOUR

Pearls swathed her throat and cascaded in ropes down her satin bodice. Her left hand played casually with one elegant strand. She wore no rings on either hand, but two individual pearls dangled gracefully from each ear lobe. Her eyes were unreadable. So was the faint smile that caught at her mouth. The artist had either failed completely to capture her personality, or he had executed it to perfection. A hidden woman. A lady with secrets so deep she let no one else know them – or her.

I had been staring at the portrait in the blue room so long, my tour guide had to come back from the next room when he realized I wasn't with him any more.

"There you are," Jonathan said. "I wondered where I lost you."

Since Christmas, I had enjoyed Jonathan's company on

numerous occasions. He was always a joy to be with, always full of fascinating local history and folklore.

"Sorry," I replied. "I got caught up in this amazing portrait."

"That's Miss Philippa Parsons," Jonathan explained. "She owned this house for more than 50 years. Lived in it all that time too – alone for the most part. You could say it was Selby's first 'safe house' for abused women."

"Really?" I responded in surprise.

"And she was the first to find a safe haven in it," he went on. "See those strands of pearls?" he pointed.

I nodded.

"They cover a wide, deep scar that reached almost halfway around her neck. He nearly slit her throat in two. No one expected her to even live – and her voice never was quite the same. She had been a particularly beautiful singer, they say." Jonathan stood silently with me as I absorbed this information.

"Who?" I finally asked. "Who did that to her?"

"They say it was her husband, Charles. He was brought to trial for it, but found 'not guilty' for lack of evidence."

"Why did he do it?" I wanted to know.

"She had supposedly gone out with friends one night to the theater. Charles didn't much go in for that sort of thing, so he didn't go with them. Instead, he went downtown to a local tavern. When he was walking home, he happened to notice the door to his neighbor's laundry house was standing open a bit and a light was on inside. Back then, the laundry rooms were separate buildings from the main houses due to the heat they generated," Jonathan explained.

"Well, he resumed, "Charles looked in from across the alley and claimed he saw Philippa in a rather compromising position with another man – no one knows if he recognized the man or not. But I say he didn't, because in those days gentlemen still practiced protecting their honor with duels."

"So 'the gentleman' tried to kill her instead?" I asked, leading him back to the point.

"It may have been Charles ... or perhaps someone he had hired ... or perhaps not. But about a week after the laundry house incident, when Miss Philippa was walking home from church one night – alone – she was knocked on the head, grabbed from behind, and her throat was cut. She was left for dead, but someone found her in time and they were able to save her life. As soon as she could get out of bed, she walked out on her husband. She moved in here and barred him from ever entering the house. He eventually returned to his family home in Atlanta.

"How tragic for her," I said, finally understanding the secrets she kept hidden behind her eyes as well as the pearls.

"From time to time, she would give sanctuary to a woman or two who suffered spousal abuse. And it was a short step from there for the place to become a sort of bed and breakfast after her death. That was sometime in the mid-1940s, I believe. Then, in 1952, the house and grounds became the Parsons Supper Club – named after her, of course – and it has remained a private club ever since," Jonathan concluded.

This impromptu history lesson occurred in the middle of an equally unanticipated tour of the private membership club that I had always wanted to visit, which was just a few blocks from my home. In fact, it had been a day defined by surprises and unexpected turns.

It had begun actually rather drearily. I had decided I had to do something about the sad looking pine straw front lawn that lay stiff and arid and lifeless across the front of my property. So, with an old leaf rake, I determinedly began removing the pine needles and piling the material at the curb.

Not long after I had started, Julia poked her head around the hedge from next door and said: "You know, I have some lawn tools that might be a better match for that job." I readily followed her to her tool shed where she handed me a sort of petit pitchfork and a stiffer type of rake.

"Pine straw's kind of tricky stuff," she said with experience. "These should work better. Would you like some help?" she added kindly.

But I couldn't bring myself to accept her offer of assistance. It was such a backbreaking, labor-intensive effort. "Oh, Julia – I really do appreciate the offer, but I couldn't ask you to do it. Besides, it gives me time to think – and maybe plan what to try next," I added hopefully.

"Maybe a professional landscaper could help?" she said casually, but with a meaningful look.

"Yes, I'm sure they could," I responded. "But I've got to sell a few more books before I can afford it."

As almost an afterthought I turned and said: "What should I do with the stuff when I get it to the curb? Will the city pick it up, do you think?"

"Oh, you won't have to worry about that," she replied rather cryptically. "Just leave it there." And she smiled and turned and went back to weeding her own garden.

When I got home, Sophie wanted very much to "help" me, too. She and I had struggled a bit to find our way together since Maggie's death. She blamed me for the loss of her sister and best friend. I mourned the loss of my "favorite." But, day by day, little by little, I began to greatly appreciate Sophie's wonderful heart and sense of humor. Her ability to enjoy life so fully. She was becoming a skilled watchdog and noticed everything – every changing bush and tree limb. She would come into the house all excited at times, obviously wanting me to follow her – a sort of "Timmy's down the well" kind of desperation about her. When I would follow her out, she would race to a fallen branch or moved flower pot and bark and bark until I assured her that all was as it should be. Once, the drill brought me out to see a new flower that had just opened on a bush in the yard. Granted, it was a rather large blossom. And this particular bush had never flowered before in her presence. I told her it was quite lovely and quite all right.

"Well," she would snort on these occasions and trot off. "As long as you know about it. I was simply bringing it to your attention," she seemed to be saying.

I would thank her and we would return to our day.

She was also growing more beautiful physically every day. Her baby fluff was turning into a glossy, flowing coat. Her ears remained floppy, but perched on top of her head. Her nose and eyes were a soft light brown – like fresh new brown sugar. She resembled a collie in form and size and coat pattern. But her coloring was a solid golden red and not quite so thick. And her nose was softly rounded. She was always "on guard" – but with a silly streak as well that never failed to make me laugh. I hoped we would bond fully one day. I knew it would take time. And that it was up to her as well as me.

Sophie had learned to use a doggy door that I had installed for her. She loved the independence it gave her to and from the house and the fenced backyard as well as the side yard where she could watch all that was happening in her world.

This day, when I was working in the front yard, however, she was quite determined she should come with me. But it wasn't fenced, and I had discovered by this time that she can be a terrible wanderer. I also hate to see dogs tied outside. In the end, of course, she won and I fashioned a sort of long leash from an old clothesline that I found and tied to her harness. She leaped and played in the pine straw, hunted and dug for moles, chewed on pine cones, made a terrible mess of the hose, got herself woefully tangled in the rope at least a dozen times, flirted shamelessly with every person and dog that passed by, and entertained me thoroughly while I worked.

Then, quite suddenly, Sophie had come to a complete halt. She had crouched low, but quivered with alertness and excitement. She was captivated by something behind me, approaching the end of my driveway. I turned just as I recognized the sound of horse hooves clacking along the pavement. There were Drew and Buddy and Hamlet in a small carriage being drawn by Trevor. Another of Drew's horses was being led behind. It wasn't his "dress" carriage – the one that we had ridden in during the Trials. This was a sort of "working" model. It had a seat for one (and room for a couple of dogs), plus a short platform behind the seat where another person could ride standing up.

"How about a drive in the woods," Drew called.

"Oh, yes, please," I agreed immediately. "I can't believe your timing. This is horrible work and I hate looking at it and oh yes, please," I repeated, dropping the pitchfork where I stood.

"I'd invite Sophie, too, but I'm not sure we can fit her on, and Buddy and Hamlet can be a bit territorial at times," Drew continued.

Turning to Sophie, I said, "Sorry, baby girl," as I untied her. "This time you'll have to stay here."

I began to lead her down the driveway to at least greet our visitors, but she decided a couple of them were awfully big and it would probably be better to watch from the safety of the other side of the fence. She gave me no argument whatsoever at not being included. I kissed her on the nose, gave her a quick hug, and jogged off to jump on behind Drew and the terriers.

"Hi Hamlet, hi Buddy," I greeted my little pals. The other horse, Fromage, gave me a welcoming nibble on the back of my shirt, and we were off, waving to Sophie and Julia next door.

We continued down the paved streets toward the woods and waved as well to all the passersby. Drew knew most of them by name. But even strangers can't resist a wave at a horse-drawn carriage – especially one with a spare horse in tow and two pups along for the ride.

Selby still has a few intersections with lights where there are buttons that can be pushed to stop the mainstream traffic flow to allow for crossing. The buttons are all placed noticeably high up on the control post. This is so riders can reach them from horseback or carriage drivers can operate them without dismounting. We pushed a couple of them on our course, and were soon at the edge of Selby Woods.

The sun was perfectly warm. The smell of horse and damp cool woods was incredibly compelling. The shade dappled across our path and Trevor's back as he kept a steady pace through the even trails.

We soon came to some small hills and Drew called back, "Hold on," as he urged Trevor into a trot to bring us up the hill with a rush of momentum. It made me laugh out loud. Going back down the slopes was even more thrilling.

Drew knows the woods like his own land. And, when we reached certain places, he let Buddy and Hamlet get down off the carriage and run a bit along side us. They came alive at the opportunity, but we all kept a careful eye on each other. There are coyotes in Selby Woods. And small dogs are never left out of sight. Buddy and Hamlet both knew this, too. They ran in relay-like fashion, ahead and behind us. But when they were summoned, they obeyed promptly and re-took their seats next to Drew.

We came upon a small clearing in the woods at one point. There was a low practice jump and a horse and rider busy with it. We watched for a few minutes. It was intriguing, rhythmic. The sound of hooves soft against the grassy ground. The horse's breath audibly expelled in a "puff," as they reached the other side of the jump. The rider's voice gently urging, instructing, rewarding. And then we drove on – quietly, not wanted to break the concentration of either horse or rider.

We circled along the north edge of the Woods, Drew pointed out private homes where the forest graduated into their lawns. Old, historic and grand, most of them. Each had a story, and Drew seemed to know them all.

When at last we came out of the Woods again, we were close to the Parsons Supper Club. He directed Trevor to take us up the circular drive and around to the side of the property behind some massive hedges.

We could hear the "click, click" of wood-against-wood even before we could see the gentleman. He was probably in his 80s, but dressed in white flannel slacks and light sweater, he could have been from any era. He was alone and idly striking a croquet mallet against a variety of colored and striped balls.

The ground was staged for play, with wickets and goals in place.

"Hey, Sterling," Drew called out. "Looking for a game?"

"Well, hello," he looked up smiling. "Yes, I am, actually. It is just too fine a day. I thought perhaps if I stood out here long enough, someone might come along and join me."

"But no takers yet?"

"Not yet. But one hopes," he replied. He placed his foot on one ball, struck it with the mallet, and sent another rolling straight and true through a wire wicket.

The side door to the old mansion opened at that moment, and Buddy and Hamlet jumped to the ground running toward the figure that appeared there. It was Jonathan.

He greeted us all with his customary charm and hospitality. And, when he discovered my interest in the history of the club, he graciously invited me in for an informal tour.

"Better take him up on it," Drew urged. "He knows almost as much about the old homes and other buildings in Selby as I do."

"I would really appreciate that," I told him. "Are you sure you have time? Sure it's all right that I go inside?" I looked down at my dirt-stained jeans and muddy tennis shoes. I didn't want to be disrespectful of this historic brick beauty, but at the same time I was very anxious to get to peek inside.

"You look just fine. We'd be delighted to have you come in. And it will be my honor to escort you as my guest," he reassured me.

I tried to straighten my carriage-blown hair and looked at Drew.

"Go. I'll take Sterling on." He walked over to him, grabbing a mallet from the rack, as I heard him say: "I've got to warn you, Sterling, I'm wicked at this game. Are you sure you're ready for me?"

Jonathan brought Buddy and Hamlet with us as he held the door for me, the sound of striking croquet mallets growing faint behind us. We entered into a bright, sparkling kitchen. The dogs made straight for a water bowl in the corner that they knew would be fresh and waiting.

We passed from the kitchen, through a large, well-stocked butler's pantry, down a back service hallway and into the main entrance hall. A large and luxurious dining room was being set for the evening meal. Off to one side was a dark-oak paneled room with leather chairs and sofa. It functioned as the bar. There were two other sitting rooms as well: a smaller one with a television, and a larger one with small tables ready for bridge or other after-dinner card games – a baby grand piano was in a bay window.

A beautifully proportioned, curving staircase led upward and Jonathan explained that the second floor was devoted to guest quarters. The rooms were there for members to house their private overnight guests for a very reasonable rate, but were not available to the general public. Wedding parties were the most common use, he said.

Each guest room was almost suite-like in size and furnishings. Each was beautifully and carefully decorated in an individualized color scheme. There were fresh-cut flowers in crystal vases, and low candy dishes filled with chocolates and mints. Each room had its own private bath, with fixtures dating back to the early 1930s at least: deep soaking tubs and huge chrome-plated showers and wide pedestal sinks; tall frosted windows, black and white tiles, thick white cotton towels overflowing the racks. Down-filled comforters spilled across the beds and there were expensive carpets underfoot.

When we entered the blue bedroom, I noticed it was slightly larger than the others. An inviting fireplace centered the room. Above the mantle hung the captivating portrait of Miss Philippa Parsons.

As we finished with Philippa's story, we walked slowly and silently into the central hallway that connected the blue bedroom with all the others. There were excellent paintings on all of the walls. Old dark-stained wood floors were deep with polished wax. At one end of the long hallway, there was another set of stairs leading upward again.

"Servants' quarters?" I asked Jonathan, indicating the third floor.

"Originally, yes. But over the years, they've also been converted to guest rooms. Although not quite on the scale as this floor, they're quite cozy and comfortable. Go on up," he invited.

We proceeded to the next floor, and I was immediately enchanted. While the level below had been perfectly lovely and warm and welcoming, this floor was charm itself. Chintz slipcovers and worn oriental rugs. Low ceilings and soft painted moldings. Even the bathrooms were more spontaneously outfitted. A skylight filled one with sunshine. A round pedestal tub sat sassily in the middle of another.

Throughout this floor, the walls were no longer graced with formal portraits and landscapes. Instead, they were covered with old framed photographs – with just the odd aging watercolor tucked in here and there. Fresh-cut flowers were everywhere here, too, but with less precision to the arrangements.

As always, I was drawn to the photos of smiling faces out

of the past. There were lots of riding parties, of course. But most of the shots were obviously taken on the grounds of this old home. They were very egalitarian: it seemed there were as many taken of staff and other workers as of the guests and people of wealth. And so much laughter. For the sad history of the beginnings of this house, I was gratified to see that Miss Philippa had established a culture of hope and happiness in it.

I stopped at one shot of three women. Surprisingly, I knew who two of them were: Philippa Parsons and Lottie Louise Faith. They were standing with a third woman between them, just at the steps to the wide porch that still wraps itself hospitably around the front and side of the house. Their arms were intertwined at the elbows and they were rocking with laughter and obvious intimacy, sharing a private joke. Who was the third woman, I asked Jonathan.

"Umm, I believe that's…" he hesitated, lifted the picture from its hook and looked quickly at the back of the print. "Yes, I'm right," he said returning it to its place. "That's Clarissa Robecheaux – René Robecheaux's wife."

Jonathan pointed out more photos that documented the obvious friendship between the three women – Philippa Parsons, Lottie Louise Faith, and Clarissa Robecheaux. But both of us were at a loss to explain the relationship. Philippa and Lottie Louise would have been much closer aligned in wealth and status. But Philippa would also have been a good 10 or more years older than either of the other women. Lottie and Clarissa were mothers of children approximately the same age, but Philippa was childless. Lottie and Clarissa also seemed to have a relationship with René in common – to what extent, was mere speculation. But there was no apparent connection between René and Philippa.

We gossiped about the possibilities as we returned to the main floor and through the kitchen to the backyard, collecting Buddy and Hamlet as we went. Drew was, indeed, beating Sterling soundly at his own game.

"Tell you what, old man," he called to him as he saw us, "I'll let you practice until you think you can take me on again."

"Oh, please, just take him away," he laughed and waved at me. "He cheats, you know."

Drew chuckled as he took Trevor's reins in hand and we moved back down the driveway.

I told Drew all about my tour on the way back. But, as I jumped down from the carriage at the end of my own driveway again, I groaned as I saw the hodgepodge of pine straw still waiting for me, half raked into piles and heaped along the curb.

"Thanks, Drew," I called sincerely. "As always, it was a fabulous time – thanks for thinking of me."

"You're most welcome, Miss Macy," He called back. "I'm sure I'll be seeing you again." And they clip-clopped down the street while I waved to Buddy, Hamlet, Trevor and Fromage as they all looked over their shoulders at me.

Sophie was beside herself to greet me again. So she joined me as I spent a few more back-breaking hours raking – leaving mound after mound of prickly brown pine needles along the front of my property. By sunset, I couldn't begin to bag it or even put it into neater piles. I could only drag myself inside for a long soapy soak in the tub and some aspirin. Blisters were already forming on my hands.

The next morning, I put on extra heavy work gloves and jeans to keep the pine refuse from poking my skin raw and returned to the front yard to attack the mess I had left the night before. It was gone. Not a scrap. Even the straggling bits I had left across the yard had been cleared neatly away. I had a few moments of self-doubt, wondering if I had, indeed, left unsightly piles of used pine straw as I had remembered. Yes, my sore muscles and blisters attested to the fact. Still in shock, I wandered down to the end of the drive to pick up the morning newspaper and noticed a note tucked into the flap of my mailbox. It was written in pencil on a carefully folded piece of lined paper, and said:

Dear Sir or Madam,

Thank you for the pine straw. We took it up this morning and hope we left everything nice and neat for you. Have a nice day.

Your friends,
Sonny and Bud

I smiled at the note as I reread it a few more times. I was quite sure I did not know any "Sonny" or "Bud," but I did remember Julia's words from the day before. As she had predicted, once piled at the curb, I didn't have to worry about disposing of it. Pine straw is a valuable commodity, it seems. And, I also discovered, anything that is put at the curb is generally considered available for the taking – from ground cover to old appliances. It was a perfectly sensible method of "recycling."

Now, all I had to be concerned about was the blotchy, barren sea of dirt and rocks and weeds that currently served as my front lawn.

TWENTY-FIVE

Spring was slipping quickly into early summer warmth.
Soon, the folks who winter in Selby would be returning north
for the next several months. The town takes on a wholly
different character during each of these two time periods.
Winter – the "in season" – is horses and sports and parties,
busy shops and restaurants and full church pews, a bit
quicker pace, and always so much to do.

One of the sure signals that "in season" is over is when the
track kitchen closes. The track kitchen serves all of the horse
people who work and live around the thoroughbred training
track. Owners, trainers, exercise riders, grooms, stable hands.
In their world, work begins long before the first rays of sun
creep up to the windows of the barn. Breakfast is important,
hearty and hot. Even for those not directly connected to the
track, it's a Selby tradition to eat breakfast at the track kitchen

at least once a season. I had been in Selby almost a year. It was time I had this experience, my friends felt. And it was only a matter of weeks before it would close for the summer.

Holly called me at 5:30 a.m. to make sure I was up.

"Are you upright?" she asked too cheerfully.

"Uh-huh," I answered from my pillow.

"We'll be there to get you in half an hour," she insisted.

"It's dark," I mumbled.

"It's worth it, I promise," she said before hanging up. "See you soon."

"You bet." It took me three tries, but I got the phone back in its cradle. I am not a morning person. Fortunately, I had bathed the night before, because I doubted if I could have found the tub in my stupor. I barely found my mouth to brush my teeth. My clothes were not difficult, but hair was another matter.

"I'm not a morning person," I greeted Holly at the door.

"I can see that," she said re-doing my pony tail. "But you'll be glad you went."

"Is there coffee?"

"Yes, dear. Good coffee." She led me down the steps and to the car.

"Good morning," Tom called out from the driver's seat.

"I'm not a morning person," I told him. "Is there coffee?"

"There will be. Incredible coffee," he replied.

"How did I ever get to know these terribly perky people?" I wondered out loud.

In a matter of minutes, we were there. In another time of day or state of mind, we might have walked. But I was starting to come around by the time we stepped up the two wooden stairs to the front porch of the old frame building.

Above the entrance hung a hand-lettered sign proclaiming this to be the "Track Kitchen." The proprietor's name was underneath, printed as boldly as the Kitchen name itself: "Patches." Just the single name, like a super model or a famous rock star. And, in this arena, he was renowned. Patches had been running the track kitchen for almost as long as most people could remember. I looked forward to meeting him.

My concern about the availability of coffee was answered before we even stepped through the door. Wonderfully provoking aromas reached us on the porch. Coffee was the top layer, followed closely by bacon, then pancakes. Southern breakfasts are never subtle.

Inside, the musky smells of horse and hay and saddle soap were also detectable, emanating from the boots and jeans and very being of the primary patrons of the place. It added a rather nice undernote, I thought.

I started looking for an open spot for the three of us to sit, but Tom and Holly pushed me toward the back. "Coffee," they both said, as we walked into the kitchen itself. Tom grabbed three cups off a stack of them and handed one to each of us. He then went over to a huge stainless steel urn and filled his cup to the top with steaming, black liquid that smelled marvelous. Other folks were doing the same. Filling and refilling their own cups.

I was doing likewise, when Tom began to talk to a tall, muscular man with close-cropped white hair working at the stove. He could have been any age. His hands were large and scrubbed several shades lighter than the rest of his soft brown skin.

"Hey, Patches," Tom said.

"Hey yourself, Mr. Tom. It's been awhile since you and Miss Holly have been in to see me."

Holly joined in. "Last time I was here was when I did that photo study of you and the place. Did you like the shots?"

A tremendous smile spread across his face – a face etched out of lines and character. But his eyes never left his work at the stove. "Go out and see for yourself in the other room," he said slyly.

"This is our friend, Macy Harris," Holly introduced me. "Macy, I'd like you to meet Mr. Patches, the owner and chief cook of the track kitchen."

I instinctively held out my hand. But he responded, "Sorry honey, can't while I'm cookin'."

"Oh, of course," I said. I remembered a chef I knew once who said the same thing. She said people were always wanting to shake hands or hug her at work – but it wasn't something she was comfortable doing working with food.

"I've heard a great deal about you and this place," I told him. He stole a quick glance in my direction. Placing two filled plates on the counter that connected to the next room, he called out, "Order up." Then he grabbed four more eggs, two in each hand, and skillfully cracked them all into a waiting skillet, without losing a sliver of shell.

"I know you," he said. "You write for the paper. Yeah, Macy Harris. I like what you have to say."

"Thank you, that's a very kind thing to say," I said sincerely.

"So, Miss Macy Harris who writes for the paper, you ready to write about the best breakfast in Selby?" he said with a grin.

"Gotta taste it first," I responded in kind.

"Guaranteed," was all he would say to that.

Tom and Holly had already left me to secure seats in the

dining area.

"Nice to meet you, Sir," I called back to Patches as I left the kitchen myself, full coffee cup in hand.

"Nice to meet you, Miss Macy Harris." He dropped a pile of chopped raw potatoes and onions into another sizzling skillet just then, and I lost sight of his face in a cloud of steam.

Tom was seated and looking intently at the menu board on the wall. Holly was standing and looking just as intently at the wall – but at a framed black and white photo. I joined her and saw it was of Patches at the stove. He was working just as I had left him. But she had caught the light dancing in a star burst off a spatula in his right hand. His left hand was balancing a plate on the tips of his fingers. A pancake was mid-air between the two. His eyes weren't even on it, but you just knew it landed squarely in the center as planned. Humor played lightly at the corners of his mouth.

"Perfect," I told her.

"Mm. Yeah. He is rather amazing."

"So are you," I returned.

"I'm not waiting to order," Tom said from his seat.

"We wouldn't have it any other way," Holly responded as she gazed at another photograph next to the one we had both just been examining.

I was torn between my appetite for food and for more of Holly's incredible photos.

"Sorry," I said as I turned to the table. "I do want to look, too – but ... bacon."

"Please, go ahead," she assured us.

Tom directed my attention to the scrambled eggs, to which Patches adds a secret ingredient making them absolutely unforgettable. Fluffy home-made biscuits. Fresh-squeezed orange juice. Bacon, of course. More coffee (as many trips as you care to make to the kitchen).

Holly soon joined us, and I was introduced to several more people as they came and went. We had also spotted Jonathan with a woman I didn't know at another table. They both gathered their coffee cups and plates and had just moved over to sit with us, when Chance and Elizabeth Montigue also came through the door.

The tables are long, with picnic benches on either side. So we accommodated everyone comfortably. Jonathan introduced me to JanMarie Longacre. She owns a large stable facility in town where she rents horse stalls as well as sleeping rooms for grooms and other short-termers during the horse season. Everyone else knew her, and she seemed extremely fun, I thought. A very "definite" personality. She's probably been born and bred around horses, and wouldn't trade places with the queen.

No one seemed to be in too much of a hurry, so second and third cups of coffee kept pace with the stories. And there were plenty of them. JanMarie contributed some of the best (and most ribald) of them all.

Just then, a group of four young men walked in. JanMarie greeted them in Spanish, and they returned the acknowledgement in the same language. She explained to us that they were Argentinean, and all were staying with her while they were in town for the polo pony auction later that day.

"Oh Lord," Jonathan broke out. "I didn't think you were still allowed to have contact with anyone connected with polo in South America?" Everyone laughed.

"Hey, I was well within my rights," JanMarie claimed with a chuckle.

"A hundred years ago, you would have been strung up," Elizabeth said only half jokingly.

"And yet, here I am – still putting a roof over their heads and counting their money," JanMarie retorted.

My blank face must have expressed my confusion, because Jonathan kindly turned to me to explain what they were all talking about.

"JanMarie stole all of the Argentinean Polo team's ponies the last time they were in town," he began.

"Wait, now – it wasn't the Argentinean team – the players were just mostly from Argentina. And it wasn't all of their ponies. And it wasn't the last time they were here. You're just telling it all wrong," JanMarie interrupted with good humored indignation. "Let me tell you what really happened," she said as she faced me.

"Most of them were staying at my place, and they had rented all of the stalls in my stables. They owed me a butt-load of money and hadn't paid me a cent. So I told the team manager – his name was Paulo – so I told Paulo that I had to have payment before the end of the day – that was on a Friday. Nothing. No money, just more promises: 'Oh, Miss JanMarie, we'll have it to you in cash by tomorrow morning...ya-da, ya-da, ya-da...' Anyway – I know they've got it, I just don't know what the big deal is about giving it to me. And meanwhile, the horses are taking up my entire stables, eating my hay, I'm paying a guy to muck out the stalls, and these guys are all staying in my house and eating my food, and it's going on two weeks and not a cent."

Chance interrupted to tell me, "That Saturday was a pretty high-goal match to be played. It's the whole reason that team was in town."

JanMarie paused to sip her coffee, and then resumed: "Now, like I said, money is not a problem with these guys. They've got it up the ying-yang. But getting this fellow Paulo to part with any of it was getting scary. So the morning of the match, all of their ponies suddenly disappeared."

Those of us who were hearing the story for the first time, burst out laughing in astonishment.

"You actually took them?" Tom asked. "You actually kidnapped a dozen horses?"

"I prefer to think of it as a shrewd negotiation tactic, and there were only eight of them," she responded. "But it was getting close to the match, and they were getting more than a little worried."

"Did they know it was you?" I asked.

"Hell, yes, they knew it was me. Otherwise, it wouldn't have worked."

"Where had you taken them," Holly wanted to know.

"Actually, to a paddock closer to the field where they were going to be playing. I was surprised no one called and told them," she said.

"But it worked?" Tom prodded.

"Paid in full within the hour," she said grinning widely.

"And they still rent from you when they're here?" I asked in amazement.

"Sure," she shrugged. "They know it's the best deal in town and that their horses will have the best. Of course, they also pay up-front now!" she said with a huge laugh.

"I still say you're lucky they didn't have you arrested," Elizabeth added, patting JanMarie on the arm as she stood up. Everyone was standing and stretching and preparing to leave then.

"Hey, you ought to go on over to the pony auction," Jonathan said to me. "It's just over at the Selby polo field. And it's going to be starting in just about 30 minutes now," he said as he looked down at his watch. "I'd take you over myself, but I've got an appointment," he explained. "Have you ever been to a horse auction?"

"No, I haven't – but I would love to go." I looked over at Tom and Holly. Tom said he had another commitment, but Holly thought she'd like to go with me. She wanted to get her camera out of the car first, but we assured Tom we could walk back to my house.

We filled the rest of the time looking at more of Holly's photos that Patches had framed and hung on the walls. She had somehow caught the unique ambiance of this place and experience. Early morning light and hushed voices. Sleepy minds and empty stomachs. Hard-working hands and good souls. The shyness of the children of the grooms and exercise riders. Grace being said. The care with which Patches prepares every meal. The good nature of the servers. Camaraderie. History. A self-contained culture.

A brief walk later, Holly and I arrived at the polo grounds where the auction had just gotten underway. A solid breeze had picked up, buffeting white pillows of clouds around a deep blue sea sky. The sun was bright and warm on our shoulders. It would be hot by noon.

I wasn't sure how late the auction would last, but a tent had been put up to provide shade for the audience and it was filled with rows of white-painted wooden folding chairs. They faced a small raised platform, where the auctioneer and an assistant were seated. Those men had a large sun umbrella providing protection, but the wind threatened to take it away before long. Two men dressed in suits and ties were standing at the front of the audience, fielding bids.

It was an eclectic crowd of young and old, worn and new, cheap and expensive. I marveled at the number of designer hair cuts and $5,000 watches – on both men and women. But there were plenty of ponytailed workmen in scuffed boots and tattered jeans and overalls as well. There were straw hats and western style and even some baseball caps. I'm learning how to tell a horseman by his hat.

Holly said the expensive hair belonged to the polo team owners. The others were the grooms and hired hands. But you could never tell who had the money at a horse auction.

It was fascinating. I rarely saw the bid, but the men in the front did. They watched for a subtle raise of a program or nod or tip of a hat brim. A couple of bidders made a loud short call – a kind of "whoop" when they bid. But even then, it was so quick I couldn't catch who it came from. It was also very good-natured. Even when it got down to two sources vying for the same horse. Chuckles accompanied the raise. And applause when the last man bowed out. There were probably no more than a dozen serious bidders that day. The rest were either selling or just there to watch. Some would throw in an occasional nod – to ride in the game just a short way before jumping off.

One young horse had been receiving spirited bidding as he stood calmly and bored at the front of the audience. But the offers had stalled, although the auctioneer was determined to get them higher, as he kept chiding the audience for more.

Just then, a major wind picked up, gusts lifted the sun umbrella off the stand, swirled it above them and slammed it down not two feet in front of the horse. Gasps came from the crowd, but the pony simply looked at it with interest and never moved.

The audience laughed and applauded, and a voice in my ear said: "That just raised his price about a thousand dollars." I turned and saw Margaret Ann Lawton smiling at me. Brooks was at her side.

She was right. As I was hugging them both hello, the bids picked back up again, and the horse brought the best price of the day.

"Come sit with us," they insisted. I looked around for Holly, but she was completely absorbed with her camera and the horses still waiting in a pen to the side of the tent.

"Brooks will make sure she knows where to find us," Margaret Ann assured me. "Come on. Monnie Belle's with us, too. We haven't seen you for ages."

I couldn't resist, and followed her to their seats to the left of the main crowd.

"Another column?" she asked about my attendance at this event.

"Probably," I answered. "I never know sometimes. I also had breakfast at the track kitchen this morning."

"Oh sweet honey, that's a whole chapter in a book," she commented. "Did you meet Patches? Lovely man, isn't he. Here's Monnie."

We slipped into some empty chairs as Monnie Belle and I greeted each other. Brooks soon followed, and said he had told Holly exactly where to find us.

It finally occurred to me to ask about why they were all

at this annual auction, and they replied that they just always come. I knew polo was encouraged and taught at Selby Academy, so that could explain Monnie's presence, I thought. It seemed rude to inquire any deeper.

We chatted about the track kitchen breakfast experience some more. And I told them JanMarie's story about stealing the polo ponies. They apparently knew all about it. Then, Margaret Ann told me that it wasn't the first time such an incident had occurred in Selby. She knew of one other time when just one pony had been stolen – and it had caused quite a furor. And … it turned out to have been perpetrated by a student of Selby Academy.

"Now, that's not exactly right, Margaret Ann," Monnie Belle cut in. "He didn't become a student of the Academy until after the offense, remember? That's why he was sent there – to try to put him into a good environment and with a strict structure."

"That's true," Margaret Ann agreed. "It should have helped, too. It really should have. He'd lost his father the year before, you see –- in an accident. Well, it was ruled an accident by the court, anyway. And it probably was."

"Oh, Macy, you already know all about that story," Margaret Ann said turning to me. "Remember? About how René Robecheaux fell off the post office dome? Well, René was this boy's father. What was the child's name?" she looked back at Monnie Belle.

"Charles … no, Charlie," Monnie remembered. Charlie Robecheaux. That was it."

Monnie Belle then picked up the narrative. "Charlie was always quiet as a boy. Shy."

"Maybe a little bit off?" Margaret Ann added her uncensored

opinion. "Of course, we all just knew him after he had become an adult. But I remember walking downtown with my father once, and Charlie Robecheaux passed us on the street. Daddy's hand tightened on mine to the point where it almost hurt. He nodded and said good morning to the man, but he kept up his pace. I tripped a bit and he just held on to my hand and kept me walking. He never said anything directly to us of course, we just sort of sensed something wasn't quite right. Children do, I believe."

"Well, Selby Academy did its best, I know. But I understand that he never really opened up enough to let the faculty and other boys influence or help him," Monnie resumed. "I'm not even sure he graduated."

"So when did the pony theft happen?" I asked.

"Oh – that was the year before he became a student. It was one of the school's ponies, as a matter of fact. One of the best. And he wasn't very clever at it. He got caught right away. But he was so young, and people felt sorry for him. His father had just been killed shortly before that. So when his mother came and asked the school if it could take him in as a student, I believe the staff were all quite receptive. After all, the pony had been returned and unharmed."

"Where do you suppose his mother came up with the money to send him to Selby Academy?" I mused. "I wouldn't think a widow's pension for the wife of a postmaster would have been all that substantial."

"Very good question," Margaret Ann quickly agreed, and seemed disappointed that she had not thought of it herself. "Do you suppose he got some sort of financial assistance?" she asked Monnie.

"I'll have to see if I can find anything in the school records sometime," Monnie responded.

Just then a gust of wind threatened to lift the entire tent, and it took our attention quite away from our gossip. Shortly thereafter, Holly joined us and she and I decided to take our leave and walk back to my house.

But the thought kept playing in the back of my mind. Perhaps someone else paid for little Charlie Robecheaux to attend Selby Academy. Perhaps one of his mother's very close friends. Someone who had wealth and influence in Selby back then. Perhaps I knew who. I promised myself I would follow up with Monnie Belle's records at the school when I had the time.

TWENTY-SIX

"One ... two ... three ... now!" Sally called as she
yanked with all her strength on the heavy iron crow bar. I
simultaneously pulled with a claw hammer at the other edge
of the six-foot long and high frame of a former closet. With
the creak of old nails, and the frightening sound of splintering
wood, the last two-by-four gave way and the entire structure
heaved forward.

"Ow!" I landed squarely in the center of the room on my
back, wood pieces on top of me.

"Oh, gosh! Are you all right?" Sally asked with a laugh as
she came over to retrieve me.

"Phoo...!" I spit dirt and grit from my mouth and sat up.

She joined me on the floor. We were both out of breath and
laughing. The room was a haze of suspended particles.

"Yea! We won," I raised both work-gloved hands in the air

305

in a victory salute.

We were in the middle of the cottage floor. Quite a few hours and a couple of weekends had already been spent reclaiming it from decades of misguided updates as well as utter neglect and abandonment.

The cottage sits behind my house at the back edge of my property. It's a small house, with one tiny bedroom, a very compact little bathroom, and a combination living room / dining room / kitchen area. Inexpensive carpeting that was dirty, dank, and must-ridden, had covered all the floors. This amateurishly over-built closet had intruded into half the usable space of the living room.

The entire main area was paneled in what had originally been quite nice, very 1950s, wide-plank, knotty pine. Everyone told me how to paint it to brighten the small space. But I was convinced that cleaned and polished, it could be rather attractive – in a sentimental, retro kind of way. I also thought that replacing the carpet with clean, cool tile flooring would further do wonders. Perhaps a redesigned bath. New curtains. Cottage furniture. I could envision it easily. In fact, it had been one of the deciding factors in my buying this particular property in the first place. But the work estimates I had gotten since then made me think it might be destined to continue to decay into oblivion.

Then, Sally had shown up one Saturday morning loaded with cleaning supplies, crow bar, hammers, wire cutters, and other assorted tools and said: "Let's do it. We can do this!"

And she convinced me that we could.

The worst was perhaps over. The horrid carpet had been removed – it had actually been glued to the double-layered linoleum floor beneath. Other ill-advised additions and conversions had been taken out. And now that this boxy intrusion was down, I could appreciate the original proportions of the room. Not large, but pleasing. Fortunately, the pine-paneled wall behind the closet remained in tact; aside from some nail holes, it hadn't suffered a bit.

We carried everything outside and heaped it on an ever-growing pile of trash. This would not even be attractive for neighborhood "recycling" I thought. Returning to the cottage, Sally began some serious "deep cleaning," while I started painting the small bathroom. Its dirty beige walls and cheap dark wood cabinets and molding were transformed by the bright glossy white paint, and the windowless room was already becoming much less claustrophobic.

"Why do you suppose they built this little cottage in the first place?" I called to Sally in the next room.

"For their visitors – their guests," she answered unhesitatingly.

"But why not put them up in the main house?" I asked.

"I don't really know. It's just the way we do it in the South, I suppose."

Yes, I agreed. That answered much about this fascinating, charming culture I had entered into in Selby. It was just the way things were done. And hospitality was as ingrained as a sense of humor. As expected as being a good cook, or telling a good story, or minding your manners. And it certainly explained the inordinate number of cottages sitting shyly behind so many main houses here. Perhaps the phenomenon was more predictable relative to the older, grander homes of Selby. And they do, indeed, have their share of guest cottages. But my house is only about 50 years old, and a very modest one at that. And yet, here is a tiny guest cottage within its embrace. Sally also has a similar structure on her property. About one out of every 10 residences in the town does. A few are rented now. But all had been created originally, and most are kept, for no other reason than to properly welcome one's guests.

Reading my thoughts, Sally then added: "Of course, a lot of times, you use your guest cottage to put up somebody else's guests, too. Like if one of your neighbors has a bunch of family in for a wedding or a funeral. Or anytime somebody's in need."

"Like when?" I prodded her to continue.

"Oh, like two summers ago, when those hurricanes hit the coast so hard. It was before you were here," she remembered. "But we had lots of refugees coming up from the low country needing places to live, and a little looking after, until they could go back to their own homes.   Mostly, those folks had family here. But when their relatives' houses and guest houses overflowed, the rest of the neighborhoods opened up their cottages – and sometimes their own homes, too."

It reminded me of what I had learned about the early days of the Parsons Supper Club and how Philippa Parsons had used it as a safe haven – first for herself, but then for other women in need. I told Sally about my tour of the place, and, although she already knew most of the club's history, she hadn't realized that Philippa Parsons, Lottie Louise Faith and Clarissa Robecheaux had been friends – as the photos I had seen in the house would indicate.

"There seems to be a real tradition of taking care of each other here in Selby," I remarked.

"Now that's a Southern thing," she replied. "And a small town thing, too, I guess. We look after one another."

"So ... perhaps that dedication to serving others would explain the giant barbecue 'temple' just outside this door," I said, only half kidding. "You could easily feed an entire block off it."

This piece of eccentric architecture was yet another feature of the house that had sold me on the place originally. The barbecue is built of sturdy red brick, and is exactly 14 feet long, 12 feet high, and four feet deep. I joked that it could quite possibly accommodate ritual human sacrifices. There is a built-in sink and electric lights, brick storage cabinets, a smooth-brick serving counter, and various other "bells and whistles." For such a small house, it was incredible. And, because it is placed in the very front courtyard of the tiny guest cottage, it seems even more out of balance size-wise. But I love it dearly, and use it surprisingly often.

"No ... that I'd call a 'folly'," Sally answered back. It was pretty well known on the street.

"But it does produce some mighty fine ribs and steaks," she admitted.

"Speaking of food, have we had lunch yet?" I asked, feeling a rumbling in my stomach.

"Not that I remember."

"Well, grab Sophie and let's go eat," I determined. "My treat."

I wrapped my brushes and put a lid on the paint as Sally located Sophie.

Sophie had been helping us all morning, but had eventually gotten bored and left when things settled down to the uninteresting tasks of cleaning and painting.

In a few minutes, Sally came back with a huge grin on her face.

"She's in her pool, she reported. "Up to her eyelids! She looks like an alligator," she laughed. "You've got to see her for yourself," and she led the way across the backyard.

We had discovered very early in her puppyhood that Sophie is a real water baby. I suspect that one of the many breeds in her vast genetic makeup may have been a fish. So Sally bought her a child's wading pool one day, and she had been spending hours reveling in it ever since. Especially now that the temperatures were beginning to creep steadily warmer and warmer. Several times a day I would find her – or hear her – out playing in it: splashing, jumping, bouncing, rolling, throwing toys in and out. But mostly, she enjoyed just lying down and lounging in it, with eyes half shut, her chin resting peacefully on one side and tail draped languidly over the other. Absolute contentment.

But this was something new. She was in the pool, flat on her tummy, head submerged up to her eyeballs, as Sally had said. When we walked up, she snorted huge bubbles and lifted her head out with a big grin.

"Playing submarine?" I asked her.

"No ... I think she's pretending to be an alligator...looking for stray cats!" Sally imagined.

"Well, if she's coming along, we need to load the backseat up with towels," I reasoned.

Eventually, we drove to the nearest deli, and I ran in for sandwiches while Sally and Sophie waited at an outside table.

In less than an hour, we were back, hard at work in the cottage again. I had purchased some self-stick white tile squares for the cottage floor and laid some of them to get an idea of how it would look. We were both pleased with the effect.

At about 6:15 that evening, Sally took her supplies and left me on my own. She had done an amazing job. I continued to lay floor while the first coat of paint in the bathroom dried. But by about 8:00 o'clock, I couldn't lift my arms above my waist. And the light was too dim anyway. Sophie gleefully joined me as I locked up the cottage door and walked the few steps to my own back entrance.

A long hot bath, and I crawled gratefully into a soft bed. It wasn't long before I was drifting blissfully off to sleep.

I am a firm believer in natural air and overhead fans. Most of the year, I love to sleep with all the windows open and listen to the soft, gentle, soothing night sounds that surround us in this beautiful, peaceful, Southern community.

It was particularly warm and balmy that night, and I was enjoying the delicate tones of a distant wind chime. Softly, I heard a small splash in Sophie's pool. I envisioned her stretched out in the cool, quiet water under the moon, and thought what a smart puppy she was. How refreshing for her after a long, busy day of doing important dog stuff. I started to slide deeper into sleep with a smile. But somewhere on the edge of consciousness, I heard the plastic slap of her dog door closing behind her. Then, slip-slop, slip-slop, soft doggy feet padding down the hall toward the bedroom. Still clinging to that lovely trance between sleep and wakefulness, I felt Sophie join me in her spot on the bed. A little "sloosh" sound as she lay down. The alarming sensation of cold water on my skin struck simultaneously with the distinct and pungent odor of wet dog fur. And suddenly, I was quite thoroughly awake.

My feet hit the floor in the same instant that my hands pulled the bedding away from the mattress. Both cats were airborne. Poor Sophie's face reflected complete surprise. I burst out laughing and finally had to sit on the floor with giggles.

This must have seemed like such a good idea to Sophie. First, you stretch out all peaceful in your pool under the stars. Breathe in the succulent floral scents released into the night air. Watch the moon shadows dance on the water. Then, you come in to share all this pleasantry with your best friends ... your family ... your pack.

Such a grand idea. Such a right idea. And, regardless of the soggy bed and disheveled cats, I had to agree.

I put the bedding into the dryer and took Sophie back outside. Then, I sat down right in the middle of her pool. She hesitated just a second before she understood and readily joined me.

Together, we stretched out and gazed up at a beautiful Carolina crescent moon. All around us was the sweet essence of pine trees and gardenias and jasmine and honeysuckle and all the other unique and delightfully Southern aromas. All the night creatures cooed and trilled and squeaked and clicked and sang just for us. We looked up at a million stars. We talked about things.

The dryer rumbled with a faraway muffled sound. "You know, Sophie, long before there were electric dryers, people used laundry houses to do their wash. Dangerous things, laundry houses. You never knew what kind of trouble they could get you into," I told her, remembering Philippa Parsons. "I wonder if Philippa had actually been the one that Charles saw that night? And if it was she, who was the other man with her?" I asked Sophie out loud. Sophie answered by blowing bubbles with an underwater snort. She then rolled on her side inviting me to tickle her tummy.

"It's not like I could actually figure it out, of course," I admitted. "I mean, it was so long ago, and about the only men I know about who lived in that time were the husband himself – 'Mean Coward Charles' – and a narcoleptic young boy named Harley, and a postmaster in love with Lottie Louise Faith. Now if it had been Lottie Louise who had been sighted ..."

I sat bolt upright, water sloshing over the sides of the small pool. What if it had been Lottie Louise? I thought about the photo of the three women together. Philippa and Lottie were of similar height and coloring. They were dressed in the same style and quality appropriate to their similar social and economic strata. No – I didn't want to believe that of either Lottie or René. My image of them was much sweeter, more innocent, more honorable.

Of course, if it had been them, that would explain a lot. Like why no one came forward at the trial to tell the truth about who had been in the laundry room. The trial wasn't about that, I reminded myself, it was about who had so mercilessly attacked Philippa and cut her throat. So maybe who was in the laundry room wasn't important.

But what if ... I kept coming back to the hypothesis that it was René and Lottie. Perhaps that would also explain the three women's friendship. No, I reasoned, that would have set them against each other. Clarissa would have hated Lottie for having an affair with her husband. And Philippa would have resented Lottie as well as René for not coming forward at the trial and at least clearing her name of scandal.

So what could have brought them together, I wondered? Somehow, René seemed to be the common thread. My mind went to the next logical thought. What if René had had an affair with Philippa? What if it had been Philippa in the laundry house as Charles had claimed, and René had been the other man? Well, it accounted for a link between the three women – but not the friendship. It might also explain where Clarissa got the money for her son Charlie to attend Selby Academy – blackmail.

Or … what if René abused Clarissa, and Philippa gave her sanctuary? And, if Lottie had found out about that, maybe that's why she ended her relationship – whatever it had been – with René. At least that all made the most sense, I thought. And it was the only one so far that accounted for the obvious fondness the women felt for one another. It had been unmistakable in the photos I had seen.

I still didn't like thinking of René in that light, though. Was this the man who had risked his life for a little boy who had fallen down a well? Was this the man with whom Lottie Louise had been such good friends? I felt sure that there was something unknown about the friendship of the women and that René was somehow the link between them. But the right insight eluded me still.

I leaned back in the cool water and tickled Sophie's ears. And thought about my "mystery" until the dryer had stopped spinning and my skin was pruney.

We returned to the house and all slept peacefully, despite my unresolved puzzle.

TWENTY-SEVEN

By July, a damp Southern heat had settled down on Selby like warm sweet syrup. Most of the town's horses were training back up North. Their stables were silent, except for the hazy buzz of flies and honey bees, and early morning song birds swooping between propped-open stall doors and windows held back by painted iron arms. Many of Selby's residents also summered up North. Others took long, slow weekends at the beach or on the lake or in the mountains, in family homes built by their great grandparents and passed through the generations like prized silver. The rest of us simply tempered our pace and entered into the peace that floated around us on the breeze of a slow-moving fan.

I learned certain ways of the South that summer. The heat of the day peaks at around 5:00 p.m., so if you must work outside, do it early in the day. Walk the dog before breakfast. Eat supper light and late. Store envelopes in the refrigerator. Spray your sheets with lavender water. Bathe at night in cool water. Keep the curtains drawn during the day. Stock the refrigerator full of ice and lemonade and sweet tea. Have at least one fan in every room. Wear a wide-brimmed straw hat in the sun. Take the newspaper in early – before its pages cling together out of dampness and are too limp to read properly and too warm to spread flat across your lap.

I also learned of the great rewards of living in Selby in summer. One of them is the concert series held in Laroque Gardens every Monday evening. There is no charge. And the music is outstanding, offering an appealing mix of styles, all expertly performed.

Most people walk over to the concerts. Some bring folding lawn chairs or small blankets tucked under their arms. Babies in strollers and toddlers on Daddy's shoulders and dogs on leashes are all welcome. Public Safety officers even stop traffic every few minutes on the busiest road near the garden gates for people to cross into the lush, cool park. Some folks bring picnic baskets or grocery sacks filled with Southern-fried chicken and Aunt Ginny's fudge to share with those around them. Fresh-picked peaches still warm from the sun are passed down the line. Glasses of wine may be exchanged.

This particular evening was a rare Saturday night performance. A well-known jazz group was playing. Sponsors had generously stepped forward, so it was still free to the public. But a voluntary collection was being taken. The proceeds were going to help build the Pee Wee football field on the northwest end of town. The field was being named in memory of Coach Dooley – Big Jake – who had coached the team for years, and had been responsible for starting this drive for a new field dedicated to the game before his tragic and heroic death, ironically not far from the property itself.

Sally and I had arranged to meet Holly, Tom and Jonathan at the base of the big cypress tree just inside the east entrance. Sally was bringing potato salad; Holly and Tom were assigned chicken; Jonathan wine. I got off with the small contribution of brownies.

The attendance was about double the usual numbers for a garden concert. There were maybe 500 all together. People were settling in all along the terraced banks on the north side of two small man-made ponds. The ponds are connected by a small stream, and tall old trees shade the waters on both sides.

On the south side of the central stream, there is a small stage. It is roofed by a large wooden arbor, draped thick by flowering vines. Small yellow scented flowers peek out from deep-green foliage. I don't know what the plant is, but its fragrance floated on the warm air that night like the colors of its blossoms across the water's smooth surface.

Jonathan, Holly and Tom were already there, and the musicians were warming with riffs and scales. We found spaces and made ourselves comfortable.

I am a relatively recent follower of jazz. But the more I learn its history and nuances, and how to really listen to it, the more I continue to grow in my enjoyment of and appreciation for it. I also have found that I really like the people who really like jazz. Tonight was no exception.

Wine bottles were passed from several groups over, and wonderful variations on potato salad were exchanged with nearby fellow music lovers. Among them were Julia and her family, Cris Demerist, and Margaret Ann and Brooks Lawton.

I even spotted the Mayor and his wife.

"Mmm, Sally said with her mouth full of one potato salad sample. That's homemade mayonnaise."

"Oh, yes," Holly said as she took a bite, "you can really tell the difference."

"Why would anyone make their own mayonnaise?" I challenged in a hushed voice.

"Taste this," Jonathan said putting a scoop in my mouth.

It was fabulous. Indefinably. And far superior to anything I had ever tasted before.

Tom said, "Don't you know that mayonnaise is the mortar of the South? And if you don't have your mama's recipe, you'd better steal one. Everybody has to have a homemade recipe for mayonnaise, you know. The South would fall apart without that."

Jonathan, Holly and Sally all nodded in agreement and utter seriousness.

I slipped my sandals off and buried my feet deeply into the cool grass and leaned back into the short chair I had brought with me.

It was just beyond dusk by this time. There was a full moon. The stars were beginning to fill the deepening sky, although gathering clouds threatened to close their dark robes across them. As much as we needed the relief of rain, I hoped it would hold off until after the concert. A hurricane was building off the coast. We might feel the reach of it.

I tried to pick out some of the constellations, but I am woefully inept at this. After confessing my shortcoming, Jonathan tried to point out some of the more obvious ones – like the Big Dipper – but they still looked simply like stars to me.

"You'd think I'd be better at this here in South Carolina," I told him. "I've never seen such night skies as we enjoy here."

"It's true," he replied. "In fact, over a hundred years ago, a famous planet sighting took place in Selby. In all the world, only four places were chosen to view the transit of Venus – and Selby was one of them."

"And – we were the only place that was successful with the sighting," Holly added.

"What's a transit of Venus?" I had to ask.

"It's when Venus passes between the earth and the sun," Jonathan explained. "And it helped scientists calculate the distance between the earth and the sun back in the late 1880s."

"Why was Selby chosen?" I probed.

"Well, one of the reasons was our clear skies and typically good weather – it took place in December. But another was because one of our residents – years earlier – had constructed a wonderful observatory and had all the necessary equipment in it. Do you know about Henry Laroque – the guy that these gardens are named for?" Jonathan asked.

I thought for a second, but then remembered the tea party at Selby Academy with Monnie Belle von Alden and Margaret Ann and their friends. Henry Laroque I recalled was the brilliant young inventor who died young but wouldn't be buried in his family's crypt.

"Oh, yes!" I exclaimed, "I do know who he was. I guess I never made the connection with the name of the Gardens and his family name. But didn't he die around 1860? Just around the start of the Civil War?"

"Yes, but he was quite advanced in most of his inventions and things. And he had left the observatory to the town. One of the town's families had taken it upon themselves to keep it up – and safe all through the war. So it was a natural to be selected for the project."

Tom added, "If you want to see what's left of the observatory structure, it's over in the corner of the Gardens. It's just a skeleton of iron now – it had originally been covered in canvas. And all the equipment has been taken out long ago, of course. But there's a stone plaque still there that tells about it, I think."

"Thanks," I said turning to him. "I'll make a point to go see it in the daylight. It sounds really interesting."

About then, a musical theme was beginning to be played on the keyboard. The drums picked it up. Then the bass. A guitar. The group's leader leaned into the microphone and introduced the members one-by-one to a round of anticipatory applause.

The featured musicians this night were older, all men, well seasoned. Their music was from the soul. There was a keyboard man, who did all the talking and exuded personality. A fellow who played both sax and clarinet, and who walked the same way he played his music – with a natural fluidity and grace. A trumpet virtuoso, whose stage presence and professionalism were exceeded only by his talent. A guitarist, whom they had just met at a local club. A bass player and drummer, who held them all together. And all of them brought a wonderful life experience as well as skill to their music – so important to really good jazz.

Throughout the evening, they allowed and encouraged local musicians to sit in and show us their style. A dozen or so played their hearts out for us amazingly well. Most were so young, still in high school, but with talent and ability that went well beyond their years. Their musicianship was impeccable. And this was a once-in-a-lifetime learning experience. Performing in an auditorium setting is one thing. But playing out in the heat of the night, with laughter and low talk all around, and strangers coming and going, improvising with musicians never before met – this is the real test, and the real tradition of jazz.

It was approaching 10 o'clock, and the warmth and humidity, which typically dissipates as the night progresses, was inexplicably still with us. Heat lightning flashed all around, but brought no cleansing wind or rain.

Suddenly, I felt several sharp points of pain on the top of my left foot. "Ow!" I exclaimed. "I think something's bitten me."

"Oh, jeez," Sally responded. "I'll bet it's fire ants," she said looking down at my bare feet in the dim light from the stage.

"Here, put some ice on it," Holly offered digging around in the cooler.

"Are you allergic to fire ants?" Sally asked.

"I don't know," I said. "I am allergic to wasp stings." The bites on my foot were beginning to sting and burn quite severely. "I know why they're called 'fire ants'," I said wincing.

"Do you want to leave?" Jonathan asked sympathetically.

"No, no," I replied. "The ice is starting to help, I think."

"Well, let me know if you start to feel weird or can't breathe or something," Sally said.

"You'll be the first to know," I promised.

The concert continued with deeply satisfying, wonderful performances from all the participants. It was an experience worthy of the night – which remained sultry and sulky, and full of magical jagged-edged flashes piercing the horizon.

By the concert's end, the performers were damp with effort and night air. My foot was numb with ice, but swollen noticeably, even in the semi dark. Fortunately it wasn't a far walk home. Sally and Jonathan carried my chair and helped me limp home.

We got back to my house, and Sophie was delighted to see her three best friends, but sensed there was something wrong with me. Sally promised she wouldn't leave until she was sure I was all right, and Jonathan told her to call him if I needed anything. I reminded him that I was right there in the room.

Sally was as good as her word and helped me change and climb into bed. Then she sorted through my medicine cabinet and found some antihistamine for me to take. She also filled an ice pack to keep on the bite area.

"You're quite a good nurse," I complimented her.

"Are you sure you're going to be all right?" she responded. "You got multiple bites, I can see now. And with that swelling, I would bet you're having an allergic reaction. Are you sure you can breathe okay? I can take you to the emergency room, you know."

"Honestly, I think I'm going to be fine. Even if I do have an allergic reaction – like with wasps – it doesn't bother my breathing," I assured her.

"What does happen?" she prodded.

"Well, mostly my blood pressure just drops," I told her.

"Oh, swell. You just go into shock. Okay, let's go to the hospital."

"And ... it usually doesn't hit for 12 or 24 hours. A delayed reaction."

She stared at me, frowning.

"I feel fine, honestly," I swore to her. "Look, if I'm not fine in the morning, you can drive me to Doc Dupree's, okay?"

"I guess," she said with a sigh. "But here's the phone, you've got my number." She plopped the phone down closer to the side of the bed.

She also left the antihistamine and some water on the bedside table and cautioned Sophie to watch over me like a hawk.

The windows were open to the night. The overhead fan in the center of the room ruffled the edges of my sheets. My foot began to throb. The bites also began to itch with an intensity unlike anything I had ever felt before – with the exception of a wasp sting. I admitted to myself that Sally might be right. I took some aspirin and another antihistamine and drifted into a fitful dream-filled sleep.

TWENTY-EIGHT

Sophie was dressed as a nurse. She was standing over me and shaking her head. Then someone began playing jazz in the background. The drums weren't quite right, though – they were loud and banging.

I awoke with a start to the boom of thunder overhead. Sophie was, indeed, standing over me (minus the nurse's uniform). The sheets were tangled around my legs and my foot was tight with swelling. It was hot to the touch.

I felt a little light-headed, but got up and hobbled down the hall leaning against the walls and anything else I could reach until I made it into the kitchen. I fumbled with the icemaker in the refrigerator and managed to refill the ice bag. Then, I limped my way back to bed, and wrapped the soothing ice pack around the bites. Sophie was lock-step with me the whole way. I took more antihistamine.

Rain was beginning to pelt the windows, but I couldn't summon the strength to get up again and work my way around the house to close them all. It seemed to be coming from every direction at once. Lightning cracked and flashed with passion. In tandem, thunder rolled and roared. I watched the bright flickering explosions in awe for a time, and then fell into a sort of half sleep. In and out, I drifted. Dreams filled my head with images of Lottie Louise wearing her giant ruby. She was laughing with Philippa Parsons and Clarissa Robecheaux. They were pointing at something and laughing harder and harder. But I couldn't see what it was that was making them laugh. Then, I was falling – backward into an old well. It was hot and dark and I couldn't stop falling. Far above me, I could hear Sophie barking and bells ringing. Suddenly, I was at the bottom of the well, and I was looking through a giant telescope back up to the opening at the top. Sally was there, leaning against the Big Dipper constellation, and asking me if I was going to be all right. She was throwing hands full of rubies down on me and telling me to come out.

"Macy!" she called. "Honey, are you all right? Jonathan and I have been calling you all morning on the phone. We got worried when you didn't answer, so I told him I'd come over and check on you. Are you well?"

"Am I down a well?" I asked stupidly.

"No, I asked if you were feeling well," she laughed at me. "How many of these things did you take?" she asked as she looked at the half-empty box of antihistamines.

"Quite a lot, I believe. Man, does my foot itch! And sting," I complained. "But I do think it's better, actually."

"Let me see," she insisted as she pulled my foot out from the sheet covering it.

"And why am I wet?" I asked, feeling my nightshirt and the top of the sheet around me.

"Oh, dear, I am so sorry!" she laughed again. "It's pouring rain out there – I've been dripping on you, I guess." She shook her hand through her hair and wet drops flew everywhere. "Didn't you notice my wet clothes? Honey, you are out of it. It's been storming all night. I think we're getting some of that hurricane that's just off the coast."

Just to prove her point, a great crash of thunder and lightning broke over us. It made the lights flicker. The phone warbled a short, silly burst. The wind gusted and shook, and angry rain struck the roof and sides of the house in wave after wave.

"Don't worry, I've closed up your windows," she said, without my even asking.

She was still frowning over my foot. "I'd really feel better if Doc Dupree could look at this. But, man! the storm is really something out there."

"Let me get up for a bit, and we'll see how I feel … and see if the weather breaks," I reasoned with her.

She helped me out of bed, with Sophie's solicitous assistance. Bathed, dressed, and with a cup of hot tea in me, I did feel significantly better. She had called Doc while I was getting dressed, and he said to keep up the course of treatment she had started. He also said if I got worse, and the storm didn't let up, he would try to make it over to my house. She also called and reassured Jonathan, and told him she would stay with me for the day.

The storm showed no signs of easing. It had its way with us most of the day. Aside from the white flashes of lightning, it was black as night even at noon. Sally remained with me the entire time. We played cards and watched old movies on DVDs and entertained Sophie with a game of tennis-ball-bowling down the hallway. I slept on and off – but without the dreams. Slowly, my foot showed signs of improving, and I think Sally and Jonathan were more relieved than even I. He had continued to call on and off throughout the day.

By evening, I was actually able to get a sandal on it and walk pretty well. Then, just as Sally was convinced she could leave me on my own, the phone rang.

"It's Monnie Belle," the woman's voice claimed. But I wouldn't have recognized her otherwise. The tone was high and strained.

"Monnie, what is it?" I asked a little frightened.

"We've had a sort of 'cave-in' I guess you could call it," she said. "The roof – it's finally given in. It's just in one end of the building – one corner, really, thank God. And it's a blessing that the students aren't back yet. But the worst part is that it's flooding the library. I'm calling everyone I can think of to come help us – we're trying desperately to save the books."

I could envision the beautiful old Selby Academy library with floor-to-ceiling shelving of carved mahogany. Some of the collections were quite valuable, I knew – all were treasures, really.

"Oh, Monnie, I'm so sorry," I exclaimed. "Sally Houseman is here with me ... we'll both come help right away," I blurted out.

Sally's immediate expression was something along the lines of: "Have you lost your mind, you idiot?" But when I explained the circumstances, she became much more sympathetic.

"I'll go, of course," she said. "But please, Honey, you stay here and off that foot!"

"Not a chance," I responded. And she was a good enough friend to let it go at that.

By the time we made our way to her car, we were both drenched to the skin. Umbrellas did nothing to shield us. We sloshed into the front seats and held our breath that it would start. Fortunately, even with the torrents of water coming down, the engine turned over immediately.

Most of the town's residents had the good sense to stay off the roads, so traffic was not a problem. Flooded intersections and gutters overwhelmed the sewer system. The dirt side roads were completely impassable. Lightning blinded us both during and after its bursts, and circled us in an unearthly eeriness. We drove with aching slowness through a town we both knew well, yet didn't recognize. Wind shuddered the heavy car like it was a paper cup. It took us at least 20 minutes to reach the school, a scant mile away.

We pulled into the gravel drive and through the iron gates. Bushes were bent and quivering. Trees were turning up their limbs in surrender. There were several other cars there, pulled haphazardly as close as possible to the building entrance.

"Oh, good, Doc's here," Sally said, spotting his 20-something-year-old, dark blue Buick. "He can look at your foot."

It took all my strength just to open the car door against the wind. I almost fell over when the gust suddenly let up as I was limping to the front door. Sally was holding on to the back of my shirt in puppet-fashion. I felt rather like when I was 4 years old, and my sister was trying to teach me how to ice skate. We stumbled up the steps, and Brooks Lawton opened the door for us before we could even ring the bell. He handed us towels and we gratefully covered ourselves in them.

"Oh, thanks so much for coming," Monnie called out with sincere gratitude, as she rushed through the entrance hall with an arm load of books. "Go on through, you'll see what needs to be done."

Brooks had already returned to the library, and we followed his example.

At the far outside corner on the north end of the room, water was running down the wall. It flowed over and through the shelves and books in its path. My stomach tightened at the sight of all those books being dealt this deathblow. The smell of it filled the room.

The beautiful old oriental carpet had been hastily thrown back away from the outer wall, and leather chairs had been pushed to the center of the room. Large trashcans and buckets caught streams from the ceiling in half-a-dozen places.

Margaret Ann was there, on a ladder. Sylvia St. Martin was on another. They were handing down book after book into the waiting arms of Brooks and Doc Dupree, who were then stacking them in the center of the room. Monnie and Cris Demerist were carrying them from there into the cafeteria for closer assessment. Ridley Knox, Drew Henderson and Jonathan were all in the latter room, performing a sort of "triage," separating the books according to their level of damage, and drying their surfaces as best they could.

Sally and I determined we could be of the most help by joining Monnie Belle and Cris in moving the books into the cafeteria. But my foot slowed me down to the point where I soon had to trade duties with Doc. He had looked quickly at my foot, and declared that I would live – at least long enough to help avert this more impending disaster.

No one spoke very much. There was an occasional joke – a sort of gallows humor. Before long, the threatened shelves were bare, and they were lined with old towels and covered in plastic tarps. Doc said he thought the storm was lessening. We all stopped to listen. Perhaps the wind wasn't quite so strong, we agreed.

Monnie Belle had put out sweet tea and cheese and crackers in the kitchen. We all went in to sit and catch our breath and talk over the next move. Monnie disappeared into a small pantry, and came back with a couple of bottles of wine. Drew took them from her and began expertly opening them, as she pulled glasses and napkins from a variety of shelves and drawers from around the enormous, yet cozy, room.

Just then, Holly and Tom came through from the front, rain gear dripping.

"Great timing," Brooks teased. "You made it just in time for the wine."

"Hey – we came as fast as we could. It's a hurricane out there, you know," Tom shot back good-naturedly, as Brooks pulled the plate of cheese and crackers just out of his reach.

"It is letting up, I think," Holly stated. Jonathan handed her a glass of wine.

"Oh, Monnie, I don't know how you can keep from just breaking down," Sally said with sympathy. "Such a mess."

"Well, I had you all to help me – I couldn't have done it alone. And we'll get it back together again" she said with surprising optimism. "Maybe we'll even get some insurance help with the new roof now – we do have good insurance coverage, I will say that. Some of the staff will be back tomorrow, and we can manage, I'm sure. This sort of thing always occurs on a Sunday, doesn't it?" She was the old

Monnie Belle again – in control and upbeat.

Ridley Knox had been finishing up the last of the damaged-book sorting. He stepped into the kitchen just as we were making ourselves comfortable, serving ourselves wine and iced tea.

Monnie saw his face first. Her look and sudden silence in turn hushed Sally, Drew, Jonathan and me immediately. Sylvia picked up on it next, then Brooks, then Chris. Tom, Holly and Doc all looked over at him, too. Margaret Ann was chatting on in the silence. Brooks shushed her gently.

We were all staring at Ridley then. He held in his hand a soft leather-bound book, a sort of journal. It was about the size of an old Bible. I thought that might be what it was, at first. But his face said it was something different. Something of a very different significance.

"What is it, Ridley?" Monnie Belle spoke first.

"Something you need to see," he responded, clearing his throat. "I was just looking through it to judge the damage, you see. I'm not sure what caught my eye. I just sort of started reading, I suppose."

"Reading what?" Margaret Ann encouraged. "What is it, Ridley? What have you found?"

"Perhaps we could … perhaps I should just read it out loud to everyone," he said. "I think it may be important. I think it could be quite important."

29

TWENTY-NINE

July 28, 1860

It came to me in the middle of the night just a fortnight
ago. I was sleeping poorly. This wretched heat has settled in,
as damp and still as anything experienced even in the coastal
cities of Savannah and Charleston. My fever has returned as
well. Along with the weakness. Nothing seems to help any
more. It's all I can do to walk to my laboratory. I have had the
servants fix a small bed for me in there. But as exhausted as I
am, I cannot sleep. Trinity brings me meals that she has tried
hard to make appealing. But it is no use. I cannot eat much
nowadays. In one of my sleepless fits it became clear to me in
a flash – it was not the single compression process I thought
it would be. It was a combination of techniques. I mustn't
put the exact formula down here. But should I record it at

all? The stones are amazing – virtually identical to those made by God in His wisdom, in the depths of His good earth. But I am not God. And yet, I have made perfect rubies – of the size and quality at my will – all in my simple laboratory. There are incredible possibilities here. But incredible possibilities for ill use as well. I must consider what to do with this invention, this knowledge.

August 17, 1860

My tests continue to prove the ruby creation process remarkably accurate. I have repeated it a dozen times or more. Always the same result – even perfect blood-reds. I have made two of them as big as goose eggs. I even replicated the inclusions that produce the star effect. The small stones can be produced in remarkable time. And, once they are cut and polished, they are all as consistent in shape and quality as peas in a pod. I am at once excited and appalled at what I have done. I have detailed the process in my notebook, but then I tore out the pages. Shall I destroy them? I know I am dying. My weakness increases. I will need to decide soon if I leave my knowledge to mankind, or have it buried with me.

August 30, 1860

The doctor has finally left me alone. I know this will be the last time I am able to write in this journal. I have decided my great dilemma, just as this oppressive heat has released the town from its grip. A great cleansing breeze has stirred the trees and cooled the air. My conscience is now just as clear as the heavens that I hope to enter soon. I confided in my great friend Anna Lucille Robecheaux. She is a good and intelligent woman. She has proven she can keep a confidence, and she is honest. I have told her to bury my discovery with me, and to come for this diary this afternoon. We have decided to hide everything – stones and all – at the bottom of the cistern near the old Quaker Meeting House. No one uses it any more, and it is deep. I believe it will be safe there. I have already told my family that I want to be buried near the old pines that stand near there. Perhaps I believe I will be able to watch over it somehow. I know my time on this earth will be done soon, and I have no more strength to resolve this by myself. Anna Lucille has sworn to me that she will honor my wishes and tell no one. I can only trust her and my God that I will bring harm to no one with my devices. May God accept my soul.

Ridley closed the book gently, smoothing the worn, water-marked leather binding with loving hands. The room was silent.

It was the last entry in the book. Ridley had had some difficulty making out the final words, they were so weakly written. The blank pages were as unfinished as the life they had reflected.

Henry Laroque had died too soon. His brilliance with him. Although he had left an abundance of inventions and discoveries to the benefit of society, he had kept this amazing process to himself. He had trusted only his friend Anna Lucille Robecheaux, and she had apparently proven worthy of his confidence. She had dutifully taken possession of his journal that same day as his last entry. He had passed away just before dawn the next morning. As was his request, he was buried near the old Quaker church in a small valley on the northwest edge of Selby – near the cistern where he and Anna Lucille had decided she would deposit everything pertaining to his revolutionary ruby creation process.

Breaking the silence, Sylvia asked, "What was the date on that last entry?"

"August 30th," Ridley replied.

"No, I mean the year date," Sylvia insisted.

"Umm…1860," Ridley confirmed turning the diary open again to the last written page.

"But it wasn't until about 1910 or so that the French synthetic process was announced," Sylvia said with interest. "Henry was, like, fifty years ahead of his time."

Holly was quick to add, "And Henry supposedly could duplicate rubies exactly – even very large sizes. Didn't you tell us that the French process was pretty feeble? I mean, that people could tell the difference and they were used for novelty jewelry, or more often for industrial purposes."

Sylvia reaffirmed Holly's remarks.

Jonathan then spoke all our thoughts and said, "It took a great deal of character to refuse the credit for such an invention just to protect the integrity of it. He knew what could happen if it fell into the wrong hands."

"I remember that the Robecheauxs had relatives in the ruby mining business. This could have ruined them as well, so Anna Lucille had a vested interest in it, too." Sylvia added.

"But I like the fact that he trusted Anna Lucille enough to confide in her and have her help hide his secret," I said, as I crossed the room and refilled my iced tea glass. "I think that speaks something about her integrity as well."

"Wait a minute," Margaret Ann stood up and reached for more wine. "Didn't that journal say that Anna Lucille agreed to hide his notes and all in the cistern? How did this journal get into the library of Selby Academy? Maybe she didn't do exactly as she was asked."

"Well, I can tell you how it probably actually got into the library, at least," Monnie Belle chimed in. "The storm broke through the ceiling just over the section where most of the books donated by Lottie Louise Faith were stacked. This journal was probably something she had tucked in with all the leather-bound classics she gave the school. It's about the same size and color."

"But how did she get possession of it? And did she give it to the school knowing what she had or by mistake?" Margaret Ann responded with raised eyebrows.

"Good question," we all agreed.

"She knew!" I exclaimed as the thought hit me. I turned to Jonathan and said, "She knew she had it, didn't she, Jonathan – she knew!"

Jonathan's smile confirmed that he agreed with what I was thinking. "Tell them," I motioned to him.

He succinctly described the photos we had seen on the third-floor walls of the Parson's Supper Club of the three women together: Philippa Parsons, Lottie Louise Faith, and Clarissa Robecheaux – René's wife. He told how they had obviously been great friends.

I then added all that I had surmised the night I shared Sophie's wading pool with her. I put forth my theories about how and why they might have become friends – what might have bonded them. I also confessed that I didn't like to think that René would have done such a horrible thing as abuse his wife, but that was the best I could come up with at the time to explain the relationship between all three of them.

Monnie spoke up then and said that she had, indeed, looked up in her records about Charlie Robecheaux attending Selby Academy. She said as far as she could tell, the money had come from Philippa Parsons. Apparently, the funds were paid for Charlie and the Faith twins and recorded on the same day. But there had been two receipts issued, one to Lottie and another to Philippa.

We all agreed, that there was definitely a connection between the two families that could account for the journal reaching Lottie Louise's possession.

Drew reasoned that perhaps Anna Lucille – René's grandmother and Henry Laroque's friend – had kept the journal herself. A keepsake of an old friend. After all, it didn't ever spell out the process itself, he pointed out. She may have felt it was innocent enough. Perhaps it was passed down in the family – as these things often are. René would have naturally taken possession of it at some point. More likely, it would have been René himself who gave the journal to Lottie, he concluded.

And Lottie, for all her scatterbrained reputation, could obviously be quite clear-thinking when she needed to be.

"In plain sight," I said then. "She hid it in plain sight. She knew what it was. And she also knew that by giving it to the school library, along with similar looking books, that it would probably be years before it was discovered – if at all. At least long after they were all gone. And she was right."

"What about the actual equipment and the process notes

and drawings that Henry alluded to?" Tom then brought out. He walked over and poured himself another glass of wine. "Where are those things now?"

"Oh, my God, I think I may know that." It was Brooks who startled us all with his quiet exclamation. "They're still in the old cistern – out by the old Quaker Church grounds – and Henry's grave." He stood up stiffly with his leg still obviously giving him trouble and looked over at Margaret Ann. "Out there where the new Pee Wee football field is going in ... the new Jake Dooley Field – the new Jake Dooley Memorial Football field."

Margaret Ann's hand went to her mouth, but she said nothing. Brooks sat down again with a sigh. She moved to his side.

"It was his leg, you see," she said as she slid her arm around his shoulders. "He had just had the accident, and his leg was really curtailing his activities. Dennis Robecheaux used to call him all the time at all hours of the day and night – usually when he had a snoot full and wanted to reminisce about high school days. And Brooks always went – always – never complained."

"It's okay, Peg," Brooks said patting her hand, slipping into his pet name for her.

"But I didn't go that night," he said quietly. "I just couldn't do it physically."

"And I wouldn't have let him if he had tried," Margaret Ann added defensively.

In response to our blank faces, Brooks continued: "The night of the train derailment ... the night coach died ... Dennis called me to meet him at the place where the new Pee Wee football field was going in. He said he had to tell me something, and that he wanted my help with something – a family secret he said. He said something like he couldn't keep it hidden any more."

After a long pause, Brooks said, "Dennis must have known about those things buried in the cistern. And he must have called Big Jake that night, too." He continued with a new light of understanding and great sadness in his eyes: "Jake hadn't answered the emergency call as a public safety volunteer after the chemical spill ... *he was already there* – to meet Dennis. He wasn't at the plant – they were both on the other side of the tracks."

"Yes," Ridley said. "Yes." He almost whispered: "... 'The blood isn't real ... tell Big Jake I'm sorry'..."

Ridley Knox was remembering then, with awesome clarity and meaning, Dennis Robecheaux's dying words.

THIRTY

The storm stayed with us for three more days. But, by the time the sky finally broke open to a few watery weak beams of sun, the story that was uncovered at Selby Academy that Sunday evening had managed to spread throughout the entire town: The Faith Ruby was never real. Dennis Robecheaux died trying to tell the truth. Coach Dooley died trying to help him.

In the weeks and months that followed, in barber shops and restaurants and on front porch swings all over town, the full story was discussed and examined, and details were added and maybe enhanced just a bit. *The Selby News* ran a front-page article about it whenever new information was uncovered or pieced together. Eventually, a national news service picked it up. But that's when everyone's mind seemed to go blank. The ranks closed at the town limits. Somehow, it was our story. A family story. It didn't need to be shared with the rest of the world – who probably wouldn't understand or appreciate it properly anyway.

This was a story that linked five generations of Selby families together in one great confidence. At its heart were two identical blood-red rubies of remarkable size and quality. It was a story of secrets, and the reason for a 50-year-old unsolved mystery. It led to the tragic death of at least two poor souls, one of whom had become a hero.

Like a jigsaw puzzle slowly taking shape, the whole picture finally became clear.

Sometime in 1860, on the eve of a war that would ravage the American southern states in particular, a South Carolina gentleman learned how to fabricate flawless rubies. They were gems of impeccable quality; virtually undetectable from mined stones. And they could be made in any size and quantity. He was a man of principal and strong character. He knew what his discovery would do if it came under the control of an unscrupulous influence. He knew his country would soon be torn in two, and he feared for both sides.

We can only guess at the wonders this man, Henry Laroque, could have achieved if his life had not been cut short by ill health. Barely 25 years old, he chose to have his great discovery die with him. He had one friend he could trust to make sure it was never revealed: Anna Lucille Robecheaux. Henry had known Anna since childhood. He had watched her work with the Underground Railroad. He greatly admired her sense of fairness, her loyalty, and her ability keep a secret. She could be trusted with this most important secret, he felt sure.

When he called upon her to help him hide his invention – the equipment, notes, drawings, all the evidence – she pledged her word and her heart to him. She, too, was a person of principal and integrity. She, too, saw the potential danger. She carefully did as they had planned. She wrapped all the materials into a bundle, weighted it with stone, and lowered it into the cistern near the Quaker Meeting House – near Henry's grave. This was a carefully chosen hiding place. Never used, almost impossible to see, grown thick with weeds and grasses. Similar hideaways were used a few years later, when other personal and community valuables were threatened by the Yankee invasion.

For awhile, everything was safe. For awhile, no one but Anna Lucille knew. But Anna Lucille probably had not anticipated the harshness of the war. The sheer length of it. The great need of the escaping slaves. The desperation. It was likely that all she could finally think about was the relief that more money might be able to provide. She must have confided in her oldest son. Somehow, she must have convinced him to allow himself to be lowered into the old cistern and retrieve one – just one – of the great twin rubies that Henry had created. Just one. It was just lying hidden there, doing no one good, and it could help so many, she must have thought. Just one. No greed, only good. Just one.

She probably took it to the largest city she could get to: Charleston. During the war, it would have been easy to find someone with the shady business practice necessary to take her incredible ruby with no questions asked. Even the closest of examinations would have proven it to be "real." But a gem of this size and no history would be more than suspect. Yet, she was able to sell it – for only a small fraction of what a real, 90-carat, "pigeon blood red," 12-point star ruby of that quality would have been worth, of course. Also quite probably, she was paid in Confederate money.

Then, it was virtually "lost" for almost 40 years. The next time it came to light was when it was bought at auction by a Charleston jeweler on behalf of a Mr. Abernathy D. Faith of New York City and Selby, South Carolina. By then, it was complete with a history of being mined in Burma. Cris Demerist tried, but even with modern research techniques, she was able to trace it back to that initial auction, but no further. No records could be found of it prior to 1900. It seems, however, that Lottie Louise's husband did buy it on good faith and paid a fair market value for it.

Meanwhile, the twin to the Faith Ruby – and proof of its invalidity – lay undisturbed, perhaps only vaguely remembered, at the bottom of an old, unused, almost obliterated cistern on the far northwest side of Selby. But children, being children, will venture exactly where their parents tell them not to. Thus, young Harley McPherson and his playmates were throwing pebbles down this very well in 1911 when he "fell asleep" and tumbled into it. It was fortuitous on several levels that René Robecheaux was one of the first rescuers on the scene. Speculation alone tells us that René volunteered to go down after the boy as much out of fear as from bravery. Fear that the secret his family had kept for three generations might be uncovered. But bravery all the same. The cistern could have crumbled in on both of them at any time during the rescue.

Quite possibly, René took the opportunity of the rescue operation to also find and pocket the second ruby. At any rate, he had it in his possession not long after that. He and Lottie Louise had become friends. That was common knowledge. To what extent that friendship reached, no one will likely ever know. But it must have been based on honesty and respect to prompt René to tell Lottie the truth about her famous Faith Ruby. It was probably long after Abe's death. Perhaps Lottie initiated an inquiry into its history. We only know that René probably showed Lottie the second ruby as proof of what he was telling her. With his devotion to her, he likely then gave the second ruby to her to assure her that the secret would always be safe. No one need know. She now had possession of the only thing that could prove her ruby was not real. She had them both.

There was a great deal of discussion, then, about how haphazardly Lottie Louise had handled her Ruby. Was it because of her scatty personality? Or, in light of this new information, because she cared so much less for the stone and its value. Doc Dupree's story of his dad seeing Lottie's twins each wearing a ruby became understandable. It must have been during the time Lottie possessed both of them.

But, on July 29, 1916, something caused Lottie to return the duplicate ruby to René. He must have been disappointed. The "secret" they shared would have been an additional bond between them. With the return of the ruby, was she saying she no longer wanted that bond? Her note to him that Drew had found in his desk drawer: "With this, I also return your heart" surely referred to the twin ruby. But beyond that, it would be speculation. He died that very night. But there was still no indication that it was anything more than a terrible, tragic, accident.

It would have been at this point that Clarissa Robecheaux came to possess the second ruby – as well as the journal belonging to Henry Laroque. René would not have had time to hide them again. She may have approached Lottie and pledged her silence as well. Perhaps Lottie refused the ruby from Clarissa, but for some reason had accepted the journal. This would have certainly accounted for their bonded friendship. And, perhaps, Lottie had simply been grateful for René's kindnesses over the years.

The connection between Clarissa Robecheaux's family and Philippa Parsons became clear when Ed Cinkowski went back in the newspaper "morgue" and found the original accounts of Philippa's attack. What common gossip had somehow forgotten over the decades was that it had been René Robecheaux who had found Philippa after the attack and had gotten her medical help. He was credited with saving her life, stopping the bleeding as well as he could, and then physically carrying her to a doctor. So René had been the central figure that connected the three women. But in a way that no one had expected. Certainly not like any of my own scenarios. It also more than explained why Philippa had paid for Charlie to attend Selby Academy. I was glad my instinctive liking of René seemed to be holding up.

René's son, Charlie, was probably also aware of his great grandmother's secret. And of the potential damage he could do with the knowledge. He seems to have been a conflicted boy – and man. Torn about doing what was right. His stealing of the polo pony from Selby Academy was probably an early crying out for someone to help him morally. But he kept himself closed so tightly against everyone at the Academy, the help he so desperately sought was unable to get through to him. What had been an "easy" secret to keep three generations earlier, was becoming more and more difficult for him. He even spent a few years of his young adulthood studying for the ministry. He had gone to China for a short time as a missionary, but ill health had forced his return. He married late, and fathered his one and only child when he was in his 40s. He was not a very likeable man. Not a particularly strong father figure for his son Dennis. When he died, barely 60 years old, Dennis was filled with unresolved questions and emotional immaturity.

The final generation to carry this secret now involving two families rested completely on the shoulders of Dennis Robecheaux. He did not carry it comfortably. The guilt he felt for his family overwhelmed him. With his father dead, and his mother soon after, he looked to a few close friends for the small bit of support and love he could find. He looked to Brooks Lawton and Big Jake Dooley. But he kept his family's secret deep inside of himself.

Then, in 1964, Dennis found a way out. The highly publicized theft of two major gems – the 100-carat oval DeLong Star Ruby, and the 500-carat sapphire called the Star of India – gave him his opportunity. More specifically, it was their return that excited him. Brooks remembered that Dennis was 17 at the time, and particularly obsessed with the case. He kept asking Brooks about it, scoured the newspapers trying to find out more details. When he heard that a deal had been struck with the thieves, and that the gems had been returned for ransom, he asked to borrow Brooks' car. Brooks gave him the keys, without any questions. Dennis was extremely nervous, but obviously it was very important to him – as well as upsetting. Dennis refused to talk about it, and Brooks simply respected that.

Apparently, Dennis had driven to Savannah, left the duplicate Faith Ruby behind the altar of a small Catholic church, and then called the police with an anonymous tip to report it. Dennis was never quite the same after that. His drinking increased. His isolation. Instead of relieving himself of his burden of secrecy and guilt, he had only added to it. He would barely speak to anyone, except Brooks and Big Jake.

When the Faith Ruby was "found" and then determined to be an exact duplicate, Lottie was still living. She was in her mid 80s, and no longer a resident of Selby. She must have understood immediately what had happened. But she never said a word about it to anyone. As close as she came to divulging anything was to Brooks. She hinted at something when he was drafting her final will. It was in 1977, and she was in her late 90s. She still trusted only Brooks for all of her legal matters. She stated in her will that the Carolina Star – also known as the Faith Ruby – was to be left to her twins to decide for themselves who would wear it. She wanted it to go to "whomever loves me best" was how she stated it in the document. Perhaps she was still thinking of René.

Brooks never found out which one of the twins took possession of the gem. Since then, they have both passed away. Neither married. There were no heirs. The whereabouts of the once fabled gem is still a mystery.

As far as the other materials that had been held in secret for so long, Dennis had kept his great-great grandmother's promise to her friend Henry. He kept watch over them in the cistern that had been filled-in so long ago. He would visit it obsessively – to check and make sure all was safe and quiet and just as he had left it last. He would also sit at Henry's grave, talking to him, bringing flowers picked from the nearby fields. His fear of discovery was so great, however, that when the location of the new Pee Wee football field was announced near there, he was convinced that the construction would uncover everything and all would be revealed. He believed he would be held responsible for this terrible secret that his family had kept for almost 150 years. He only knew to ask for help from two friends – Brooks Lawton and Big Jake Dooley. Only Big Jake had come that night.

To bring a final end to the debates, the old cistern out where the original Quaker church had once stood was located and dug up. Nothing was found in it.

EPILOGUE

Reverend Ridley Knox leaned in closely to the small stone grave marker. He carefully arranged a bouquet of handpicked field flowers in a plastic vase next to the name carved in the marble. Then he pulled up his trouser legs and sat down on the ground next to the still-mounded grave.

There was no need to look around him. The small cemetery just behind the First Presbyterian Church in Selby was empty of visitors. It usually was. The autumn sun was clear and bright and warm. The colored leaves of the trees around him gave off a spiced scent that Ridley breathed in deeply.

Ridley clasped his hands around his knees, rocked back a bit, and looked down at the grave. "Hello, Dennis," he said. "I thought I owed you a visit. I wanted to tell you that I'm sorry I didn't understand what you were trying to tell me that last day in the hospital. I'm even more sorry that I didn't understand your pain while you were still living. I wish so much that I could have helped – that I could have done something to help you."

He shifted a bit and looked right at the stone. "I thought you'd like to know that the secret's out now – no more need to keep anything hidden. You might also like to know that we actually did open up that old cistern. And you know what? We didn't find a thing. Now, here's what I think ... I think your daddy cleared it out long ago – long before you were born. I also think he may have disposed of it all when he went to China as a young man. Here's the thing, Dennis, China has just now announced a process for synthesizing rubies so perfectly that they're almost impossible to tell from the real thing. So what do you think? Coincidence?"

Ridley chuckled out loud. Then he sat very still for a while. With a sad, warm smile on his face, he reached out his right hand and softly placed it on the grave before him. Then he raised his hand above it in benediction. And he forgave Dennis Robecheaux. He forgave him on behalf of Big Jake, and on behalf of Henry Laroque, and on behalf of the town of Selby, and in the name of God.

"Peace be with you, Dennis. Peace."

THE END